MOTHER'S DAY

A whistling gal and a crowing hen,
they both will come to a no-good end.
—Ma Barker,
1879-1935

MOTHER'S DAY

By J. M. RYAN

PRENTICE-HALL, INC., ENGLEWOOD CLIFFS, NEW JERSEY

TO BETTE

I had four sons, four lovely boys.
Then, in 1927, a policeman got killed and they come after
my boy Herman, and surrounded him.
I had told him not to give up.
He killed himself.

My boy Lloyd was caught robbin' the U.S. Mails.
He's in Leavenworth for twenty years.

Little Arthur, who I call "Dock" got arrested for the murder
of a night watchman at a hospital. They never proved a thing
and anyway the watchman was old. Dock is in prison for life.

Freddie, who's my youngest and my baby got caught in a
little job of burglary and got locked up in the Kansas State Pen.

Now I'm alone.

What's a mother to do?

BOOK
ONE

The gun is a Thompson submachine gun, latest model 1928, carved handgrip forward, round piepan drum, rate of fire 300 shots a minute, .45 caliber, muzzle velocity 920 feet per second. He props it muzzle-up with his left hand, his right holding open the door of the new 1934 Chevrolet as lights out, engine off, it slides through the luminous fog along the sandy lake road.

A faint squeak of brakes as the dark shiny sedan rocks to a stop under a mass of vague blurry palm trees looming out of the mist. He sits stiffly in the front seat, listening. He loosens his tie. Dripping from the damp fog rolling off the lake, the palms hang motionless in the blue smoky light. It is five o'clock in the morning, January 16, 1935, Lake Weir, Florida.

He drops out onto the road, holding the door for four others, shadowy, featureless in the gloom, all in dark business suits and hats, swinging submachine guns and automatic rifles that glitter in the dim bluish light. They wait in silence beside the dark Chevrolet and out of the thick drifting fog behind them rolls a gleaming new 1934 Ford sedan, wire wheels, high spade-shaped grille, big flat headlights above its wide sloping fenders.

Five men dismount, five more submachine guns.

A black '32 Chevrolet phaeton, canvas top glistening wet, stops behind the Ford. The men swing heavily down from the running board, crunching across the road under fifty-round drums slung from shoulder straps, canisters of tear gas grenades and bulletproof vests.

Fifteen men are now gathered in the fog under the shadowy palms, all armed with submachine guns, shotguns, .45 automatics and rifles. Collected around the first group, they are ready to begin the search.

They have come to find the Barker-Karpis gang in this tiny lakeside village in Florida and they are the Special Field Detachment of the Federal Bureau of Investigation.

•

A mile away, the dark second-story window is almost hidden in the palms and drifting mist.

The woman's voice is raspy and tough, the accent southern. A bullchested caller of hogs, an old lady gunnery sergeant.

"*What* in thee god damn hell was *that?*"

"Nothin'." A man's voice, high and nasal. The Ozarks.

"Nothin'! Don't yew tell me nothin'!" she says. "Somebody messin' around the *yard.*"

"Dammit, Ma, it's that foolish pig by the garage. Maybe his rope got loose."

"Git *rid* o' that pig, Fred."

"We gotta keep the pig 'til Karpis gets back." He laughs. "Go blow hell outa old *Joe.*"

"Honest to *God*, Fred . . . you an' Alvin Karpis."

". . . git that ole alley-gator, blow his damn head off." He laughs again.

"Freddie, sometimes I believe yore mean enough to stomp a unborn child . . ."

•

The lead group of agents waits in the shadowy fog beside the Ford. A scout returns to report.

"The trouble here is the houses all look the same. There's at least five of them with boat docks."

An agent fingers the safety on his submachine gun. Click click. On safety. 300 rounds a minute. 920 feet per second. Penetration into white pine at ten foot range, seven inches. Penetration human flesh, unlimited.

"Knock on a door and ask somebody."

"Suppose it's *their* door?"

•

Fred Barker rolls on the squeaky castiron bed. From days and nights of alarms, packed suitcases and loaded guns, the anxious life on the edge of the bed, he sleeps in trousers and greasy BVD tops, bare skinny arms folded back over his face like a cat. As he struggles awake, he scratches his ribs, his bony head turned toward the faint predawn light from the window.

4

"Ma, you goin' fix some coffee, huh, Ma?"

Ma's massive silhouette fills the rocker, remote and mysterious, a mountain in the dark.

"No. Wait'll the *coon* gets here. He's paid money to *cook*, let 'im *cook*. I'll turn on the light for ye, Freddie," Ma says.

"No. Leave the damn light off," he says. "I got me a real ballbuster of a headache."

"What is it, Fred, honey?"

"It's my eyes, I reckon. The light only makes it worse."

"It's the cops houndin' ye done it, Fred."

"I suppose that's so, Ma."

"Always after yew."

"Yeah, Ma."

"It's a nervous headache."

"Yeah."

"Your whole head aches because of yore nerves."

"Yeah."

"Yew got nerves inside yore head, y'know."

"Yeah, Ma, fer crissake shut up now."

"Take some Asefetida pills. Snuff fer pleasure, pills fer pain."

"Them pills make me puke, Ma."

"Maybe yew feel better ef y'puke up."

"Aaaah," he says.

"Poor little Fred. Ole head achin' away."

"M-m-m."

"Fred, it ain't the booze, is it?"

"Ma, I swore on The Book."

"I know ye did, Fred. I'm proud ye did."

"I never touch it Ma. You know that."

"Bless ye, Fred."

Fred yawns, rubbing his rounded, stubbled jaw. A hangover in Florida in the wet goddam fog. Every remaining tooth in his head aches. Two streaks of pain slide up from his incisors and collide at the center of his skull. Where the hell did he leave that bottle? Behind the stove? Could it explode back there?

"What the hell time is it?" he says. Old Ma will start to rock soon.

5

"It's early." The rocking begins. "An' stop that all the time cussin'."

Ma Barker, superFagin of the Ozarks, short, pudgy mountain of a woman, jowly, her soft sagging features carry at times a look of cruel humor, a jolly murderess. At other times, a permanent expression of remembered pain and disappointment twists her thin cracked lips. She treasures past hurts. Pinched little eaglebeak of a nose. A man-eating puffin. A carniverous hen.

Eyes of an alert pig. Sparkling brown, moist little pig eyes. Her frizzy hair has been dyed red, and in the bluish-gray light of predawn looks purple.

But Ma's most memorable features are her eyes. Glittering quick little brown eyes encased in fortresses of fat.

The chair creaks and groans under one hundred and ninety pounds of maternal muscle, the lioness awake in the dark.

•

Out in the fog, on the sandy side road, two more dark sedans roll silently to a stop, more agents dismount. They scuttle across the gravel into the mass of tropic shrubs where the others, misty shapes in the gloom, are gathered. Submachine guns gleam in the soft bluish light. It is unexpectedly chilly. An agent takes out a cigarette, remembers and puts it away.

They are reinforced by twenty local Florida lawmen, sheriff's men in big hats carrying shotguns and rifles. A deputy chokes back his morning hacking spell.

The agents are cold, wet and on edge. Sixty days ago, two agents, friends of theirs, were killed by the Dillinger gang in a Wisconsin ambush. A week ago in Chicago, a Barker mobster came out of his room shooting and had to be chopped down with auto-rifles. And the word is around that Alvin Karpis is here in Florida, holed up with the Barker gang, tommy gun and all.

They watch as John J. Lafferty, agent in charge, assembles his troops. Unfortunately, the local village idiot, a man in a cowboy hat who never sleeps, has joined their army. He knows where everything is and who everyone is at Lake Weir.

He has never heard of the Barkers.

•

Upstairs in the back bedroom, Ma lights a cigarette, holding it between her teeth, the way her daddy smoked cheroots. She rocks in the dark in the creaky chair, coughing in her barrel chest, sparks spilling over her massive bosom, as she studies the shadowy form of her scrawny son sprawled across the bed.

"All the time cussin'." Ma pulls deeply on the cigarette, coughs, sparks flicker onto the rug. "I do believe it's them northern wimmin got you boys all messed up. Northern wimmin."

Fred has heard all of this many times before.

"Knock it off, Ma," he says. He squeezes his forearm trying to make out the tattoo in the gloom. He would like to have one o' them northern wimmin here right now, Ma or no Ma. Fix a hangover.

Like the platinum blonde with the great big beautiful knockers. She never could get enough and neither could he. Twenty-three years old, pretty as a movie-star, naked around the house all day, Ma's worst enemy. "Fatwitted," crazy name, wild woman. Platinum blonde with the most beautiful body he'd ever seen. Have her here right now. Fix a hangover quick.

As he turns toward the faint blue-gray light from the window, Ma gazes upon the face of her baby.

With his large, bulging staring eyes, Fred Barker looks like a skinny lemur gone mad. His damp black hair is parted in the center and combed straight back from a ragged widow's peak at the upper reaches of his round oily forehead. His sharp nose is too large for his face, his mouth is small and petulant and his chin rounded and receding. He looks nose-heavy. The scars and welts across his forehead and cheekbones give him a sad, exhausted look that might come from extreme sorrow or uncontrolled booze. Or amateur plastic surgery.

"Nobody among my people ever cussed," Ma says. "Never said a blas-*phe*-mous word . . ."

The cigarette glows in the dark, bobbing as she shifts it around between her teeth. The rocker squeaks as she shifts her weight.

"Ever time there was a revival meetin', my pa took me along on our mule . . ."

•

7

The mule stepped carefully over the wet fallen logs steaming in the bright yellow sunshine, between the charred stumps, racoon berry and hog apple, over jagged boulders wedged in the red clay, following the hackamore, yanked along by the lean angry dark-bearded man in the shabby frock coat, his face shadowed by a battered wool hat. Pa chewed savagely at the hunk of Indian Maid in his left hand and spat between his yellow teeth. Ticks in his beard, moonshine in his belly, and a skullful of paralyzing hatred for everything north of the Ozarks.

Sitting side-saddle, rolling easily on the bare back of the mule, little Kate half listened to her father, half listened to the distant hymn-singing from the hollow. Keep on the sunny side, always on the sunny side, keep on the sunny side of life.

Pa stumbled and swore, squinting in the sunlight, splashing brown juice against a splintered stump. The chorus from the meeting was louder.

"Pray to the good Lord, Kate, keep ye from sin." He slid sideways in the red mud and yanked at the rope.

"Keep to the sunny side, Kate."

Kate smiled, singing softly along with the congregation.

"Keep ye from sin," he rasped. "Keep to th' sunny side, Kate." The dark man stumbled down the slope, scattering rocks, yanking at the rope, the bottle of white lightning sloshing in his coat pocket.

"Kate, when you was but three years of age, ole Jesse was murdered . . . ole Jesse James . . . he robbed from the rich . . . an' he give to the poor . . ."

The familiar recital.

"He did, Pa," Kate said.

"Damn'f he didn't! He robbed from th' *rich* an' he give to th' *poor*. When ole Jesse he seed a ole man a'shiverin' in the snow, why Jesse he'd shuck off his own coat off'n his back an' he'd give it to that pore ole man, just *like that!*"

He tripped on a root and slipped across a wet rock.

When he spoke of Jesse James, his scratchy voice rose an octave. Pa was his own evangelist and his stumbling hillside recital a fragmented, gasping sermon hotter than the hellfire and

8

damnation that the preacher would deliver down in the hollow.

Kate listened to the singing.

"He did, Pa," she said.

"You bet yer boots he did, Kate. Jest like *that!*" He stumbled again and swore.

"Many's the time Jesse he'd show up jest as some Yankee coward was agoin' to foreclose on some morgidge and ole Jesse he'd holler, 'Hold *on* there, now, Yank! Hold on.' An' he'd give the bluebelly the morgidge money . . ."

He paused to kick through dead branches.

". . . and he'd hand the widder a *ree*-seat and he'd boot his tail outa there! Later, out on the road, he'd stick a gun in the Yankee an' git that money back an' give it all to the *widder*." He choked with satisfaction. He jounced and slipped, yanking on the rope, pulling the big-eared mule down the slope.

They struck the trail, working through wet stunted pine, maple stumps, buckhorn brake, nightshade and rosebud, yellowish green leaves of May apple and steaming dead black oaks.

"He robbed off the rich an' he give to the poor. Never a one like ole Jesse. God's own Christian man!"

He glanced back at Kate, his black eyes glittering.

"It's too bad you ain't a boy, Katie. I often wished you was . . . You know, fer a gal, you ain't the best lookin' thing around."

He laughed and bit off a chew. "Ugly as home-made sin." His boot heel caught in a rock and he stumbled.

"Sonofabitch," he said, spewing amber slop across the rocks. The singing from the hollow was louder. Keep on the sunny side.

"Ole Hangin' Jedge Parker, there was a Yankee fer ye . . . He saved up his pris'ners 'til he had six of 'em . . . Then he hung 'em all at once . . . Called 'em his 'terrible examples,' Fort Smith, Arkinsaw . . . Right out o' the devil's brimstone works . . . Ole Jesse had to shoot this feller, I don't recall his name, never amounted to shucks as an outlaw, woulda died o' the gallopin' consumption anyhow . . . brung in the body in a tumbleweed wagon . . ."

He tore off a chunk of Indian Maid in his yellow teeth.

9

"Th' Pinkertons blew up Doc Samuels' house . . . The bomb tore the arm clean off ole Jesse's poor mother, greater injustice was never done . . . Jesse suffered a great vexation of *spirit*, went to *traveling* again, shootin' down the bluebellies what *done* it . . . Never killed a man in his entire life wasn't a Yankee or had did him a wrong . . . Hangin' Jedge Parker hung up eighty-eight men, six on one single morning . . . Better off t' shoot yerse'f if the law grabs ye . . . Beat 'em to it . . ."

He pressed his thumb against his large nose and snorted.

"Slam a bullet right through yore punkin!"

Blackbearded Pa stumbled along, chewing and spraying the rocks, shaking his head in wonderment.

With "Keep On The Sunny Side" yowling up from the hollow and Pa rapping his hard-breathing creed in her other ear, little Kate's head was spinning and her young heart was full.

•

In the dark bedroom in Florida, the hand-cranked Victrola scrapes along, the thick old blue-label record is worn from years of *Keep On The Sunny Side*. Freddie Barker's head has begun to throb to a beat of it's own.

"Ma, turn that crap down."

"Now, Freddie, you don't mean that. That's a bewdiful song."

"I heard it ten million times. Stuff it."

"You jes listen careful, Freddie. You'll feel a sight better."

"Turn it down then, Ma . . . Hey." He sits up suddenly and the movement jolts his head. "Where's the *machine*gun?"

"I shoved it underneath the bed, Freddie. I tripped on it an' near busted my big toe."

Freddie is on his knees grunting in the dark as he claws around under the bedspring. His face and throat are soaked with sweat.

"Don't leave that big old gun layin' around, Fred." She puffs and her owl eyes are lit by the glowing tip.

He cradles the submachine gun and slaps the butt plate. "I gotta clean it today. Goddam damp *ruins* a weapon. This goddam Florida is damp all the *time*."

"It ain't either damp."

"It's damp since I been here."

"You ain't been here but a coupla months, Freddie boy."

"That's long enough."

"I don't see why you can't use a pistol anyways, like everybody else does."

"I like that Thompson gun, that's why."

"Ole Jesse got along fine with a plain .44."

"Stuff ole Jesse."

"Now Freddie, you know you don't mean that." She rocks and puffs, rocks and puffs, balancing the cigarette between her teeth.

Freddie is a great talker. If the cops could only just leave him alone, he'd be a right nice boy. Not so high-strung.

•

Outside, the FBI search through the fogbound village has begun. The agents have stopped a fisherman out early for bigmouth bass.

"Federal officers. We're lookin' for a family, haven't lived here long, probably renting. A woman, middle-aged, two men, late twenties, early thirties. They most likely are on the lakefront, have a motorboat."

The fisherman shakes his head.

"There may be more people with 'em," Lafferty says. "Possibly even quite a few people."

•

A mile away in the upstairs room, Ma has finished her cigarette, ground the butt into the rug and is now well into her coughing spell. She coughs as if her heart will surely break. A tear of self-pity rolls down her sagging cheeks.

"Sometimes I think maybe we was better off back in Tulsa, Freddie. Just you an' me an' Alvin . . . In Tulsa."

Watching the shadowy ceiling, the submachine gun across his belly, Freddie croons, "Take me back to Tulsa, I'm too young to marry."

"You gotta admit we lived right good when the cops wasn't botherin' us too hard. A small bunch o' boys bringin' in the money. Any time there's trouble, I could always talk the dumb coppers out of it. Jest go down the po-lice station an' throw a fit . . . 'Those boys would be good if you cops would jest let 'em alone.' Never failed."

"That's right, Ma."

"Before Mr. Dunlop went and lost his mind."

•

Arthur V. Dunlop, a tall, uneasy man with wavy gray hair, had been in his time a card-shark, house painter, professional gambler and a bill poster. Now, in what he was sure was his prime, he was companion and nonpaying roomer with Ma Barker. Around Tulsa, in 1931, there was no word for "kept man." Arthur called Ma "Kate," cooked, washed dishes and served nervously through the long nights in the wallpapered bedroom to keep 190-pound Ma placated.

Ma thought Arthur was truly handsome, loved his double-breasted suits, his old-fashioned tenor voice, his boiled collars, his shirtstuds and subservience and, when she could find his occasional hidden bottle, kept him alert enough for the bullring. He shared a number of her tastes. They had their picture taken together. They visited Oklahoma City. He took Ma to dances in Aurora, the picture show in Thayer. Courtly, red-eared, gentleman bill poster. He knew all the words to her favorite song. (He could have been on the radio, everyone said.)

"It will help us every day, it will brighten all the way," he would wheeze, "if we keep on the sunny side of life," and Ma would smile.

Now on a warm day in May, reasonably happy (the last tornado had passed no closer than Wichita) dressed in his best suitpants and undershirt, he crouched before a bureau mirror festooned with snapshots and souvenir postcards, spreading his fifty-three-year-old jowl with thumb and forefinger as he carefully edged the long straight razor into the creamy suds under his full sideburn, wondering as he always did whether this time he might slice off his ear.

"Hey . . . ARTHUR!"

"Freddie!" He grabbed the top of the dresser. "Baby Lord Jesus, boy, don't sneak up on a man that way! Criminee, Fred, I dang near cut my throat!"

"That ain't a bad idea, Arthur." Fred Barker watched him, bulging brown eyes glittering. "Ole turkey neck Dunlop. Slice yer damn ole *gullit!*"

"Gee whiz, Freddie, you shouldn't oughta talk like that." Arthur shook the razor into the basin. Fred sneered.

"Where's Ma, dumbell?"

"She's upstairs, I reckon, Fred."

"Well git yer ass upstairs an' git her."

"Sure Fred, right away!" Arthur started for the door. "Hey, Kate!"

"Cut that out, Arthur! Don't you go a hollerin' after my Maw like that or I'll bust yer goddam head fer ya. Now you git on upstairs an' tell her Freddie is home. I got Alvin Karpis with me."

Wiping his red face with the hotel towel, sliding his suspenders up over his flabby shoulders, Arthur V. Dunlop trotted up the stairs.

"Bastard," said Fred.

Alvin Karpis stepped into the room from the hall. Fresh from time in Kansas State Penitentiary, 5'9", 130 pounds, lifeless brown hair over a long sullen pimpled face, squirrel-jowls and querulous mouth and the eyes were blue and flat. "Old Creepy," the fish-eyed petty thug at twenty-two. Cowboy belt buckle and J.C. Penney fedora. Burglary 2nd degree at seventeen, reform school escape, larceny-auto, safe blower, transferred to Penitentiary at twenty-one to serve 4, paroled at twenty-two. He had met Fred Barker at Kansas State and decided to join him when paroled. An interview with the Barker group, a forward-looking organization with just the sort of initiative and drive to intrigue an ambitious young man anxious to improve himself and perfect his craft. Alvin Karpis at twenty-two stood a long way from All-City Marbles Champion and still some distance from

Public Enemy Number One. Today, a cherry orchard of acne had not helped his disposition.

"Who is that bird?" He snapped his thumb after Arthur.

"That there is Mister A.V. Dunlop. The sap hangs around. He ain't worth a damn though."

Alvin Karpis ran his hand over a lump on his chin.

"I thought he was yer pa."

"Arthur? Christ! He ain't my paw. My paw is over to Joplin. He cut out years ago. *He* ain't no good *neither*. Maw keeps Arthur around for laughs. The *bill poster!*"

"Huh?"

"That's what he done. A *bill* poster! Now he's good at cleanin' guns. That's about all he's good at."

Redfaced Arthur reappeared, wiping his knobby hands on his undershirt. "Yore maw will be down in a minute." A sick old man grin. "She's fixin' up to see ya."

"Put a shirt on over yer tits an' git some coffee on the stove, Arthur."

"Surely, Freddie, right away." He trotted back to the kitchen.

Ma Barker smeared a blood-red lipstick across the rice-powdered cracks in her thin lips, rubbed a spot of dead pink on each sagging cheek and blinked her pouchy brown eyes. She clumped down stairs and deliberately paused at the newel post, holding her heavy arms stiffly, her square-fingered hands clenched at her left flank like Garbo in "Anna Christie." She wore a draped, green silk dress with an orange sash across her barrel-like belly, beads the size of crabapples and flat brown leather shoes with imitation diamond buckles. Her finger-waved hair fit her round skull like a cap and was stained a deep orange red.

"Ma, I brought home a buddy. Alvin, this here's my maw."

"Well well! So you're the one. Out in the free world again, huh? You're Alvin."

"Yes mam. Alvin Karpis."

"Karpis. What kind o' name is that?"

"It's American."

"It's a funny soundin' name."

"Ole Alvin says he'll stay a couple days, Ma."

14

"Why that'll be fine, Alvin. You can move yore stuff right on in."

"I ain't got any stuff but what I got on."

"When you git out?"

"Yesterday. They gimme ten bucks an' this suit o' clothes. I had to swipe the belt."

"We'll fix that up, son. I reckon Dock's clothes're a little small but maybe Fred has got some'll fit ye."

"Yeah." Alvin stared at the floor.

"Ole Alvin's a card, ain't he, Ma? What's fer chow?"

"I got a chicken, Freddie. We'll celebrate. How 'bout that, Alvin? We'll celebrate yer gittin' out."

"Yeah. That's swell."

"Fried chicken . . . tomorra we'll maybe git to work."

"Work?"

"Ma is figgered out a job er two."

"There's a real easy one in town. A snotty ole jewelry store. They bin askin' fer it fer some time."

"You figgered it out? You did?"

"Sure! I figger all my boys' work. We do all right, don't we, Freddie?"

"You said a true word there, Ma."

Karpis smiled warily.

"Cast in thy lot among us," said Ma. "Let us all have one purse."

"Ole Ma is a real bible student. She knows all them things."

"Yeah?" Karpis said, "I know one, the golden rule. Do unto others before they do it to you." He rubbed a red lump on his chin.

"That's blas-*phe*-mous boy, but the spirit is correct. You'll fit in just fine around here."

"I told ya he was a card, Ma."

•

Sunday morning, church call, Ma wore her imitation fox fur (Oklahoma coon pelt) and a brown cloche hat that made her look oddly like Red Grange.

"Come on boys, we don't wanta be late."

15

They scuffed across the carpet, each determined to be last.

Ma paused by her standard home wall-reproduction of the young Jesus.

"Ye know, He wasn't sech a bad-lookin' young fella."

She sighed.

Karpis followed Fred out to the '27 Ford touring car.

"Ma, that same cop is lookin' at me again," Fred said.

"Don't you pay him no mind, Freddie," Ma smiled.

"He's lookin' at me, damn him. You know that gits me on edge."

"Don't swear on the Sabbath, Freddie."

"You know what that lookin' at me does, Ma. You know it makes me break out."

"Don't you mind that ole cop, Freddie. You cain't help it ef you're odd lookin'."

"He's still a'lookin', Ma."

"Start up the car, Fred."

"Yeah," Karpis said. "Let's go if we're goin'."

In the simple frame church, the congregation roared out "Keep On The Sunny Side." The collection plate was passed. After the bald sissy retrieved it and moved on, Alvin flashed Fred the handful of coins he had palmed. Fred doubled up. Ma shushed the boys with a prim iron-toothed smile and a wave of her threadbare glove. Fred giggled to himself, with a look of heartfelt admiration for Karpis. Alvin the working crook, Fred the killer. The eagle and the hawk.

•

The snotty jewelry store was robbed. Fred managed to hit the jeweler with his pistol and broke his nose but the new Barker team lacked polish. Fred and Karpis were in the hands of the police before they got halfway home.

Ma put on her black dress and did her routine for a weary judge. He had listened to Ma Barker dozens of times.

Having practiced with a mirror, Ma was more professional with her part than the boys had been with theirs.

"I swear on my pore husband's grave!" she cried. "They're

only childern! None o' this is truly their fault! It's the neighbors, all the time after 'em 'til they get arrested fer things they never did, always blame the Barker boys, jest pore but honest God-fearin', church-goin', hymn-singin', Christian boys, but that's *too much* fer *some* people, always after 'em, can't leave us alone, can't leave us live in peace. They bore false witness against my righteous childern, yer honor! I'm a woman alone, your honor, a widda . . ." (27 miles away, George Barker paused in a corn-field and looked up) ". . . tryin' to jest bring up her childern in the only way our Savior give us to do, an' my pore boys jest tryin' to help out, doin' a little honest hand-to-mouth work here an' there so's to make both ends meet when they ain't ac-tually doin' church work and helpin' the poor."

An old man sitting at the back of the courtroom applauded. A fortuitous shaft of sunlight haloed Fred and Karpis. Ma stabbed her thick finger at Karpis.

"That boy, yore honor, is a orphan I took in to raise as my own, out of Christian goodness! A pore orphan boy, alone in this world!"

(In Kansas City, Karpis' mother and father felt a chill.)

Karpis' flat blue-eyed stare caused the judge to look away.

"Lift up the poor and the lonely, and the Lord rejoices! It's not easy, yore honor, not easy at all, but the Good Lord knows we pray three times a day and we try to do God's work . . . Never missed a Sunday, never missed a revival meetin' from the time they was born, yore honor, some folks that ain't as truly *good* as them, they become mighty *jealous*, they make all *kinds* of trouble for my poor boys . . ."

The judge tried to cry.

Outside, Ma and the boys laughed as they rounded the corner of the courthouse, free. Fred slapped Ma on the rump and she giggled and lumbered after him to frog him on the arm. He cackled.

"Ma, you really laid it on that old judge."

Ma gasped for breath, popeyes bulging. "Freddie, I truly *had* to tell him."

Karpis smiled faintly. Ma was a real talker and a real live wire. She had a way with cops.

•

Under the bright blue open sky, ten miles out of Tulsa, Alvin Karpis whipped the .45 Colt pistol around and fired. As the echoes broke across the red clay hillocks, Ma grinned, the juices began. Fred fired four fast shots with the revolver. Ma laughed at the noise, the sharp smell of gunpowder. Her pulse quickened.

"Practice makes perfect, boys."

She settled herself on the hardwood kitchen chair beside the 1927 Touring T. Arthur Dunlop brought out fried chicken wrapped in newspaper. Ma bit into a leg, spat newsprint.

"I never seen the paper!" she growled. "It's so confounded greasy, ye can look straight through it." Arthur apologized.

Under a rain of gunfire from Alvin and Fred, quickly arranged groups of cans and bottles exploded off fence posts. Ma slapped her heavy thigh with her broad hand. (Pa let her fire the musket.) "You gotta do better'n that, Alvin. Stronger'n *that!*"

Karpis reloaded with fresh shells from an old candy box on the hood, seven in the magazine, one in the chamber. The Barkers had a good bunch of weapons.

"Come on, Freddie!" Ma cried. "You ain't gonna let Alvin beat yew out, are ye? Yew got any guts at all?"

Freddie swore.

Arthur V. Dunlop, wearing his best gray double-breasted suit and his Ponca City Cravat, stood back of the parked touring car, handing up more fried chicken from a battered cardboard Quaker Oats box. Orange pop and Dr. Pepper. One Nehi. Fred finished a Doc Pepper, belched, tossed the bottle in the road and cracked off two quick shots. The bottle exploded in sparkling shards of glass. Echoes scattered away over the red clay hills.

"How about that, Ma? Huh?"

"Do better'n that, Fred. Brother Dock is a better shot than that. He'd a clipped it in one."

Ma, grinning, took a chicken leg from Arthur without looking around and sank her teeth in it.

"Oh, Lordy, that's good grease!"

Fred exploded a bottle.

"That's just beautiful, son." Gummy chicken caught in her bridge. She fished at it with her thick forefinger. Her brown eyes bulged.

Arthur Dunlop ducked back around the car. Karpis fired a precise group into a fence post. A strand of rusty barbed wire parted and dropped in the weeds.

There was a screech of brakes and Karpis spun around. A dusty pickup truck. Foreigner. Model T Ford, "Tulsa County Sheriff's Office" painted across a large star on the dented door. The cops. A fat constable leaned out the driver's window.

"What's goin' on, Kate?"

Ma's massive features settled in solemn hate.

"Jest a fambly picnic, Boyd, why? Is there a law aginst decent Godfearin' Christian famblys havin' a picnic?"

"OK, Kate. Jest askin'. Is that there Freddie or Dock?"

"Which one?"

"That boy right there."

"What ye wanta know fer? You got a warrant er somethin'?"

Ma ripped off the last of her chicken leg and threw the bone under his truck. "Why don't ye go bother the real criminals insteada houndin' my boys all the time? Fer instance, why don't ye go round up a few nigger *rapers* once in a while insteada houndin' these decent young boys?"

"Now, Kate, don't let's start in on that stuff. I only asked which one of the boys that was."

"You oughta know, Boyd. You ain't arrested him in almost a year, have ye?"

"I was jest curious, Kate."

"You're damn curious, Boyd."

"All I asked is who is that strange boy there."

"That's all you asked. He's a friend. And he's none o' your damn business. He's a fambly friend. Old friend from Aye-rorah."

"What ye got all them high power guns fer?"

19

"Huntin'. How else you s'pose we eat?"

The sheriff sighed. "All right, Kate, enjoy yourself. Hey, ye got a extry wing there? Bottle o' dope?"

Arthur Dunlop took a wing from the box, Ma grabbed his arm.

"Nope. Ain't got but bare enough fer jest us poor folks."

"OK, Kate . . ." He squinted his bloodshot blue eyes and sighed. "Well, see ye later."

"Yeah . . ." Ma watched the truck over the rise out of sight. "Feed that sowbelly cop! He's always pokin' around . . . writin' down license numbers. Gimme a piece o' bird. One with some juice on it."

"Sure, Kate," Arthur said.

Karpis lounged in the back seat, feet on the top of the door, chewing a greasy leg.

"Alvin Karpis, you handle a gun right well," Ma said.

Fred sneered and jammed six rimmed-cartridges into the cylinder and swung it back into place. He sprawled along a front fender, toes on the running board, revolver steadied against a headlight.

"It takes a worried man/ to sing a worried song," he crooned through his prow-like nose. "I'm worried now, but I won't be worried l-o-n-g."

"Purty, Fred, right purty," moaned Ma, snuffling chicken.

Ma wiped her fingers on her skirt. "This is the best ole picnic we had since the boys got *out*, Arthur."

"Sure is, Kate." Arthur gazed dolefully in the direction of Tulsa.

Four shots ripped out from in front of the car.

"Cheer up, Arthur. You bin skulkin' around here like a suck-egg mule."

"Oh I feel fine, Kate. I surely do."

There was a barrage of rapid fire and a peach can jittered across the road.

"Open me a dope."

"Comin' up, Kate."

"An' don't try openin' it with yore teeth, neither."

"You know I couldn't do that, Kate."

She laughed. "Gimme a kiss now."

Glancing at the boys, both reloading, Arthur complied.

"Lordy! That's a real barnburner! Save yer strength, Mister Dunlop, the pistol shootin' has made me restless."

Six new ones in place, Fred looked over the broken bottles and perforated cans. Suddenly he scrunched down behind the headlight.

"Hey, boy!"

A black eleven-year-old, attracted by the noise, stopped dead in his tracks. One knee was missing from his daddy's overalls, his bare feet were the color of the dust.

"Boy!"

"Yas suh?"

"C'mere, boy."

Ma grinned. That pickaninny was trembling comically.

The boy could actually feel the fear. It was the Man. A young one, but from the look of that gun, the Man, all right.

Fred smiled. This was his favorite moment from the picture show. The lone rider had cornered the bad guy. Jesse James and the nigger Yankee. The boy dragged slowly across the road.

The noise struck the boy like a flat board.

The noise was the loudest the boy had ever heard. Dirt spray from the road stung his bare ankles. A faint smear of blue smoke above the gun. The Man's crazy eyes were almost closed.

"Hold it there, boy."

Ma bounced happily on her chair. Arthur Dunlop loosened his cravat and steadied himself against the spare tire. He concentrated on his left shoe. Karpis watched lazily over the doortop from the rear seat.

Fred aimed the Colt at the sweatshiny black face.

"How quick are you, boy?"

The Man was starting to think. The boy's fright increased.

"I dunno."

"You dunno what?"

"I don't rightly know, suh." The fear was swelling inside him like a balloon.

"You just bet you don't know, boy."

The boy wet his overalls. Fred grinned with satisfaction.

"Boy, I bet you're real quick."

Fred aimed carefully with both hands on the revolver. His right forefinger slowly squeezed the trigger.

Ma smiled in a distracted way, her bulging brown eyes blinked rapidly. She clutched at her beads.

The gun went off with a deafening report. She jumped. Dirt spattered the overall legs.

"Move it, Sambo!" she yelled.

The boy turned and ran, bare feet scarcely touching the road, aware of the explosions and the pebbles and his heavy wet pants and the knowledge that he would be dead when one of those things went through his back and then he was past the hill and down in the brush at the creek.

Fred swung the empty cylinder free and blew through the barrel. "Coons are yellah. There's one won't bother no white gals."

Ma twisted the beads and wiped her palms.

"Freddie does have a temper. A spirited boy. Oh he made that rascal move. He made him move." Her heart was pounding, fine beads of sweat glistened on the pudgy nape of her neck.

In the back of the Ford, Karpis finished a wing, sucked a bad tooth and fingered his ear.

Ole Fred was mighty impressive.

Fred slammed one into the chamber.

"We got any more bottles?"

"That's all we got left, Fred, just that one." Arthur mopped his purpled forehead with his Oklahoma City silk handkerchief.

"Shoulda popped that ole Boogie," Fred said.

Ma sighed, stretching her fat arms.

"Let's go, Arthur. I'll help ye pick up all the leavings. I want ye to save yer strength fer later."

"Sure, Kate."

She stood up, yawning. "Them boys really fired them guns . . . they really cut loose."

•

Fred wanted badly to cut loose in the West Plains, Missouri department store, particularly when the lounge-lizard floor-walker screamed. But coolheaded, practical Alvin insisted on emptying the cash register instead and they hurried out through the paralyzed Christmas shoppers and the skinny Santa with the bell and Fred gunned the stolen Chevrolet down back alleys and out of town.

Ma was waiting, big brown eyes sparkling, chewing her lower lip with excitement.

"Put the money in the purse, Alvin, honey." She held the bag and the coins chunked among the crinkly paper and packs of fifty. Christmastime at a department store can bring true happiness, she was sure.

THE POOR IS HATED EVEN OF HIS OWN NEIGHBOR; BUT THE RICH HATH MANY FRIENDS.

"Jesse used a grain sack. I use this big ole purse. My lucky purse."

•

Two days later, a local sheriff following a routine tip on a minor robbery case spotted the boys in the Texas Star garage. They were strangers to him. He started toward them and the shorter of the two made a move for his leather jacket and for the sheriff a small alarm sounded. The punks wanted to argue.

"OK, boys, stand still and put your hands up!" he yelled, pawing at his gun.

The first shot struck him in the stomach with a sound like a batted ball. He felt himself going backward, sliding on the grease, the noise racketing off the galvanized iron walls seemed to lift him, and the second shot struck him in the chest, missing his badge (which he always knew would save his life some day) and the third shot struck him in the eye and his big flabby useless body went skidding into the galvanized iron wall and lay still.

The boys cut across the concrete floor, Alvin stuffing his unfired gun into his shirt, Freddie laughing at how easy it had been, sniffing powder, thinking he was short three cartridges, better reload as soon as possible.

The car started easily and Alvin turned the corner and headed north. A man stepped off the curb, mouth working soundlessly, pointing toward the garage.

"Backfire!" Alvin yelled, and away they went.

•

The 1930 Nash sedan stood in the yard next to the porch. A squarish, blocky machine, thick wooden-spoked wheels, spotlight on the driver's side, one white side-walled tire.

"Right classy," Arthur Dunlop said, stumbling under the weight of Ma's fattest suitcase, his handsome face perspiring, his sloping shoulders draped with Ma's souvenir wall pennants.

"Get that crap in the car and shut up," said Fred.

In the tiny wallpapered living room, Ma gathered the last of the Kewpie dolls and snapshots, the Manger of Bethlehem in the glass jar which snowed when you shook it up and she held an orange and blue souvenir postcard close to the light.

"The only time I was ever to Oklahoma City . . . Hotel Cherokee."

She put it with the others in the Farina box and smoothed a wrinkled photograph of a 1916 Oldsmobile roadster.

"The first automobile the boys ever took by themselves. I was proud . . . Herman was twenty-three, Fred was but sixteen, a little child."

Fred kicked the screen door open and he and Karpis struggled out onto the porch with Ma's cedar chest.

"That's what happens when ya leave fingerprints layin' around. The cops are lookin' fer ye," Fred said.

"*Me* leave fingerprints! Hell, you shot the guy."

"You left the prints, Alvin, an' they're lookin' fer you."

"Let 'em look."

Ma waddled out carrying her hand-colored print of The Young Jesus and an Oklahoma City Kewpie doll, an enameled baby wearing sixgun holsters and a plaster sombrero. Ma wore her traveling costume; orange hair, green hair ribbon, low-waisted blue middie-jumper with orange scarf, purple pleated skirt and new tennis shoes.

24

She smiled girlishly at Karpis, watching the muscles leap in his thin arms as he and Fred stowed the heavy chest.

"Alvin, you're too valuable to mess around with these two-bit coppers. I got plans fer ye. We're goin' to St. Paul."

Fred was back out with two automatic rifles.

"Come on, Arthur, shake it up!"

Arthur struggled across the porch with a 4-ton suitcase.

"I don't see why we're all the time movin'. We just got nicely settled down," he mumbled.

"None o' yore beezwax," said Fred.

"Yeah, but how come we're movin'?"

"Look, dummy, somebody told Ma they found a fingerprint in the garage. They're lookin' fer Alvin Karpis, so we're gonna take a vacation."

"Who told ye they found a fingerprint?"

"None o' yer business Arthur," Ma said. "Jest stow them suitcases and let's go to travelin'."

"Ole Arthur, he's a nosey one, ain't he?" Fred said.

Karpis laughed.

"Now, boys . . ." Arthur said, folding his Texas Buckaroo Men's Shoppe pearl gray suitcoat and placing it over the seat where Fred couldn't get at it. He looked out the window at the weedy yard, the frame bungalow. Goodbye to Tulsa.

Fred drove, Ma settled herself with a cold leg of chicken in the front seat, Karpis in the back with Arthur Dunlop who, worried about his piles, sat sideways across a suitcase and Ma's Victrola.

"Watch out fer them records," Ma said.

Arthur nodded.

They passed Bartlesville and headed up Route 75 for Topeka.

"Flatten'n a nun's tit," said Karpis, staring out the window at the countryside.

"You wanta stop off in Kay Cee and say hello to yer folks?" Freddie said, grinning.

"Hell no," Karpis said.

Arthur Dunlop stirred.

"Why not?" he said.

"Did somebody ask you?" Karpis said.

"No. No sir. Nobody did." Arthur leaned back against Ma's hatbox.

They sang three verses of "Keep On The Sunny Side" as they drove north, Fred socking the wheel with the side of his hand. Karpis kept time by waving the Colt .45.

"Watch that pistol, please," Arthur said.

"Huh?"

"You pointed it right at me."

"No shit?"

Ma patted Freddie's tattooed arm.

"Fred, you swiped a right good one this time. I do enjoy a sumptuous automobile."

As they rumbled across the Verdigris River bridge outside Neodesha, Kansas, Arthur loosened his collar.

"Could you go a little slower, Fred? I do believe I'm becomin' carsick."

Fred ignored him.

"I coulda got a better car but I didn't have time," he said to Ma. "I wanted to pick up a Ford. They're faster'n grease lightnin' on a pave road."

"This one is a real jimdandy, Freddie boy," Ma said.

Fred watched the farmlands sliding past, the occasional crossroads store.

"We might just stop off an' nail a gas station or two."

"Not around here," Ma said. "These blockheads ain't got any money worth takin'. Wait'll we git north. That's where the fat ones live. More than enough gold to go around. Keep yore eye on the road, Freddie."

"I ain't hit a dog all morning."

"Fred, you do an' I'll bust yore head, so I will."

"Lemme jest clip th' ole lame ones, Ma."

" 'A *righteous* man *regardeth* the life of his beast; but the tender mercies of the *wicked* are *cruel.*' Chapter twelve, number ten."

"It ain't my beast, Ma. Why do I have to regard his life anyhow?"

26

"Save yore fire fer people, Fred. They're the ones that deserve it. They can do ye ten times more harm in five minutes than any animal can in ten years."

The overloaded Nash sped north across Kansas, heading through the long afternoon shadows for the Nebraska line. Ma slept, her jaw slack, lipsticked mouth open, hands folded on her lap. Fred kept his bloodshot gray eyes fixed on the long straight unending road, habitual anger fighting headache in a war of attrition inside his narrow skull.

In the back seat, Arthur Dunlop stirred uneasily. Karpis was staring at him again.

•

Harry Sawyer, the Man to See in St. Paul, looked across his desk at Ma and laid down a thick screen of cigar smoke, his tested tactic for disarming a new customer. Harry had been around the rackets for years. He had come up the hard way. His predecessor had his legs blown off when he started his car.

"This is what we call the St. Paul system," he said in his deep irritating voice. "You come to town, check in with me, I get you a place to stay, you don't cause any trouble, I see the coppers don't bother you."

Ma blinked at him stolidly through the smoke.

"It's a nice rest, just so you behave yourselves," Sawyer said. "I got people in the police department let me know what's goin' on, just so long as my clients don't raise any hell while they're in town. You keep your nose clean, they leave you alone, fair enough? That way, in St. Paul we got no crime problem at all, and for you, it's a nice quiet place to visit."

"Yeah," Ma said. She glanced around the office at the framed affectionately inscribed photographs of civic leaders, cloche-hatted chorus beauties arm in arm with Harry Sawyer, Chief of Police shaking hands with his real pal, Harry, *Country Club names membership chairman, H. Sawyer*, Harry Sawyer at Police Lt. testimonial dinner.

She glanced at Sawyer. What race is Sawyer? He doesn't look American. A poor woman alone, chased by her oppressors can't be too choosy. A dear friend back in Joplin had told Ma about

27

northerners and how they often changed their real names to American names so no one would know they were foreigners. A gentlewoman herself, Ma was heartsick at such an idea. But a poor woman alone, chased by her oppressors can't be choosy.

Harry studied her, fingering his broad flat nose, tugging on the waxy cartilage of his left ear. What part in any mob could this fat old broad play? These hayseeds. The refugees from Tulsa were getting more improbable every time. Gypsies. Dressed like a fortune-teller. She looked like she might be part-Indian.

"Okay," Ma said. "We need a place to live. Somethin' quiet."

Harry Sawyer stood up. He took a slip of paper from under his telephone, folded and handed it to Ma.

"I got ya a nice spot in a rooming house. 1836 North Imbert Street. Ya can come an' go pretty much as ya please."

Ma grunted.

The mud-spattered Nash waited in the alley back of Harry Sawyer's "Green Lantern" bar and grill. Ma woke up Freddie and read him the address.

"We got a place, now we can get to work," she said.

"Where are we?" Arthur Dunlop groaned.

"Shut up," said Fred.

•

Wearing caps and newly stolen sheepskin jackets, Fred, carrying the secondhand violin case, and Karpis a paper bag with a .38 in it, tiptoed down the carpeted hall toward the glass oval front door. From the shadows back of the stairs, Mrs. Reinhardt watched them. New roomers and odd ones. Had to have a phone in the room. In a depression you take in all kinds.

She moved out into the hall.

"Mornin', boys."

"Howdy, mam," Karpis said.

"Goin' for your lesson early today."

She glanced at the battered case.

"Huh?" Fred said. "Oh yeah. Yeah that's right."

"Violin? My husband played the violin."

"Yeah. The violin."

"Don't the cold affect the wood?"

"Nah," Fred said. "When I play this baby, it warms right up."
He nudged Karpis who laughed.

The door slam shook the frame house.

Mrs. Reinhardt stared after them.

"I wish they'd be more careful o' that door."

Her son, Mike, chewed his Wheaties and swallowed hard.

"What's all the racket, Mom?"

"It's the Blackburn boys from ID. They stamp around all hours o' the day and night."

She closed the heavy kitchen door carefully, sighed as she sat down and dipped her toast into her cold coffee.

"You know something, Mike? I don't believe that boy plays any violin at all."

Mike leaned his head low over the oil cloth, reading the Wheaties box. His mother insisted.

"That boy don't look musical."

"Huh? Yeah. He's double ugly all right. Hunchback o' Notre Dame."

He spooned a soggy mound of Wheaties and chewed solemnly. His mother narrowed her eyes.

"You know, Edward G. Robinson, carried a violin case in the movie, and it wasn't a violin at all, it was a machine gun."

"Paul Muni, Mom. You mean 'Scarface.' That's Paul Muni."

"Well, whichever. I bet those boys are *gangsters*."

"I bet they *are*, Mom. Goin' out right now to take some rat stool pigeon for a ride and *bump him off!* Ratatat-tat-tat!"

"Well, it's not funny."

He wiped his lips on the dish cloth.

"Gotta get goin', Ma, I'm late."

He pulled on his leather jacket and padded cap, earmuffs down against the April weather.

"Pick up a mag on the way home, Mike, the radio's busted."

•

Ma recognized the picture, read WANTED FOR MURDER in loud black letters and she was frightened. At the same time she was proud. Freddie, her own little boy.

The posters were similar. The boring inventory. Alvin Karpis

#7071, received State Industrial Reformatory, Hutchinson, Kansas, Feb. 25, 1926, Crime, burglary 2nd degree, sentence 10 yrs., escaped Mar. 9, 1929, returned March 25, 1930. As Raymond Hadley #17902, arrested Police Dept. Kansas City, Mar. 23, 1930, larceny-auto, release to Reformatory, Alvin Karpis #1539, State Pen., Lansing, Kans., as George Haller, #8008, arrested Tulsa, delivered Police Dept. Okmulgee, A. Karpis #1609, arrested June 10, sentenced 4 yrs. State Pen., paroled.

Stuff nobody but cops cared about, why plaster it all over the walls in a public place?

Crucifying a young boy. Wrecking his whole life with shameful persecution. Still, she thought, nothing on his sheet as good as Dock or Freddie, larceny-auto, 1918, for instance, murder night watchman for another, or, Lloyd, robbery U.S. Mails. My boy Lloyd hit the Federals.

Ma hurried out of the post office.

The damn bastards were sending these printed sheets all over the country! She blinked back the tears. Now, by the Lord Jesus, it was murder. Little Freddie. For one fat old sheriff.

She trotted across the street and caught a cab.

•

She slammed the bedroom door behind her and tossed her coat on the bed.

"You know what they got plastered up in the post office? Big as life? Pictures! Great big pictures and rewards. $5000 each."

Fred poured himself more coffee.

"Just for killin' that jerky old sheriff?"

Ma was livid. "Why do they keep *houndin'* you boys? Why can't they let bygones be bygones?"

"Alvin, we're famous."

Karpis yawned. "Yeah. Ain't that some riot?"

Ma gnawed on a doughnut. "They *never* let up. Make your life a livin' hell. These're sorry doughnuts, no grease."

"Ma, we'll go on down tomorra an' swipe a pair o' them posters fer the sittin' room," Fred said.

Ma stared out the window at the wintry street, chewing vigorously.

"They got some nerve. They never *proved* anything about that sheriff *anyhow*."

"Which picture did they use?"

"That old one from the Kansas Pen." She took the last doughnut. "It's not a good picture at all."

Good gray Arthur V. Dunlop appeared and Ma's voice lowered.

"I'll tell you about it later."

"Howdy Kate, howdy boys." Arthur set a bag of groceries on the dresser.

"Hel-lo, Mister Dunlop!" Ma said. "Where you *been?*"

•

Mike Reinhardt flipped the new detective magazine open to a green halftone picture layout, dotted line across garage floor to Maltese cross marking the spot, a title that shouted for vengeance, an artist's representation of a prehistoric mad dog turned dragon with a particularly foamy case of hydrophobia. Large official government portraits of two young men, numbered and everything.

"Lookit this, Mom!" Mike said. The landlady put on her glasses.

> Mad-Dog Fiends Are On The Loose. YOUR OWN LIFE IS AT STAKE. *WAKE UP, AMERICA!* Fred Barker and Alvin Karpis are here in rotogravure.

"Ohhhh." She closed the door, a dead look on her face.

"It's them. It's them. Ohhhh . . ."

"Mom . . ."

"They're right here in the house! They killed a man and they're livin' right here in my house! I *told* you they were gangsters!"

She fumbled for her handkerchief and Asefetida tablets. She shook her head.

Mike started for the door. "I'll call the cops."

"No! Wait!" She choked, took a breath and whispered. "We better wait. Wait 'til tonight! I'll go next door and call the police. That way they can catch 'em asleep."

Mike locked the door and slid the bolt.

"When they're asleep," she whispered. ". . . Otherwise, they'll kill ya. They'll kill us both. I knew it. I knew it when I *looked* at 'em. They killed a sheriff, they'll kill us."

She sat down, her eyes wide. She hugged herself and rocked back and forth.

"We'll wait 'til the middle of the night and call the police to come get 'em."

"Mom . . ."

"Don't make a sound."

•

When the clock said two, she called the police.

"It's Alvin Karpis and Fred Barker, wanted for murder."

The cop listened and called another number immediately.

"Alvin Karpis and Fred Barker, wanted for murder."

Harry Sawyer in his pajamas, sat on the edge of his bed, picked up a stale cigar and called Ma Barker on the phone in her room.

"Karpis and Fred Barker wanted for murder."

Ma, with her orange bathrobe tight around her barrel belly, scratched her ear.

"Who says so? What ye *talkin'* about?"

"The police got a tip from a guy that your boys are in town," Sawyer said. "Some punk is hungry for the reward money. Ten grand is a lot of dough."

"Who was it tipped 'em off?" Ma said wearily.

Her gaze rested on the framed picture of Jesse James beside the Tulsa Kewpie.

Ole Jesse found he couldn't trust even his closest friends. He took Ed Miller out an' shot him. Then Dick Liddill played ole Jesse false, had to shoot him too. Traitors, foulin' the nest . . . that dirty little coward/ I wonder how does he feel/ For he ate of Jesse's bread an' he slept in Jesse's bed/ Then he laid poor Jesse in his grave. . . .

Arthur V. Dunlop stood in the Oklahoma City sunshine with his arm around Kate Barker and the photographer snapped the picture. Sweethearts.

"I dunno," Sawyer droned on. "Somebody called up on the phone. The call came from your part of town."

Ma blinked her moist brown eyes and licked her thin lips.

He ate of Jesse's bread an' he slept in Jesse's bed/ Then he laid poor Jesse in his grave. . . .

•

By 4 A.M., the Nash sedan was packed. Ma looked around the room, slung her possum fur around her blocky shoulders and snatched up her lucky purse.

"Let's go, boys," she said.

Arthur Dunlop took a last sip of coffee from the fresh pot on the burner as they moved out.

"Leave the cup," Fred said. "That's stealin'."

"Always movin'," Arthur said. "Movin' out in the middle of the darn night."

"Come on Arthur, stop swilling that slop. It's bad fer yer nerves."

"Might's well take the crullers. I bought 'em fresh." He hugged the package under his arm. "I oughta comb my hair."

"Let's go, Mister Dunlop," Ma said. "Quit stallin' around."

The Nash hit a country road and bounced along over the ruts in the dark. The suitcase on the roof bucked and pulled at the clothesline holding it fast. Arthur Dunlop hung on to the strap at his rear window.

"Arthur, ya look worried," Karpis said from the front seat.

"Worried lookin' man," Ma said, close beside Arthur.

"He's got the worried man blues . . ." Fred said and laughed.

He sang the verse.

It takes a worried man/ to sing a worried song.

Ma joined in from the back seat.

It takes a worried man/ to sing a worried song.

Mother, Fred and Karpis sang together, laughing as they went.

It takes a worried man/ to sing a worried song.

He's worried now/ but he won't be worried long.

Arthur grinned feebly, staring out at the dark trees flashing past his window.

33

"Come on, ole man," Ma yelled. "Join in!"

Arthur managed a sick smile and took up the chorus. *He's worried now/ but he won't be worried long!*

He did have an excellent voice, diminished now by fatigue and rising fear. Ma cuddled up to Arthur Dunlop and slid a thick arm around his neck.

"Careful of my suit," he said.

"Sure, honey," Ma said. She playfully poked his cheek with her stubby finger.

"You know, Arthur, it's awful fer a person to become greedy."

He nodded half-heartedly.

"Too bad, Arthur. Too bad." She planted a kiss on his cheek and grinned at him.

"You were a good ole boy," she said.

Ma opened the fresh crullers with her free hand, jammed one into her mouth and chomped it around.

"Would ye like a cruller?" she said to Arthur's face.

"I don't believe so, thanks."

She fumbled one from the package. "Have a cruller."

"I really ain't very hungry, I guess."

"Have a bite."

She held it against his mouth.

"Go on," she said.

He managad a small bite, chewed slowly and laboriously.

"Swallow," she said.

He tried.

"Kate," he said. "I cain't swaller. I don't feel real well at all." There were tears in his eyes.

"How come?" Ma said. "How come ye don't feel well?"

"Maybe I ain't been gettin' enough rest."

"Well, maybe we can fix that, Mr. Dunlop."

They coasted down a smooth grassy slope and Freddie yanked the Nash to a stop. He killed the engine. They sat in silence. Gasoline whomped around in the tank. Silence.

Ma moved first. She opened the door for Arthur and stood waiting.

"Come on, worried man. You're worried now, but ye won't be worried long."

"What? What we doin'?" He stumbled out onto wet grass. A chill breeze was blowing off the lake. It was almost May, the seasons were changing. He would never get used to the north.

They marched from the car down to the shore, Ma in the lead, a soft dreamy smile of fulfillment on her pudgy face.

I ALSO WILL LAUGH AT YOUR CALAMITY; I WILL MOCK WHEN YOUR FEAR COMETH; WHEN YOUR FEAR COMETH AS DESOLATION, AND YOUR DESTRUCTION COMETH AS A WHIRLWIND; WHEN DISTRESS AND ANGUISH COMETH UPON YOU.

"Welcome to Lake Freasted," Freddie said.

"Where's that?" Arthur said.

"You know what?" Ma said. "It's right chilly out here." The crullers were stuffed into her sweater pocket.

At the water's edge, they stopped and then old Arthur turned to run and Fred had him by the arm. The boy was unbelievably strong. Arthur was sweating, his dobby cotton broadcloth shirt would be a mess. Woven color stripes, ocean pearl buttons.

Like a grizzly in her heavy sweater, Ma stood facing him, a foot away, one cheek bulging with cruller.

"Now *wait* a minute, Ma!" he yelled. "You're *kiddin'* me, aincha? Yer jest *foolin'*, Kate . . . Katie?"

Ma, chewing and swallowing, watched him, her eyes focused somewhere beyond his head.

"I'll show ya how much I'm foolin'."

She was very quiet. Karpis watched, wishing Arthur Dunlop would stop yelling. Arthur nearly fell.

"Kate, yer *wrong!* You're makin' a big mistake! Gimme a chance, fer the Christ sake!"

Ma shook her head, smiling faintly. A fresh cruller.

"Nossir, Mister Dunlop, my mind's made up. Once my mind's made up, I can't back down, can I? What kind of example would that be fer the boys? I gotta be a good mother, don't I?"

"Kate! What ye *doin'* this *for?*"

"Mister Dunlop, you went and told the *po*-lice on us fer a miserable ten thousand dollars."

"Kate." Arthur held out his hands. The shirtstuds glittered. "Wait a minute. Wait a darn minute, Kate. Them *boys* made this up!"

"Don't you dare say anything against my boys!"

"Kate, yer *wrong!*"

She ripped off a bite and chewed. "Yer goin' fer a swim, Mr. Dunlop. Git them clo's off."

Fred scuffed his shoe nervously, his arm quivered. Karpis took out his gun. He supposed he would be called on.

"Kate," Arthur yelled. "I never said a word to anybody!"

"Yes you did too."

"I never *told* no cops." Arthur sounded tired. "I never told *nobody*. Kate! Why would I do a thing like *that?*"

"Mr. Dunlop. I'm not gonna argue with ye." She daintily wiped her fingers on her sweater.

Fred clicked off the safety on his gun. Karpis did the same with his.

"Kate! You got things all wrong!" Arthur yelled.

"You told the cops on my boys."

"No. I never neither! Why would I do a dumb thing like *that?*"

"Because yer a dumb nogood miserable lowdown stool pigeon. Because you were gonna take all that money and run off somewheres with it. Who with, Mister Dunlop? Did ye have somebody all picked out?"

Fred raised his gun.

"Kate, you're plumb crazy!" Arthur yelled.

"All right, Mister Dunlop. I won't argue with ye."

Freddie shouldered Karpis aside and crashed two bullets into Arthur Dunlop at a range of inches and Ma blinked and grinned and a deafening third shot cracked through Arthur's handsome head as he fell over backward and two more shots tore into the dark lake beyond and Arthur fell full length in a foot of water with a solid thunking splash and a soft gurgling left thick bubbles and little patches of foam bobbing on the ripples.

36

"Git the clothes off him, boys," Ma said in a tight voice. "It'll take these rubes longer to figger out who the weasel *was*."

". . . The coppers git a look at Arthur with no clothes on, they won't *want* to know who he was," Fred said.

The last cruller disappeared into her wet mouth. ". . . Put holes in at ole boy the size of goose-eggs."

"His ole eyes was as big as foxgrapes," Fred said.

"Damn if they wasn't," Ma said.

"Did you see his shirt on fire before he fell down?" Fred said.

Karpis stared at the water. His heart was still pounding.

"Ole Ma is a hard one, ain't she, Alvin?"

"Yeah. She is."

"Oh, he jumped," Fred said. "He jumped three feet!"

Karpis nodded.

Fred sloshed out into the water, chuckling. Ma walked lightly back to the car as the boys took the last of the clothing from Arthur's slippery corpse.

•

Fred stood out in the water, ankle deep, motionless, arms close at his side, his bony head bowed.

"What ya doin', prayin'?" Karpis said.

"Huh? What? Prayin'? I'm takin' a piss," Freddie said. "*Prayin'* . . ."

He finished and they trudged up the slope dragging the soggy bloodsmelly store-bought clothes of A. V. Dunlop, ladies' man.

"The most important thing in life is to get even," Ma said. "That's the most important thing in life." She felt light-headed and pleasantly dizzy.

She threw a heavy arm around Freddie's thin shoulders as he slid in behind the wheel. He fumbled for the ignition key and Ma was unable to keep her hands off him.

"Freddie, you was jest bewdiful! I could really jest love you up fer that!"

"Hell's fire, Ma, it was a pleasure."

"Fred, you was jest wonderful the way you faced right up to that lowdown bastard an' let him have it . . ."

37

Freddie giggled.

"My own little boy," Ma crooned. "Lemme give you a great big ole hug and a kiss . . ."

Alvin Karpis sat alone now in the back seat as Fred started the car. Ole Ma sure was a loving mother.

•

The police pulled up in front of 1836 North Imbert Street back in St. Paul and the officers surrounded the boarding house.

> THEN SHALL THEY CALL UPON ME, BUT I WILL NOT AN-
> SWER; THEY SHALL SEEK ME EARLY, BUT THEY SHALL
> NOT FIND ME.

One hundred miles away, Ma bounced along in the front seat of the speeding Nash, watching the cold pink sun rising beyond the sliding row of dark bare trees off to the left. A cloudless day and they were headed back south. There was no singing this time. The night had been a long one.

At 7 A.M., they went through Osseo, Wisconsin. "What a dumb name," Ma said. Abandoned gas stations in the shivery dawn.

They raced past the Burma Shave signs, no use reading them damn things, they make no sense, past Chamber of Commerce billboards: KEEP MOVING, THIS MEANS YOU, WE CAN'T TAKE CARE OF OUR OWN. 1932 was a tough year. For rent signs and boarded windows.

A man in overalls stood on a frosted rise in a meadow and watched as they passed.

Sometime during the morning, they would cross the Mississippi below La Crosse, over into Iowa, heading for Kansas City. Sawyer had given Ma a number to call. For a fee.

Karpis took the wheel from Fred who crawled into the back and fell asleep.

"Poor thing, he works so hard," Ma said.

They raced through green rolling farmland, cows moving across the misty fields. Below Guttenberg, Iowa, Alvin drove the Nash down into a wild stretch of trees and brush on the west bank of the river where he and Fred washed off most of the mud from Wisconsin. The splattered, encrusted sedan was noticeable even among pickup trucks and farmers' Fords. Best not to look like travelers. Just in case the state cops had telephones. With Arthur gone, the suitcase from the roof and the boxes from the running boards could be moved inside the car. A set of Iowa license plates might help. For now, Fred rubbed a handful of mud over the old ones from Missouri.

The bloody rags from fashion plate Dunlop were drowned in the Mississippi. Oklahoma City's finest department store. Arthur had insisted on high cushion shoulders, crescent shaped pockets, pleated trousers with back buckle-strap.

A quiet splash, ripples and slathers of brown water washed the sodden mess down out of sight.

"That's a right ugly lookin' stream," Ma said, scratching her massive belly. She shook out the paper bags. No more doughnuts.

Fred fell into the back and Karpis drove.

"Can't be sorry to leave St. Paul," Ma mumbled. "That boardin' house mattress lay there like a bag o' walnut shells."

"Yeah," Karpis said, watching the long straight highway, telephone poles rushing past.

Ma smiled.

"Back in Aye-roarah now, I had me a right nice quilt . . . Star of Texas, Irish-chain, saw-teeth, sunflower, shell, nine-diamond and checkerboard! . . . fit fer a king . . ."

Karpis was sure he could still smell gunpowder from the night's shooting.

•

Back on the shore of Freasted Lake, Wisconsin State Police found a woman's glove. In the shallows, the body of Arthur V. Dunlop floated face down. The hair fanned out. The officers noted that whoever he was, he was getting a little bald.

•

The Florida predawn fog is still as thick as ever. Under the shadowy palms, the FBI, submachine guns and rifles ready, in company with the armed men from the local sheriff's office, moves slowly along in the predawn gloom searching for the house where the Barker gang is holed up. They stop a local Negro on the sandy beach road.

"... middle-aged woman, her two sons. They haven't been in Florida long, they're renting a house on the lake, they have a motorboat."

The Negro nods his head vigorously.

"Sure. Mrs. Blackburn. Her son lives with her."

The other agents crowd around. A sheriff rests his shotgun on his hip.

"Blackburn. What's her son's name?"

"His name's Fred. Fred Blackburn."

"Anybody else?"

"Yeah, there's lotsa people lately. There's a feller named George Haller. Fred calls him Al, tho. Alvin."

"Alvin and Fred. Do you know the people?"

"Sure. I work for 'em. I'm the cook."

"You're the cook, huh?"

"Yes sir. I'm the best cook in Marion County. Mrs. Blackburn don't like to cook. I rake leaves, I drive the car for 'em. I'm the chief cook and bottlewasher you might say."

"Yeah, yeah, yeah, which one is their house?"

"I'm goin' there now. I'm a little bit late as it is."

With a rattle of bolts, the sheriff's men load their rifles. Lafferty motions to his men.

"Come on Charlie. It looks like we found 'em. OK, boy, you show us the house."

•

The new house in sunny Kansas City needed a marker, a souvenir. For luck.

With Ma directing, Fred at the wheel and Karpis sprawled in the back seat, the travelers drove in their newly acquired 1930 wire-wheeled Hudson (the owner, an Ottumwa doctor, objected and Alvin hit him with his fist and competitive Fred slugged him with the .45. "That's the way you do that, boy") to Union Station, Kay Cee Mo, where Ma knew the best souvenirs were available.

In a rack of multi-colored pennants, Kewpies, ashtrays and pillows stood the button-eyed teddy bear, KANSAS CITY lettered across his round belly.

"Kan-sas City!" Ma said. She snapped her thick finger against the furry navel. "I'll take this one." Got a gut on him like Arthur himself.

The clerk, green eye-shade and steel-brimmed glasses, smiled at his first sale in two days. "Ya wanta eat it here or shall I wrap it up?"

Another smart aleck.

"Boy, you're too goddam funny to go on livin'," Ma said quietly.

The clerk reached for yesterday's *Star* to gift-wrap the bear. "Sorry, mam, jest a little Kansas City pleasantry."

"Well, you keep all yore pleasant little ideas to your own self, Jasper," Ma said. "Or I'll turn the boys loose on ye."

Fred and Alvin gave the clerk their best midmorning hard-eyed look.

"Well, sure, mam," he said. "I never meant no . . ."

"Shut up," Ma said.

•

Holding her teddy bear, Ma was gracious to the realtor.

"Country Club Plaza distric'," she said sweetly. "My idea is to rent a nice place in a high tone neighborhood."

"Splendid," the realtor said. "I know what you mean."

Cute gray hair, Ma thought. Just like whatsisname.

•

The apartment (wall bed behind glass doors, stucco Spanish walls, imitation-candle wall lights with orange flame-bulbs) was the best yet.

"The cops never look twice at ye if you're in the right part of town," Ma said.

Fred grunted, dragging the 4-ton suitcase into the bedroom.

The teddy bear joined the Tulsa Kewpie, Jesse James and the young Jesus on the simulated timbered mantelpiece over the gas burner (plaster logs) in the mission-archway fireplace.

"Right nice," Ma said, patting the bear. "Right nice. Big fat belly like Arthur V. Dunlop."

41

She fell into the big chair by the Florentine end-table.

"Alvin, you're now my son. You boys are in the *in*-surance business. You move around a lot."

Karpis grinned, standing the automatic rifle in the corner.

"Sure, Ma."

Fred stumbled through with the washtub loaded with clothing and .45 caliber ammunition.

"Clean the auto-rifle, Fred. The barl is clogged up with dust balls bigger'n dogs."

He dropped the tub with a crash. There was an instant knock from the tenant below.

"Sure, Ma."

"I gotta think about a good job. A payday."

She opened the bag of cream puffs and bit into the first one.

"You know, this is right nice! All new furniture! Two red chairs and a nice green lounge! Oh it'll be grand. We'll get a livin' room set . . . a davenport . . . a settee . . . a chase . . ."

Fred, on his hands and knees, rummaged through the cedar chest for the rifle rod. "Ma, maybe we oughta forget about banks and just hit furniture stores," he said.

"Yore jest funnin', aincha boy?"

"Yes mam. Jest a joke."

He took the automatic rifle from the corner and sat down, the weapon across his lap.

"Run the rod down that barl an' lemme see it. Disgrace lettin' a high-class gun dirty up that way."

●

Ma and Arthur V. Dunlop stood together in the bright sun at Oklahoma City. The snapshot was turning brown. Ma took aim with her sewing shears and lopped Arthur off the left side.

"I never did have much luck with fellas."

She slipped the altered version into the dressing-table mirror. A woman alone.

"That's a right attractive pho-toe."

●

Alvin Karpis sat in the tub of soapy water, lathering his skinny arms, scraping away the grime of the past three days.

"Pureefied in the blood of the lamb! Alvin Karpis, ain't you the *clean* one, always soapin' up an' bathin' away."

Ma stood filling the doorway, thick arm resting against the jamb, grinning like a fat old cat.

"That's right, Ma, a bath ever' two weeks."

"I'll soap yer back fer ye."

"You don't have to," Karpis blushed. The Barkers were a funny bunch, all right.

"I always do fer Freddie." Ma was at the side of the tub. He couldn't very well get up and run.

"Yeah . . ." He thrashed around in the suds. "Hell."

"Whatsamatter?"

"I dropped the soap."

"I'll find it." She leaned over him, sleeve rolled up her fat arm.

"I'll find it, Kate." Their hands collided underwater. Her body had a faint sweet smell. She felt around.

"It's right here somewheres," she sighed.

"That ain't it, Kate."

"I *know that*, Alvin."

She giggled.

"Ma, yer a caution." She truly was.

Her heavy face was close to his. "Alvin, you know somethin'? You're a right handsome young boy. You know that?"

•

Karpis stood at the mirror in his BVDs, combing his wet brown hair. Fred appeared at the door.

"Goin' out to a picture show. You comin'?"

"Naw, I just took a bath. I'm gonna hang around."

Fred turned away. "Ma?"

"No Freddie, I'm tired. Too much travelin'. I'm goin' to bed early."

"OK, Ma. See ya later."

He crossed the living room.

"Don't come home too late, Freddie."

"OK, Ma."

"When ya come in, knock first, huh? It might be the cops."

"Oh sure, Ma. Like this . . ." He rapped the shave-and-a-haircut-two-bits.

"That'll do fine, Freddie."

She took the cap off her lipstick.

•

The "breakfast nook" was so small that Karpis sat in the hall, his plate balanced on his knee while Fred sat at the stove and Ma, determined to live graciously, wedged herself in against the wall, the built-in board threatening to cut her in half. She wore her Ruth Chatterton negligee trimmed with imitation ostrich and her marcelled orange hair in a blinding green ribbon. Her square, pudgy feet were bare. "Mules" were for northern women.

"Ma, these pancakes are crappy," Fred said.

"Jest eat 'em and chew 'em good. They'll go down ef ye try."

"We shouldn'ta shot Arthur."

"Now that ain't a nice thing to say," Ma said.

Karpis chewed the black charred discs in silence. Black lace pancakes, black lace underwear. Last night had been the nuttiest thing he'd ever been through. Ma Barker was not like anyone he'd ever even heard of. Sometimes she seemed eighty years old and then she'd get going on some crazy idea of her own and you'd swear she was more like sixteen. Well, thirty-five. He shook his head.

"Any more, Alvin?" Ma said.

"No thanks." He glanced up.

She looked at him dispassionately and waddled back to the kitchen.

No thanks, ma, no more.

"Boys, we had enough hittin' stores and such. We need money."

"Goddam right," Freddie said.

"It jest breaks my pore mother's heart to think of dear brother Dock rottin' away down there in the pen while we mess with penny ante jobs."

Fred laid out the auto rifle and the two Colts, ripping a surplus Dunlop shirt for oil rags.

44

"The God's truth is it's gonna take some real dough to spring him."

Freddie stroked oil along the wooden stock.

"There's gonna have to be some sizeable payments made to git him back."

Freddie spilled oil down the chamber, rubbing furiously with the shirt rag.

"Sawyer is lendin' us some new men and we're goin' where the money is at. We're gonna touch up a bank er two."

"About fuckin' time," Freddie said.

"You stop that there, er I'll wash out yore mouth with this here soap," Ma said, cracking a dish against the sink.

"Sure, Ma," Freddie said, sighting along the barrel. "Pow."

•

The next day Ma was gone. At noon, Karpis wandered into the kitchen dragging on a cigarette. Fred sat in his underwear in the breakfast nook, eating layer cake.

"Ma is window shoppin'," he said.

"Huh?"

"She goes out to a likely town, walks around lookin' at banks, readin' the cash assets on the windows. She's a real good jug-marker."

"How about these new guys?"

"They're on the way. They're some St. Paul peckerheads Sawyer's got sittin' around doin' nothin'."

"What do we need with 'em?"

Fred flashed his older-boy, troop-leader sneer, enhanced with chocolate frosting.

"Alvin, we need extra help on a bank job. You're not hittin' ten cent stores no more, boy. This here's the big time."

•

The Sawyer reinforcements, four free-lance professionals with bank experience, trooped into the Kansas City living room.

Ma bobbled a cigarette in her teeth and grunted hello.

An unimpressive quartet, even for Sawyer.

Wilding, a redhaired man in his forties who spent his time

yawning and nibbling his fingertips, a nameless young leather-jacketed acne case, Racetrack Bobby Hatton the driver, and one Harold Beesemeyer.

The usual batch of lopsided faces seen on post office walls.

"I thought we was gettin' Harvey Bailey," Ma said.

"He's too high price," Wilding said, yawning. "He's around town but he don't work on small stuff."

Ma bit her tongue.

As they pulled chairs up to Ma's new mahogany table, Beesemeyer, a thick-necked young man with a dented nose, snatched Ma's Kansas City teddy bear off the mantel and began a vaudeville bear-with-a-small-pecker routine. Freddie, the Grip of Steel, took him by the left bicep and the milky look in Freddie's feral eyes told Harold he would do better to keep his hands in his pockets.

Beesemeyer subdued, the work at hand proceeded. Ma made sense to the pros and well-planned jobs were hard to find in 1932.

Alvin spread the leaves on the expandable table and Ma unfolded the gas station maps and opened a school composition notebook. *My trip to the country*, by Ma Barker, age fifty-three.

"I got a good one," she said. "A nice fat bank. Fort Scott, Kansas. The county seat banks are where the money is. I walked in an' told the saps I wanta open up a savings account."

"Jesus, that's a hot one," Harold said. Wilding yawned.

"I looked around fer the vault," Ma said, her pencil skimming over the paper as the floor-plan took shape. "They don't have but one, right there in plain sight."

The men leaned closer.

"It looks to be a good one, though," Ma squinted, puffing a fresh cigarette. "Right good country-style bank."

"How about the roads, Ma?" Fred said.

"Ole Jesse would always pick a town with at least five exits and nice straight roads leading to the state line. That's so the dumb cops can't follow ye across."

Karpis smoothed the gas station map and located Fort Scott.

46

Wilding lit a cigar as Harold Beesemeyer watched over his shoulder.

"Fort Scott, Kansas," Ma said. "One mile from the Missoura line. The best road is Route 54, north and south there's Route 69 ("Sixty-nine," said clever Harold Beesemeyer), straight as an arrah. You could go up to Hammond and cut over, or you could take it south and cut over to Garland just across the line. Best idea, plan on usin' 54 east, that's Wall Street, and git right outa there and cross the state line. Once yer safe over the line, take 71 north and yer home. If the little boys in blue come pokin' around, you were at home all the time."

Ma grinned and puffed her cigarette.

"I *know* you was because I was right here all the time."

Cigar smoker Wilding nodded. He yawned.

"What's the trouble with you?" Ma said. "Is all this puttin' you to sleep?"

"No, no, not at all," he said. "I'm always like this before a job. I can't help it. I guess it's nerves. I always yawn when I get nervous."

Ma grunted impatiently. Harry Sawyer and his big-city help.

"When you go into town," she said, "you gotta make a strong *impression*, right off. Ole Jesse'd always snap off a few shots at the rubes standin' around. Make 'em move. Put the fear o' Jesus Christ in the dumbbells. "Smite a scorner and the simple will beware.' Proverbs, ex-eye-ex, twenty-six."

She dropped her cigarette butt and ground it into the rug with her heavy heel. Karpis reached down and tossed it in the flowered waste can.

Harold Beesemeyer decided to ask a question. He was a live one.

"What's all this Jesse James? We gonna ride horses?"

Ma tapped her iron tooth with the pencil. She studied Harold's eager blond face.

"You *smart*, honey?"

"Only foolin' Mizz Barker."

"You ain't funny."

"I guess not, Mizz Barker."

47

"This here is serious business, boy."

"Yes mam."

"Freddie, you better put the smart aleck there on somethin' easy. Maybe he ain't got good sense."

"Sure, Ma. I'll use ole Harold fer a human shield."

The men bent over the map again. Wilding stifled a yawn. Ma glanced at Harold Beesemeyer.

"I thought we was gettin' perfessional help! Horses . . ."

•

The big time at last, thought Karpis. A professional undertaking with skilled technicians, experienced workmen.

The Fort Scott bank looked just like Ma said it would and Freddie went immediately, pistol in hand, to the uniformed bank guard and struck him with all his might. As the old man crumpled, Karpis yelled, "This is a stickup, everybody down! On the floor!" Grabbing the first executive type he saw, Karpis pushed a gun in his face and together they went to the vault which was opened at top speed. Harold Beesemeyer stood guard over the customers on the floor and Freddie slid along the window scanning the street for town cops. Out to the curb and the waiting car went Karpis and Wilding the cigar smoker. Freddie kicked the disarmed guard on the floor (who reminded him in an infuriating way of Arthur Dunlop) and then the entire gang was aboard and Bobby Hatton raced the engine and Freddie took up a gunner's position at a back window.

Freddie had fired four careful shots at store windows when, speeding east on Wall Street, the Nash struck the St. Louis, San Francisco tracks at sixty miles an hour and bounced in the air, Freddie's .38 went off and after the yelling stopped inside the car, Harold Beesemeyer had a flesh wound in his left buttock.

"Barker, you dumbbell!" cried Hatton, swerving around a farm wagon.

Fred aimed his .38 at the back of the driver's head. Karpis pushed Fred's hand away. Fred fired out the window, breaking a window in an empty store.

Harold Beesemeyer moaned and clutched his injured, blood-soaked ham.

He wiped his fingers on the seat.

"Hey, goddamit!" Fred cried. "I got this goddam car from Sawyer. I ain't gonna have you fuck up the upholstery!"

"I can't help bleedin'," said Harold.

"Sit on the floor, bleed on the floor!" Fred yelled.

"It's too hard," Harold said.

"You're spoilin' the moohair!" Fred yelled.

They argued.

Karpis had his first small doubts about Fred Barker.

•

From the gothic depths of the Stromberg-Carlson, Amos 'n Andy *awaahed* to a finish. Ma flipped it off.

Freddie, Karpis and the St. Paul men were back home from work in the Jayhawker State. With a triumphant grin, Fred dumped the suitcase on the floor.

"Here it is, Ma! Everything worked like a charm."

"Well, ain't that nice!"

"We run it off like you said. Right on the schnozzola. Old Harold caught one."

"That's too bad."

Ma threw back the lid and ran her chubby hands through the packets.

"He won't be with us fer a while," Freddie said.

"Small blessings," Ma said. "Harold . . . he's too smart fer his own good. A natural born damn fool."

The St. Paul men sat stiffly on the couch. They were exhausted. Too tired to yawn, redheaded Wilding stuck a cigar in his sagging mouth and left it unlit.

Karpis took a drag on his cigarette and leaned forward in his chair.

"Ma, you know twenty-five grand is pretty fair dough."

Ma smiled.

"Boy, it's very good. It's perfessional. It's about time, ain't it?"

•

In the heat of the afternoon, Ma sat in her club chair wrecking the second layer of a Whitman Sampler, chomping through the cocoanut brittles, nut nougats, molasses crunchies, cream

49

dips and caramel nut-tops (when the chocolate-covered cherries touched her iron tooth, a bolt of pure lightning shot to the top of her skull) as she traced with her square-tipped finger the words of her latest letter from son Dock at Oklahoma State.

Freddie strode through the living room. He wore knickers, wool stockings, Bobby Jones sweater and a large flat cap. Alvin in similar disguise, followed, lugging the golfbags.

"Little exercise, Ma," he said.

Ma's jaw sagged.

"What the hell you wearin', Fred?"

"This is what ye wear, Ma. Knickers."

"Them's short pants."

"Nah, Ma. It's knickers. Pretty sharp, huh? Snazzy." He studied himself in the gilded foyer mirror.

"Little Lord Faunt-*Leroy*!" Ma yelled. "Ye look like a real sissy!"

"Ma, fer crissake, this is what the dudes wear playin' golf. We're suppose to be rich guys, we should oughta dress up like 'em."

"I suppose . . . Only don't go wearin' that foolishness around the house. Ye look like a real Yankee cookie-pusher."

"That's what we're suppose to *be*, Ma. Country Club Plaza. *In*-surance."

Ma shrugged and dug back into the creams. A cherry center squirted between her chubby fingers.

"Lord God."

•

Alvin Karpis slowly brought back the club, shifted, pulled down hard and slammed the little white ball a satisfying clout.

"Hey, Bobby Jones," Fred sneered.

Fred whipped his driver into the tee and six pounds of turf rose and fell back. "Shit," he said.

Karpis walked over to the bags.

"It don't make no dif, Fred. I seen ya cheatin' on the last four holes anyhow."

Fred burned. "I never cheated. Who the hell has to cheat playin' this pansy game?"

50

"You was cheatin'." Karpis was becoming a pain in the ass for a punk kid.

One leg of Fred's knickers sagged badly, wrinkling his Navajo pattern stocking. His fifteen-dollar golf shoes were soggy from sloshing through the water hazard. He had lost six Kro-Flites and his temper. He spat in disgust.

"Ah, fuck this crap," he said. "Let's go get a slug. I know a speak over on Prairie Avenue."

Karpis took hold of the bags and lifted.

"Cripes! What you got in there? Fatty Arbuckle?"

The auto rifle was stowed with the irons. Fred jammed his muddy driver in beside it.

"You don't want to git caught without a rod o' some kind," he said.

•

Ma stood at the dining room table, an apron over her green silk dress, covering the pink sash, the pink bow on her rump and the heavy crocheted roses spread across her abdomen.

Fred, slightly drunk, weaved to his chair unnoticed by Ma, herself reeking of chocolate after an afternoon of caramel and creme delights.

"Chow is on."

"Boy, that looks good, Ma!" Karpis said.

Fred stared at his plate and rubbed his red face. "Fried corruption."

"Now there Fred, don't git sourcastic. That's real tenderline meat."

"Looks OK to me, Ma," said Karpis.

"Dig in Alvin. Sidemeat!" Ma was going to the picture show tonight. Ruth Chatterton was her favorite.

The funny little doorbell sounded again and again.

"Them damn kids playin' in the hall," Ma said, when the door burst open and Harold Beesemeyer fell in.

"They grabbed Wilding and Bobby Hatton!" he said. "I think Harvey Bailey, too. It was cops of some kind, they coulda been Federals. Wilding was two holes ahead of me on the nine-hole

51

course when they grabbed him. I took off. I don't think they seen me."

"Let's go boys." Ma started for the mantel; the souvenir dolls and pennants. Ruth Chatterton could go screw herself.

"Get the suitcases, I'll pack the kitchen stuff," Karpis said.

"Boy, it's lucky I'm a lousy golf player," Harold Beesemeyer said. "By the way, my ass is a lot better. I took the bandage off."

"Ever two weeks we gotta hit the road," Fred said.

Beesemeyer rubbed his bottom.

"They woulda grabbed me too, only I fell behind."

"Get the extra drums fer the Tommy gun!" Karpis yelled from the bathroom.

"It was that close," Beesemeyer said.

"Some day I'm gonna kill me a Fed," Freddie said. "Bam! Right in the punkin!"

Karpis tossed a new rifle and the Colts on the couch. "Here, bring these around the back door. I'll get the car."

Fred wrestled a strapped suitcase to the door. "Half the stuff wasn't unpacked from last time."

"Hurray! We're one up on 'em." Karpis ran for the stairs.

Harold straddled a chair, favoring his battle-scarred rump. "Boy, am I ever lucky!"

Ma cleared the last of the Kewpies, swept the pictures into a box of linens. "It's the Fort Scott *bank*, I reckon. Better not to be around when the questions start." She slammed the cover on the box. "They're just not ever gonna leave us alone!"

Harold whistled. "Just think! They was that close to grabbin' me!"

Fred was back again, red-faced, panting.

"Freddie, whyn't you take the biscuits along?" Ma said, spilling the last of the chocolates into her bandanna. Fred's hangover started. He turned to Harold.

"Come on Ironhead, git off that chair. It's goin' along with us."

Harold stood up in slow motion. "Where ya goin'?"

"China."

"Aw. Yer kiddin'."

The table lamp with the realistic fire scene in its base jiggled as Ma hurried through the room.

"Come on Fred. Let's git the pillows and my Kewpie dolls," she said, seizing her battered shoebox. "My nice pho-toes o' my pore little fambly."

Karpis was back. "The car's ready. I got a rifle under the front seat. Gimme the suitcases. Let's go!"

He straightened up with the double load and staggered off down the hall.

"All my nice new furniture," Ma said.

Fred hefted an enormous wicker basket packed with blankets, hot water bottles, Bisodol, Dr. Walter's corn-remover, pile suppositories and rectal ointment, Murine for Ma's egg-like eyes, a balloon spray douche and a bedpan from the Arthur Dunlop era, a hardwood crutch from the time Ma stepped on Arthur's foot, a quart of Approved Russian Mineral Oil and Ma's souvenirs.

Beesemeyer held out his hand.

"I just want ya to know there's no hard feelin's about you shootin' me in the butt. It was a accident."

"Git outa my fuckin' way," said Fred.

Ma followed him through the door, a caramel stuck in her molars.

"How can I ever make a decent home fer you boys?" she lisped.

Harold Beesemeyer sat alone on the couch in the empty apartment.

The door stood ajar.

He uncorked a flask.

"Boy, am I ever lucky."

•

Back to St. Paul. This time no boardinghouse, no big-eyed landlady. The weather was scorching in town; Harry Sawyer suggested a lake cottage. He knew just the place.

"Nice neighborhood, neighbors just like yourself."

Professional people with means.

Mrs. Hunter and two sons. Or would it be Mrs. Claypool?

Mrs. Vandervanter. Matinees with Ruth Chatterton were invaluable to Ma.

Harry Sawyer stood on the porch with Ma watching the sailboats out on the sparkling blue water. He glanced at Ma out of the corner of his eye.

"What happened to Dunlop?" he said.

"Arthur? He went home to Thayer. He had to visit with his sister. She's bin poorly fer months and months."

Sawyer said nothing.

"Oh, months and months," Ma said.

"Well. That was smart to dump him in Wisconsin but don't try anything like that around here, Kate, because I can't guarantee protection on a rap that serious."

"I got a letter from Arthur jest the other day," Ma said.

"Yeah," Sawyer said. He turned and walked back to the road where his gleaming maroon Auburn Speedster was parked under the dark pines.

"That's a right nice aut-toe," Ma said.

"I'm gonna git me one o' those sometime," Karpis said.

"In a pig's ass," Fred said.

"I'd betcha on it only you'd welsh."

"Says you," Fred said.

Ma lumbered off to the kitchen.

"This is the life, ain't it?" Karpis said, swinging his thin arms in the sunshine.

"Yeah, only a coupla broads would make it even better." Fred paced the wooden porch. "Ma stuck us out here for a reason. No bimbos around. No poontang."

Karpis watched a sailboat across the lake making a turn in the sun. Freddie rubbed his tattooed arm.

"Ma can't stand wimmin around and she can't stand booze," he said. "She's got some goddam hillbilly notion they're the root of all evil. It gets to be a pain in the ass after a time."

He scaled a stone out into the water.

"She's the best mother a boy could want."

Freddie stood staring across the lake. Two tiny figures appeared on a boat dock on the far shore. Girls in bathing suits. Big beautiful knockers.

"It's too bad the Federals grabbed ole Wilding and Bobby Hatton," Karpis said.

"Yeah, it's a shame. It busts my heart. Dummy up, Alvin. It's more dough for us," Fred said.

Across the lake, the girls slid into the water.

"Anyhow . . ." Fred yawned. "That's what ye get, usin' escaped cons. The Federal men was out lookin' fer them boys."

"Well at least the Federals ain't after us," Karpis said. "We just got the local boneheads to worry about."

"And a good hot piece of ass," Fred said. He walked into the cottage. "Hey Ma!" he yelled. "When the hell's chow?"

•

Ma sat in the blue canvas deck chair, rubbing her fat wrists and fishwhite arms. Heat rash spread over her flabby biceps like red gravel.

"I b'lieve I'll burn myse'f in the sun so's I look like a high-tone nigger lady," she chuckled.

Time to get to work. Money to spring brother Dock. After a month of enforced relaxation at White Bear Lake, Freddie was showing unmistakable signs of restlessness. Good. The boy believed as she did. Idle hands and work for the devil. Freddie was anxious to put his shoulder to the wheel. Thank the Lord the boy didn't drink. And no women either. Freddie was just a baby after all.

Ma assembled her findings from her latest trip, this time to Kansas. The best looking prospect had been the Cloud County Bank at Concordia, Kansas. Good fast roads, different state to avoid local cops, fat vaults yearning to be set free and help a poor old woman hold her tiny brood together. Thirty miles from the Nebraska line, Rte. 81 N and S, 9 E and W. This time Sawyer had promised really professional help. No more bumble-fingers.

•

Harry Sawyer made the introduction brief ("This is Jelly Nash. He's one of the best workmen in the country") and then he left.

Talking with Ma Barker brought on digital ague and the roaring trouble in his ears.

A small bald man with a large warped nose and a limp, the famous Jelly Nash smiled shyly. "Please t'meetcha, Missus Barker."

"Like-wise, Mr. Nash." Ma smiled faintly. "Funny, I thought you were a younger man. Anyhow, Sawyer tells me you're a real perfessional."

They burst out laughing.

"Jelly, how the hell are ye? Still avoidin' honest work?"

"Kate, it's a pleasure t'see you again."

"How d'ya stand it in the north?"

"It's rough," Jelly laughed. "But the money's here."

"Lord I ain't seen you since Joplin," Ma said.

"Was it Joplin?" Jelly grinned. "My my. You did the plans on many a good one back there."

"What about this bird Sawyer?" Ma said.

Jelly Nash shrugged and lowered himself into a deck chair.

"Harry Sawyer is a buddy from way back. He throws me a little job now and then." He smiled.

"Yeah. Well, I don't know about *you*, Mr. Nash, but it's time *we* got back to work. The damn cost o' livin' is breakin' my back. We got a hat full o' bills that gotta be paid."

"I know what you mean. Things are tough all over."

"You can't very well say 'stick 'em up' to the *landlord*. Ever once in a while you need some cash money."

"Don't I know it though," Nash said. "Everybody's complaining. With what I pay Sawyer fer protection and just plain everyday living expenses, I got nothing to show at the end o' the year."

"Ain't it the truth! We hafta move every couple o' months with the way the coppers been pickin' on us. It adds up. It ain't cheap."

"It's rough."

"Rougher'n a cob," Ma said.

"A job that pays dough is a hard thing to come by. Even for the kind o' experience I got."

56

"Everybody tells me you got a right good name here in the business."

"Oh, I know a couple of things, I guess."

"I got a spot comin' up we could use some smart help on."

"Yeah?"

"An' by Heaven, there's no reason why Johnnie Dillinger has to git all the money in the country. It ain't as if he could spent it *all*."

"Ole Johnnie runs a real good bunch. He's a right smart man fer a northerner."

"What kinda name *is* Dillinger?"

"Damn ef I know, Kate." Jelly rubbed his warped nose. "He's jest awful good at it."

"Well, anyhow, I got an idea on somethin' good, you might work in."

"I got some time. I ain't real busy right now."

"That's fine, Mister Nash, lemme show ye what I got in mind."

Ma sketched the bank floor plan from Concordia, Kansas.

"You're handy as ever with the pencil," Nash said.

Ma laid in the surrounding streets.

"Yeah. I coulda bin a real picture drawer."

She unfolded an Automobile Club map. A business traveler should avail herself of services.

"I figger it's time to touch up a country bank. Better to find these fat farmer banks out in the country an' knock 'em over and get away, than try to hit a branch bank in a big city full a cops, streets crowded, ten zillion people standin' around lookin' at ye."

Nash nodded. "Yeah, but how d'ya find 'em?"

"Leave that part to me."

Fred and Alvin slumped into chairs. Fred had his own reference material, a battered copy of *Film Fun*.

Ma concentrated on Jelly Nash. "Best thing is a country bank at a county seat, with nice straight crossroads and located near the state line. Another thing, you never know in a big city whether they're diggin' up the streets or you might get stopped by a auto wreck or some fool thing. Out in the country you don't have all these troubles. And there ain't so many cops either. Once you're over the state line, you're home free. Country banks are a sight *easier*. Why look for trouble?"

Fred had found the Toby Wing bathing suit layout. He wondered about Toby Wing.

Across the room, Ma recognized the forbidden source of inflammation.

Toby Wing had platinum hair. Great big, beautiful. . . .

"Put down that book and pay attention, goddammit!" Ma yelled. "Don't you want to improve yoreself?"

Fred turned to the truss ads.

Jelly Nash thought the bank looked very good.

•

Tuesday, July 26, in the middle of a 108 degree summer, the new Barker gang, Freddie, Karpis, Nash and two Sawyer men, hit the little town of Concordia, Kansas. A burst of warning shots were fired up and down 6th Street, citizens scattered, and a St. Paul man took position on the sidewalk with an auto-rifle, the big 8-cylinder Chrysler ticking softly at the curb. The boys clattered across the hard slick floor of the Cloud County Bank with rifles and handguns at the ready.

Two local farmers and a very pretty cosmetician from the yellow brick beauty shop next door were the only customers and nobody moved.

Karpis and Jelly Nash went for the valuables by way of H.F. Bard, bank vice president, and a fascinated farmer, O.J. Stutz, who were both slugged with a pistol.

Film Fun Fred, with an eye for the girls, selected two bank stenographers and the beauty shop operator as hostages for the ride out of town. When Jesse James hit Northfield, Minnesota in 1876, local riflemen almost wiped out his gang, and bankrobbers since had lived in horror of another such armed uprising on the part of villagers. Town girls riding on the running boards could shield the workmen from any Concordia eaglescouts eager for Rotary Club heroism awards.

There was fast, intelligent work and very little noise on the job. Ma's planning, with a few knowledgeable refinements by Jelly Nash, moved the gang with precision. $19,000 available in cash.

"Let's have the securities," Jelly said.

Freddie wanted to hit H.F. Bard again. Jelly pushed him aside.

Holding a handkerchief to his head wound, the bank official cooperated. The securities were registered; they couldn't be disposed of. Let the hooligans think they had made a score.

Jelly Nash, the banking expert, took the available cash and loaded up Karpis and Stumps McDonald (a nervous young gorilla on loan from Sawyer) with $220,894 in securities, and they stumbled out to the car with $240,000 worth of loot. Karpis then stopped Freddie from letting any shots go for fun by rushing his feminine charges out onto the boards, and, with the other Sawyer man driving, they took off.

Concordia's six thousand scattered inhabitants were hardly much opposition on a scorching Tuesday in July and the pilgrims roared out along tree-shaded Lincoln, U.S. 81, at a brisk fifty miles an hour. The speed caused cotton skirts to lift and Freddie was heading for trouble of another kind. The beautician's white uniform was loosely buttoned in the heat of mid-summer and the gaps fanned the glowing coals of his Film Fun starlet-blasted mind.

As he concentrated on the beauty shop operator's dark red hair and lush white skin, years of Ma Barker gang discipline evaporated. He noted the whiteness of her thighs and the movement of her bosom as the Chrysler jolted across the Missouri Pacific and Sante Fe tracks and he suddenly realized in his primitive way that this pretty young girl was actually in his power.

They were out of town almost immediately. Two old men fishing near the Republican River bridge, looked up at the three bouncing girls on the running board and marveled at the endless capacity of Concordia's young to find new and exciting ways to have fun.

A few miles north, the driver slowed the sedan and pulled off 81 on a dirt road into a vast field of corn rippling in the sun.

"End of the line," he called. The girls, windwhipped, weary

and badly frightened, dismounted. The silence and the heat were oppressive. The beautician ran her slim hand through her rumpled hair.

"Wait a minute," Fred said, climbing out. "This won't take no time at all."

Karpis took the wheel. He was sweating.

"Come on, you jerk, let's go," he said.

"Wait a goddam minute, we got plenty o' time," Fred said, his bulging brown eyes riveted on the redhead's chest and the line of buttons down the front of her uniform. One vigorous rip and she'd be naked as his hottest fantasies. Toby Wing in Kansas. He rubbed his big nose vigorously.

"We better move," Nash said. "We got $240,000 in the case."

"Yeah, yeah," said Freddie.

"We gonna wait while he digs a hole in that Kansas bimbo?" Nash said. "We got too much dough here. We're hotter'n a pistol right now."

"Fred, I'll leave ya," Karpis said and gunned the motor. The radiator bubbled in the heat.

"Come on Fred," Nash said. "We're late as it is."

Freddie hesitated. The girl, trembling, stared at the black dirt.

"Don't hurt me," she mumbled. The Chrysler began to move.

Fred glared at her then jumped aboard and the Chrysler swung around with a roar and scattering of dust and the three girls were standing alone in a sea of waving corn tassels. The redhead began to cry.

In the speeding Chrysler, nobody said a word for fifteen miles. Karpis found himself suddenly exhausted as the tension dissolved. One of the Sawyer men dozed, his shotgun clasped between his knees. Fred sat rigidly jamming his feet against the hot floorboards, the muscles working in his bony face.

"Did ya see the gams on the redhead? I tell ya Karpis these Kansas bimbos are dyin' for it!"

Karpis watched the road ahead, shimmering in the heat.

"Keep your mind on the dough, Fred."

"Too friggin' bad . . . I have a broad like that practically

under lock and key and have to let her go without bingin' her one
. . . Free nookie, achin' fer it . . . That's a cryin' shame. I
coulda drove it right through her."

"Pay attention to business," Karpis said.

"Karpis is right," Nash said. "Get the loot an' move out. Ye
don't want a rape charge on ya. That could get these rubes *really*
up in arms."

"Don't tell *me*, baldy. You're along fer the job. Don't gimme
a lotta shit-head advice."

Nash smiled. "I'm just tellin' ya boy. Save that stuff for the
cribs. The amateurs are all trouble."

"Yeah?" Fred spat out the window. "You talk a good game,
Jelly."

"Freddie, when we get back, I'll take ya down to St. Peter
Street. There's more hookers along St. Peter and Jackson than
they got in Juarez, Mexico."

•

A swollen vision of 1933 high fashion in her shantung beach
pajamas, Ma went to the cottage door and there he stood, 5 feet
4, large, dark staring eyes like his mother's, a dapper handsome
little man in a gray suit, smiling nervously. Softer looking than
rattlesnake Fred, finer featured than Ma.

Dock Barker, little Arthur, was home.

Ma sprang heavily at him and the little fellow struggled to
keep from falling over his suitcase. He blinked his big eyes happily.

"My baby!" She threw a headlock on him. He tried to keep
his slick dark hair from getting mussed as his hat rolled in a circle.

"Oh, Dock," she cried. "I worked so hard to git ye sprung,
ye'll never know!"

He saw the living room set, the rugs.

"My own little Dock . . . I cain't believe yore free. God
A'mighty, Dock, it cost me a fortune!"

He took in the drapes, the Florentine carved table.

"Dock, you're my own little boy."

His soft milky face was covered with meaty kisses.

61

"Come on Ma, fer cryin' out loud . . ." Grinning with embarrassment, he thrust an arm against her massive chest and scooped up his hat.

"Great God, where'd ye git that?" Ma yelled.

He twisted the silk-lined black derby on his forefinger.

"Chicagah, Ma. Ain't she a beaut?"

At the hall mirror, over the flowers on the venetian table, he carefully recombed his shiny black hair straight back from his high pale forehead and straightened his tie. Then he placed the derby on his head.

Ma was aghast.

"Dock, boy, that prison went and *ruint* ye. You've gone foolish!"

"Criminee, Ma, I thought you were glad to see me."

Ma hurled a thick bare arm around his neck.

"Dock, I'm as happy as only a real mother could ever be. Only I jest cain't say I'm all fired happy about that *hat*."

She kissed him loudly on the cheek.

"It's class, Ma. Don't wanta look like a hayseed forever. Looks classy, don't it?"

He glanced back at the mirror. Ma dragged him toward the sitting room.

"Dock, you're too *puny* fer a hat like that. It makes ye look like a circus midget."

"Naw it don't, Ma. Cost me eleven bucks."

"Well, I'm glad yore home, Dock. I can see you've surely missed yore old maw. When did the sonsabitches let ye go?"

"Four days ago, Ma."

"Praise th' Lord."

"Ma, get this! They let me out on the condition I never go back to Oklahoma no more!"

"Great God A'mighty!"

"Ain't that a hot one?"

He perched on the flowered settee and looked around the room.

"Pretty snazzy, Ma. You must be doin' pretty good."

"We'll do a sight better, now yore here."

62

"Goddam," he said. "Yes sir. Hey, how about a little snort. Ma? Got any white lightnin' in the jug?"

Ma was serious.

"Dock, I don't allow no booze of any sort. None atall."

"You don't?"

"It's bad fer the boys. We got a right good bunch now and there's jest two laws. No likker and no wimmin. An' that's that."

"I'll be damned," he said mildly. He gazed out the screen doors across the lake. "I just thought I might have me a little snort o' mule."

"Dock, honey, I can see you've missed yore old maw."

•

Fred tossed his jacket in the corner and faced his brother.

"Well look who's here. They let ya out, huh?"

"Hello banjo-eyes," Dock said. "You still tryin' to act tough?"

"Shorty, you better git on the ball here. You better dummy up. Times changed since you was in the pen."

"Fred, don't tell me what to do. An' lay off that 'shorty' crap."

"Don't call me banjo-eyes."

Ma looked from one to the other. Her two precious boys.

"Oh, I'm jest s'glad we're all together again," she said. "Our little fambly."

•

Romney Daley arrived by street car. Old Tulsa boyhood pal of Freddie and Dock, fellow alumni of Oklahoma State, small-time thief, responding to Ma's offer of employment.

Romney (who claimed to be a full-blooded Cherokee for Tulsa status) was a big-jawed cheerful young man with a great shock of wavy hair and prominent ears. He wore a heavy green cap, rodeo boots and a thick buttoned sweater, and his luggage from the bus ride was a paper bag containing a candy-striped shirt he stole in Ponca City on his way north.

"I sure am grateful to you fer takin' me in like this, Missus Barker," he said.

Ma leered.

Freddie showed Romney where he could fix up a nice cot for himself in the garage. Dirty picture calendar on the wall, don't get your stuff mixed in with the rakes or hoses, Ma is particular about the gardening tools.

"If ya gotta jack off, go out in back."

Romney was grateful all over again.

•

"Ma, Glenn Leroy sent a bill fer legal services. He wants his dough."

"I don't see the sense in payin' good hard-earned money to a lawyer. Why in thunder should he git all that money when God knows I truly have need of it, keepin' a Christian home together fer my boys . . . Ye know, anyways, he didn't work all that hard on gettin' brother Dock outa th' pen."

Ma smiled, tongue pressed against her new bridge, cracked lips wet with pleasure, moist brown eyes sparkling with inspiration.

"Ask him to the course fer a round of golf."

Freddie hefted the golf bag. Take out half a dozen Kro-Flites and all the irons and the Thompson gun would fit in right well.

Sprawled in the fat new two-tone velour club chair, in the soft orange glow from the brassplated bridge lamp with imported bead fringed shade, Ma read the Bible. Her woman's heart found vindication, page after page. The lyricism of the ages warned her of tribute exacted by the unworthy for inglorious service rendered. They that labor not as the shield of righteousness shall duly be rewarded with the flaming shaft of a just wrath.

The Book was such a comfort to a woman alone. Pestered by lawyers.

Smart aleck shyster. A city boy. Double breasted suit and carnation. Served him right. Dude. Now for a man who had real style, there was Arthur V. Dunlop. Lover Boy. Always clean linen. Religious about that. In summer, he wore Fancy Striped Madras Nainsook underwear suits, triple stitched seams and specially tailored double-section seat. A real gentleman. A victim of his own greed. The tragic failing of so many.

Ma yawned mightily and her moist brown eyes closed.

•

"I brought a souvenir fer yer collection, Ma."

Ma was napping in the chair with her mouth open when Freddie returned. He flashed a signet between thumb and forefinger.

"I woulda brought ye his necktie, but he got somethin' *on* it when I let him have it."

"*Freddie*." She rubbed her sticky eyes. "For Mercy's *Sake!* Yore jest *terrible!*"

She tried to force the ring on her stubby finger, settled for her fat pinkie.

"I *never!* . . . Freddie, yore a devil. You truly are . . . It's a right nice ring."

A good big wet kiss for Freddie.

•

Ma and Romney Daley walked arm-in-arm to their train gate in Chicago's Union Pacific station. For once a redcap could wrestle her baggage, just like they did for hightone rich folks.

She wore her new super quality all-wool cashmere suede-velour coat with genuine Canadian beaver oversleeve cuffs and high collar. She had told the little store clerk that if he was lying about the Canadian beaver she would kill him and he laughed. For the trip to California, Ma had selected a lavender beret, to set off her orange hair and a silk tweed daytime frock.

As she clumped along in her kidskin one strap shoes with imitation diamond wings on the sides, several people turned to look. Ma smiled. They obviously knew a lady when they saw one.

Romney trudged along resplendent in a hip length black leather coat with sheepskin collar, varsity model cheviot bell-bottoms, two-tone shoes and a stunning gray fedora with a six-inch crown and a three-inch brim.

He chewed gum.

"Are you full-blooded Cherokee, Romney? I b'lieve I might have a drop o' Cherokee, myself."

"I think I'm full-blooded, OK."

"I reserved a lower berth. Isn't that somethin'?"

"This sure is nice o' you Missus Barker, I surely do appreciate it."

"The train takes five days to get out there, Romney. We can play a lot o' cards. D'you play cards, Romney? Five whole days and nights. Don't that seem like a long time? We'll think up ways to pass the time."

He grinned modestly.

"Romney, you know somethin'? You're a right handsome young boy. You know that?"

"Why thank you kindly, Mrs. Barker."

•

With Ma out of the state, White Bear Lake was quiet. Karpis had just stretched out on the couch, when Fred burst through the twin screen doors with a lumpy, dog-sized package.

"Sawyer says one of those Kansas bank guys died," Karpis said. "In Concordia."

Fred snorted. "Yeah? That's too bad. So did my Kansas hard on. Anyway, boy, Sawyer is a bullshit artist. Dummy up."

He dropped the package on the settee, tore away the string, elbowed wrapping paper aside and straightened up cradling a black oily Thompson submachine gun, M1928. His crazy eyes were bulging out of his bony face.

"How d'ya like *this* baby?"

Karpis whistled.

"Man. That's real class. I never seen one o' them up close."

"Three hundred rounds a minute," Fred said tapping the fifty-shot drum. "Ya can sock fifty rounds through a dumb cop while he's still tryin' to haul out his cap gun!"

"Where in hell d'ya *get* it?"

"The cops! Ain't that a *riot?* Sawyer got his stooge on the Force to rent us a *tommy gun!* Don't that beat all? We just ain't supposed to use it around *here!* Outa state only! And the blockhead has to have it back by Monday morning or he'll get in trouble!"

He tossed the gun to Karpis who balanced it with his right hand on the trigger grip, slipped his left hand around the thick wooden forward grip and aimed carefully at Jesse James on the wall.

"Ho, Mama," he said.

•

After a Wonder Baker's chocolate cake and a fifth of bourbon,

Fred wandered into the big room for a serious talk with Dock and Karpis.

"Whatya say we pick up a little dough?"

Karpis was shaving out of a basin. "How?"

"Hit a bank. Hit one around here," Fred said.

"Around here?"

"Hell yes. How come we gotta drive eight million miles every time?" Fred said. "Christ, them drives're beginnin' to bust my balls."

"We ain't supposed to hit anything close to St. Paul." Little Dock tossed his newspaper on the floor. "You know damn well what Sawyer said."

"Sawyer. What's that craphead know?"

"I dunno about workin' around here," Karpis said. "Anyway, Ma ain't here neither."

"Let's blast one off without her, fer once," Freddie said.

Karpis shrugged. "What ya got in mind?"

"Minneapolis. The Third Northwestern Bank."

"Jesus. I dunno about that."

"Come on, fer crissake. We're cooped up here an' Ma is out livin' it up in California. Let's go pick up a little loot. Christmas is comin'."

Dock ran his hand over his shiny black hair. "Does Sawyer know about it?"

"I wouldn't tell that bum the time o' day. He might sic the cops on us."

Fred tossed the new submachine gun on the couch.

"Come on boys, let's try this ole beauty out. I gotta have it back to the dumbbell by Monday morning."

•

Friday afternoon, the 16th of December, Fred, Karpis, brother Dock, a reluctant Jelly Nash and a non-Sawyer man from Chicago started out in two sedans under the brown wintry sky through streets hung with Christmas decorations. Freddie brought a pint for luck and, of course, the shiny black Thompson.

They stopped in Como Park, stashed the smaller car and rode

67

together in the Buick down Lexington to Marshall, west to the Lake Street Bridge and the die was cast.

A tinsel-sequinned MERRY XMAS sign stretched across the grimy street, faded red paper bells, weather-stained and mis-shapen, wobbled on their wires. JOYOUS YULETIDE 1932.

"Merry Christmas, Freddie," Karpis said.

"Up yours," Fred said.

An endless line of men in overcoats and leather jackets, caps pulled down against the cold, shuffled slowly along the curb next to a shabby brick warehouse. A stiff breeze was blowing.

"Lookit them jerks," Fred said.

"A goddam breadline," Dock said.

"Why don't they swipe a rod an' go to work?"

"They think Roosevelt is gonna *feed* 'em. They're nuts."

"Goddam bums," Fred mumbled. "Freeloaders."

"Go easy on the sauce," Dock said.

"Don't tell me nothin'," Fred said.

Jelly Nash studied the street signs. "Prosperity is just around the corner, boys," he said. "There she is! Prosperity! The Third Northwestern Bank."

The kaleidoscope began. Fred tore the paper bag off the Tommy gun, hit the sidewalk running and nearly fell on his face. Jelly Nash scooted around him and Karpis, Dock and the Sawyer man followed him through the double glass doors. Fif-teen customers stared in silence as the gang cut across the floor fanning out to the walls, a woman yelled once and Fred yelled "Let's go baby, this is a stickup! Keep your hands all the way up or I'll blow your head off! Up! Get 'em up!"

Her hands shot up, she dropped her heavy purse and bent to retrieve it.

"Leave it alone!" yelled Fred.

"I've gotta pick it up!" she screamed.

"Goddam it, leave it where it is!"

"I can't!" she yelled.

She was on her hands and knees, fur coat flopping, determined to get the purse off the floor, Fred determined to break her skull with the Tommy butt, Dock shoved Freddie away, Jelly Nash was behind the counter, a gun shoved in the vice president's pale blond face, somebody's rimless glasses were stepped on with a rasping crunch, Karpis had the bag open and Nash shoved everything loose down into it; the floor woman couldn't lift her bag with both hands, Freddie broke loose and kicked her hard on her bottom and she began to cry. Dock thought this is the day I go crazy, this is the one and Nash and Karpis yelled at a thin man with glasses wearing old-fashioned garters on his sleeves to open the vault and Karpis stepped in and smashed foureyes across the head with the heavy flat .45 and blood sprayed over the fancy shirtsleeves and the slow bastard got the vault open immediately.

The rest of the customers stood frozen, watching.

"Everybody down on the floor!" Dock yelled. "Lay down!"

A woman clasped her gloved hands over her eyes. "Don't shoot me!"

"Calm down, lady, or yer gonna get the works!"

"It's just like the picture show," an old man said.

"Shut up and flop!" yelled Dock.

The civilians folded gracefully onto the marble floor.

Dock held his gun on the collapsed customers, spread over the floor like so many fallen leaves.

"May I get up please?" A fat bird in a dark cheviot overcoat, black homburg.

"No, stay right where you are."

"I'm afraid I'll have to get up, please. I have a bladder condition . . ." The man was rolling slowly over to get his legs under his fat belly.

"Shut yer mouth," Dock hissed.

"I'm afraid I've soiled myself . . ." Fatso groaned and Dock stepped back in horror.

"The bulls!" yelled Fred and Dock saw them, two of them, squad car pulled up at the curb, peering through the big dirty window and Fred stuck the barrel of the submachine gun against Dock's face and the whole world cut loose in a great flaming blast that brought the window (Third Northwestern Bank in block letters backward) crashing down in sections and Police Officer Lew Carey was killed instantly and his partner Joe Birsky slid across the bloody sidewalk coughing bright red foam from his lungs.

Fred hung on to the stuttering Thompson and it ripped a line of shots straight up the window moulding and over the ceiling, hitting a great orange overhead ball lamp which exploded like a bomb.

"Jeez, ya see that?" yelled Fred. "Right up inna goddam air, busts the goddam light!"

Karpis and Nash ran through the rain of glass lugging the heavy stuff from the vault, the Sawyer man hopped over a yelling woman on his way to the door, Dock backed off from his portly wet friend on the floor who now lay on his face, homburg clutched over the nape of his neck and Dock grabbed Fred by the arm and they cut through the swinging glass doors out to the sedan.

"I gotta learn how to control this baby. Right up inna air!" Fred stood on the slippery sidewalk and sprayed the buildings in a circle. Windows shattered on the second floor across the street. People ran screaming for cover.

The driver roared the engine and Dock yelled at Fred. Fred swung aboard and the sedan lurched off up the street and around the corner.

One cop lay on his back, his chest and arm torn to shreds. The other cop tried to move. Glass tinkled in the splintered window frame and the floored customers shielded their faces.

Out at the bloody curb, Patrolman Joe Birsky stopped trying.

•

Anton Kuhlberg had been sick for a year. Twelve months out of work. Now in December of the third year of the Great Depression he was recovered enough to get out of bed and he had to find work. A wife and two children. They lost their own house; they had all moved in with his wife's parents. A fight every night, arguments at noon, trouble in the morning. He looked for weeks with no result. Something just had to happen right for a change. Then his friend Norman Dickson told him about a possibility downtown in St. Paul. A few jobs, nothing much, selling Christmas wreaths. Yuletide season, people would surely spend a little something to celebrate Christmas. Can't afford a tree, how about a Christmas wreath? Twenty-five cents. Don't celebrate Christmas, you don't go to heaven. Two bits. His friend Dickson had earned three dollars. Bundle up, Anton, because it's cold as anything standing out on the street.

Anton got the job. His wife saw him happy for the first time in a year as he left the house and drove off with Dickson in her father's old Essex. Anton Kuhlberg was a gentle man, helpful to a fault. Always lending a hand to the neighbor with the car that wouldn't start, shoveling Mrs. Evensen's driveway, knocking himself out for others.

"It's a break," he laughed. "A new profession. Our bum luck is changing."

Friday evening would see the best business of the week; payday night for the working stiffs, seven more shopping days to Xmas. Get your wreaths here, twenty-five cents. Strange occupation for a law-school graduate with no practice but times were rough. It's only temporary. The Governor and the Mayor saw things looking up right after the first of the year. Everyone did. New president in March. F.D. Roosevelt.

"Take it through the park, it'll save a few blocks," Dickson said.

Anton Kuhlberg swung the old Essex onto the curving concrete roadway into Como Park, past the kids playing in the snow, the tangled barren trees and back near a side road he saw the two cars stopped.

"Somebody's stuck," he said.

"Looks like a flat," Dickson said.

"Lousy tires, likely worn out," Anton said and braked to a stop.

"Let's not stop," Dickson said. "We're late for work."

"Lend a helping hand," Anton said. "Hell, I got a job now, I should show my appreciation."

He smiled at the man in the heavy green cap, bent over by the larger of the two sedans.

"Anything wrong?" he called.

"Ah, just changin' a tire," the man said, ducking his head.

"Can I help?" Anton had his hand on the door handle.

Fred Barker raised up in the back seat of the larger sedan and fired a burst from the Tommy gun which killed Anton Kuhlberg instantly.

•

"What ye do *that* for?" Ma crumpled the black headlines and threw the paper across the room.

Freddie grinned in a sick way.

"He was copyin' down the license number."

"He was?"

"Well, he might have." He smiled up at Ma. "Anyway, we got twenty grand."

"That's not enough! And whatya go an' bust a bank around here fer? We're suppose to lay off."

"It wasn't St. Paul, Ma. It was Minneapolis."

"Minneapolis," Ma said. "Boy, you got yore father's brains."

She leaned forward, both hands on the arms of Fred's chair. She shook her head slowly. Her heavy face was sad. Dock got up, motioned to Karpis and they went into the other room and turned the radio on loud. Dock jammed a cigarette in his mouth and struck a match. This damn foolishness was still going on years after they grew out of being little boys and Dock was powerless to stop it. He heard the first slap over the noise from the radio.

Ma swung the .45, wrapped in a towel, against Freddie's bowed head and grunted with the effort. Freddie closed his eyes tight and clasped his hands.

"I'm helpin' yew, Fred," Ma said and swung again. Freddie swayed on the bamboo beach chair and kept his eyes closed.

Ma cranked up the Victrola and started "Keep On The Sunny Side." Glancing at herself in the wall mirror, she stopped and renewed her vermilion lipstick. She wrapped the .45 more securely in the dampened towel and spread her sturdy legs, taking a position in front of her seated son.

It will help us every day/ it will brighten all the way, sang the Victrola.

72

"Foolishness is bound in the heart of a child; but the rod of correction shall drive it far from him," Ma said and swung the heavy .45.

•

When her temper cooled, Ma set to work lining up a sound, practical, planned bank job to make up for the disaster at Third Northwestern. Something similar to the Concordia job, a small town on straight roads, near a state line. Her fears about big city crime had been confirmed. Back to the sticks. Harry Sawyer sent some recruits, others came from Chicago and St. Paul, attracted by the gang's growing reputation. $240,000 from the Cloud County Bank. They had definitely reached the big time. The $220,894 worth of Kansas securities had been sold near Minneapolis to the bank's detectives for $15,000 cash but that was a minor detail. $240,000 was a respectable day's haul.

In addition to Karpis, Fred and Dock, Romney Daley, their old buddy from Tulsa, Jelly Nash, Al Buford the money changer, Ross Coleman and Eddie Green would make the trip. This time the target was Fairbury, Nebraska, farms and poultry, county seat of Jefferson County on the Little Blue River, ten short miles from the Kansas line. The National Bank was waiting.

Ma took the train down to Fairbury. Picking her iron tooth in railroad dining cars, staring out the long window at the sliding fields and barns, the countryside of Iowa tumbling past. An average, pudgy woman with Manchurian Wolf-dyed dog furs, Enna Jettick shoes and cloche hat with cabbage roses; the recently widowed clubwoman, Mrs. A.J. Claypool, from Joplin, Missouri.

You see, I only have just what dear A.J. left me and I'd hate to have anything happen to my pitiful little savings. I don't know a blessed thing about banking. You mean that little room with the funny door is what do you call it, the vault?

Sharp brown eyes noting distances, 14 feet to the main doors, two guards, both elderly, one on duty at a time, the white-haired bastard looked safest, hit the place when he has the duty.

A faceless, completely ordinary woman asking harmless dumb female questions about the bank. No one would ever remember her. Invisible.

She worked a month on maps, driving schedules, bank layout, bank personnel schedules, ideal time for the hit. The drivers went down to Fairbury and practiced their timing. Eight men in two cars should do it just about right. The boys were keyed up and ready.

From the moment they piled out of the cars in Fairbury, Dock was aware only of a great deal of noise, shots ripping up and down the business street, the smell of fresh brickdust and a bank lobby a mile and a half across peopled with yelling Nebraskans and bumping into Fred whose pistol the dumb guard nearly picked up; earbusting shots crashing out inside the echoing hard-surfaced room, rifling drawers, grabbing heavy canvas bags and everyone running like hell again out to the cars where a path had to be forced through the dumbbell townspeople who gawked around like it was one big free circus. There was more shooting as they pulled out of town, racing south for Kansas on a miserable road, both cars careening all over the highway and Ross Coleman bleeding like a red waterfall all over the back seat.

Coleman couldn't stop yelling and he couldn't stop bleeding so at Powhattan, Kansas, his friend Eddie Green took one car with Buford and Daley and drove Coleman to Verne Miller's in Kansas City and the nearest friendly surgeon.

"As long as we're right in the area," Freddie said. "What say we swing back to Concordia and I throw a fast one in that beauty-parlor broad?"

No one answered. Bald Jelly Nash gazed out the window, Karpis drove a straight line for St. Joseph and Dock settled back for a nap, his .45 bulging in its holster.

"Shit heads," Fred said, wondering if they could stop at a hook shop in St. Joe.

"$151,350," Jelly Nash said. "Fair."

•

Washing supper dishes, Fred had a brotherly talk with Dock.

"Where was you in there? D'you just come along fer the ride?"

74

"What're ya talkin' about?"

"I didn't see any gun action outa you, Dock."

"You were too busy beating up on the old ladies to notice."

"Two jobs in a row, boy. You better git with it, Dock. The fellers are beginning to wonder."

•

Jelly puffed on a cigar as they spread the riches on the dining-room table.

"This here's a good haul, Ma. You figured this one right well."

"Now boys, ain't that a sight more like it?" Ma was gnawing fried chicken. "You jest hafta let your Ma handle these things."

•

Ma shoved past the headwaiter in his dude tuxedo and bulldozed her way through the sliding crowd on the slippery dance floor.

The Hollyhocks was packed with the rowdy Saturday night bunch from St. Paul. Whiskey served in teacups, toasts drunk to Prohibition, Lester Lustgarten and his Harvest Moon Hotshots, moon over Lake Minnetonka painted on the base drum, a flat-chested vocalist with tight blonde curling-ironed hair bawling "By a Waterfall" into an unconnected microphone.

Harry Sawyer at a wall table, looked up, saw Ma approaching and took a quick drink.

"I'm tryin' to find out where the hell the boys are!" Ma shouted above the band. "They ain't been home since Wednesday!"

"Sit down, Mrs. Barker, take a load off, ah, have a chair, that is."

Ma stood.

"Where the boys?"

"Ah, the boys. Kate, the boys are down at the St. Peter Street *re*-sorts gettin' a little. You know. They figure they oughta relax between jobs."

Ma leaned across the table to Sawyer. Her green-gold festoon necklace and ropes of Senorita pearls spilled free and swung to and fro and she roared at him.

"I told those dumbbells *no women!* You can't *trust* women! Ever last one of 'em is a natural born *stool pigeon!* Ye go five hunderd miles, make a real score, get away with it and then blab it all to some *fe-male!*" Ma snorted. "*No women* and *no booze!*"

Harold Teen and Lillums at the next table paused to listen, grinning at the real life dialogue, as good as the gangster movies. Ma glared and they went back to their Wauwatosa pretzels and Golden Wedding doubles.

"I told the boys *once*, I told 'em a *thousand* times," Ma said.

Sawyer shrugged. "Boys oughta get their ashes hauled now an' then."

"Sawyer, don't you tell me what's good fer my boys an' what's not!" She stared at him as she sucked her iron tooth. "Don't you even dare to try."

She bumped the dude headwaiter hard on her way out.

•

"It's a chance to make some real honest-to-God money fer once," Harry Sawyer said. "An' I for one think we oughta grab it as soon as we can. It's too good to let lay there."

Clouds of smoke from his hardworking Cremo filled the air above the table. Fred, Alvin Karpis and Dock nodded glumly and waited.

The Hollyhocks was a peculiar place for business meetings but the call from Sawyer had been urgent so they sat under the blaring guns of Lester Lustgarten's Hotshots and listened as the plan unfolded to the thump and crash of "Everything I Have Is Yours" and "Did You Ever See A Dream Walking?"

Jack Blauen, a former rum-runner, had an idea about a kidnapping. Kidnapping was a new field to the bankrobbing Barkers and Blauen explained. You didn't necessarily have to kill the guy and chop him up and the payoff could be enormous. Gardner G. Hart, heir to a local brewery fortune seemed a logical choice. Sawyer would provide a bit of police protection and useful information from inside the department once the snatch was made.

Karpis thought the kidnapping could be a chance to make some money for once without the Barker family sideshow, which had begun to pall a bit. Shouting Ma, the boy-slugger, had lost some of her early charm.

Dock welcomed money as a means to double-breasted suits, English shoes and the kind of polo coats Gary Cooper wore on the screen. Anything that might make him look taller than 5 feet 4.

Fred toyed with a cup of whiskey and watched Wilma Lustgarten's wooden bottom and wondered if she put out.

Sawyer had brought along an eastern professional to work with the Barkers. At last they would meet the supergangster the boss had been extolling for three straight weeks.

He stood at Sawyer's elbow, a remarkably handsome man in his early thirties. Dark blond wavy hair, blue eyes, straight perfect nose, flaring nostrils, cleft chin and dimples, Dark Oxford Gray Worsted suit with aristocratic cushion shoulders, six-inch lapels, handsewn collar, twenty-inch trouser bottoms, Florsheim perforated wing shoes, broadcloth shirt with British stripes and an honest-to-God carnation in his buttonhole. He glowed.

"Boys," Sawyer said. "This here is Fred Goetz, Chicago. Goetz was with Al Capone in '29." Goetz smiled like a famous movie star and hurried around to their side of the table.

Karpis and Dock shook his hand and Fred stared at Goetz and kept a firm grip on his whiskey cup.

"These are the boys I told you about, Goetz," Sawyer said. He slapped everyone on the back and trotted over to the bandstand to coax Wilma Lustgarten to sing "Annie Doesn't Live Here Anymore" or suffer a broken arm.

Goetz was almost everything the Barker warriors were not. A self-admitted war hero, flyer, outstanding athlete at University of Illinois, fraternity man. Also, arrested 1925, attempted rape, seven-year-old girl. Skipped his mother's $5000 bail, eventually got his historic job as a Capone gunman and soared to the heights on St. Valentine's Day, 1929, when disguised as a policeman, he machine-gunned six Bugs Moran men in the legendary garage massacre.

The unsuccessful affair with the child was not widely known

although Goetz was hardly reticent about the rest of his career. Parts of it he even improved with his great natural talent for embellishment and a deep and sincere desire to give his audience the larger-than-life heroes he knew they wanted.

Dock Barker saw Goetz as a guide to fine haberdashery, Alvin Karpis was impressed by such an Olympian example of success and enterprise in the profession. Goetz did seem to be a celebrity. He wondered if Goetz could actually have had time to do all he said he did. Fred Barker saw Goetz as a distinct pain in the ass.

A northern big city dude. A non-stop mouth. An instant friend and sissy-looking self-appointed buddy whose handshaking, arm gripping, all around pawing was definitely non-Ozark.

Goetz bought Fred Barker a drink which Freddie accepted without comment. Goetz decided the hardfaced boy, Alvin Karpis, might enjoy a few of his tales of Old Chicago.

"One time Di and me . . ." he began.

"Who?" Karpis frowned.

"Di. Dion."

"Dion?"

"Dion! Dion O'Bannion!"

"Oh. Who's he?"

"He was merely a very big man in Chicago, that's who."

"Oh," Karpis said.

"Yes sir. A very big man."

Fred was interested.

"Tell me about the Great War, Goetz. Is it true you killed eight hundred Germans?"

"No, no. I was in the Air Service. I was a pilot."

"Then you was the Ace of Aces, huh? With a hat-in-the-ring painted on yer aeroplane?"

"No, no. That's Rickenbacker. Captain Eddie."

"You're pretty smart, Goetz. You went to college, didnya?"

"Yes sir! University of Illinois. President of my frat."

Fred winked at Karpis. Karpis nodded.

"Fellows, I like the sound of this Hart business," Goetz said.

"Yeah?" Fred drained his cup.

78

"Yes sir. I could use some moolah right about now."

"Funny words," Fred said.

"Yes sir." Goetz ordered a drink. "I've got a champagne appetite on a beer income."

He waited for applause.

"Let's go home, Al," Fred said.

·

Ma saw Ruth Chatterton in "Once A Lady" with Ivor Novello. Ma never cried at the movies. She ate chocolates from an open box on the seat beside her. "Once A Lady" was good for two layers of nougat cremes and cherry crunches.

Goetz, the new man from Sawyer, was bringing his wife over to meet the Barkers after dinner so she came directly home from the matinee to begin the evening meal for her little family. Chicken swimming in grease, the same grease, carried in a Folger's coffee can, that traveled with her like the Kewpies and pennants. A self-perpetuating touch of down home.

She burned the chickens to a crisp, humming "Keep On The Sunny Side" as she reheated the breakfast biscuits.

Freddie had a spoonful of cough medicine before dinner. Another. Three in all. Poor little Freddie and his cough. Ma's bulging eyes misted over. The goddam cops hounded that boy until his very health was breaking.

After dinner, Fred and Dock cleared away the dishes and Karpis dished out the ice cream. Goetz and his wife were due any second. Ma clenched and unclenched her stubby right fist.

Viola Goetz was a completely stunning young woman in her mid-twenties; blue-black hair, velvety white skin, great sad dark eyes and full red lips. Long beautiful legs, a sensual figure dominated by the most perfect bosom the boys had seen this side of the Bijou or even the stage show at the Oriental Theatre. She dressed in a way no broad around Tulsa had yet thought of. She was fitted into a dark two-piece crepe suit with an open jacket which allowed her delicious bosom necessary freedom to move on its own.

Ma's ears went flat and she nearly hissed. She squatted on the

79

edge of her green velour club chair like a great horned toad and prepared to demolish the distracting visitor while Goetz and the boys slouched back to the kitchen to expedite the ice cream.

"Hurry back now, heah?" said Viola in a mock southern accent which struck Ma as a peculiar way to talk.

Five foot two, eyes of blue, can she, can she, can she woo . . . sang Freddie in the kitchen, tilting his shopworn refill bottle of cough medicine.

"Ma don't like broads hangin' around," Dock said to Goetz with a grin. "No booze, no broads."

"Is that a fact?" Goetz clicked his glass and downed a shot.

"Your wife is some looker," Dock said.

"Huh? Oh, well I tell ya, Dock, she's not my wife. Not really."

"What?"

Goetz smiled.

"I'm not married. I tell people Viola's Mrs. Goetz." He lit a cigarette. "A wife is a damn good front for respectable neighborhoods. If they think you're married, the neighbors are satisfied. They're less likely to call the cops than if they thought you were living with a broad."

He tapped his ashes in the sink.

"Don't get the straight-laced folks stirred up," he said.

"Why doncha just *get* married?" Fred said.

Goetz smiled again.

"I don't believe in it," he said. "She lives a good life. She doesn't mind."

The northern ways of big city gangsters were new and strange to simple country boys.

"If you get holed up with a bimbo," Goetz said, "get yourself a ring at the ten cent store." He flashed his in the light. "It's a great cover."

"Well, Ma don't trust women," Dock said. "Natural born stool pigeons. They're bad fer business."

"Broads are bad for business but good fer what ails ya," Freddie said. "So is this." He downed a shot, had another small coughing spell which he extinguished with a drink and leaned against the wall, grinning.

"Speaking of business, one time Dion O'Bannion and Al Capone . . ." Goetz began. The ice cream slowly melted.

In Ma's expensively furnished living room, Viola Goetz found a cut crystal goblet and poured herself an ounce of gin from her monogrammed flask.

"Don't put yer feet on the furniture, honey," Ma said.

"Sure, Ma."

"And yew should keep yore knees together."

"Yowsa."

"No real lady drinks likker, ye know."

"That's too bad, Ma." Viola's dark eyes lazily fixed on Ma over the glass. "I'm glad I'm not real. Think what I'd be missin'."

Young Mr. Goetz, personable, likeable, dimpled, wavy-haired, clothed in Kuppenheimer's finest, brushed aside Ma's beaded curtains and joined the ladies.

"Well now, you two been getting acquainted?" He smiled. "I've been telling the boys about my experiences."

Beautiful Viola turned to deal with her mate.

"That's all that bird does," she cried. "Business all the time!"

Ma yawned horribly without knowing it.

Fred sat down, staring at Mrs. Goetz.

Viola recrossed her long perfect legs, managing somehow to shift her mid calf hem to mid-thigh before the skirt settled and the action stopped.

Fred gulped.

Husband and wife played a familiar scene.

"Goetz, honey," Viola said. "I get goddam tired of 'when I was top gunner for Mr. Capone' and 'Bam! they bounced like duck-pins when I leaned the old chopper into 'em in the garage on St. Valentine's Day.' Goetz, you got a one-track mind like Mr. Coolidge said."

"Well, gee, honey, it's all true. I can't help it if I'm famous."

"Well, gee, Goetz, old Viola gets tired of listening to that junk day and night. Big shot fraternity man, big shot athlete, big shot war hero. You've really got a big shot mouth. That mouth is gonna be the death o' you yet."

"There now, honey, you'll be OK when you sober up."

Viola's beautiful face flushed.

"Don't you call me a boozer, Fred Goetz, or I'll tell the folks about the time you were a big shot lifeguard. About the time you saved Little Orphan Annie from drowning and the cops had to save *her* from *you!*"

Goetz smiled and shot his cuffs.

"Don't get carried away, Viola. When you start dreaming out loud, you're not funny anymore."

"The all-American!" She spread her arms and her bosom rose. Ma choked. "The all-American! Oh, we had it rough over in France!" Viola cried. "I was president of my fraternity, see my ring? The only university man at the St. Valentine's Day Massacre!"

"OK, Viola . . . beddy-bye." Goetz took her arm. "We're getting a little raucous, baby. Time to re-tire. Put on your Dr. Dentons and light your little candle."

Viola stood up, balancing on her showgirl heels.

"Don't push, Sgt. York, I can get there myself. G'night everybody, I'm please t'metcha all."

Goetz turned and waved from the door.

"G'night Mrs. Barker, fellas, see y'tomorrow."

"Goodnight Goetz," Ma said. The boys stared at the closed door where fantastic Viola Goetz had stood just a moment before.

Ma snorted and stubbed out her cigarette.

"Goodnight! There ye see it, boys. Wimmin, whiskey and too much talkin'. I wouldn't trust that gal from here to the lamppost." She lit a cigarette and puffed furiously. " 'It is better to dwell in the wilderness, than with a contentious and angry woman.' "

"Boy, she's some looker, ain't she Alvin?" Fred mumbled.

"She's some broad."

Ma frowned through her smoke.

82

" 'Thine eyes shall behold strange women, and thine heart shall utter perverse things.' Git yore mind outa th' gutter and on higher things. Read The Book now and then. 'Proverbs'."

Fred pulled his new overcoat from the closet and shrugged his skinny shoulders into its silk lining. Viola and her lace underwear leg-crossing had upset his precarious libido.

"Goin' to the picture show, Ma."

"Which one? Not one o' them nasty chorus-gal movies, is it?"

"Nah, a cowboy pitcher with Hoot Gibson."

"OK then, Freddie. Don't be out late now."

Ma puffed earnestly at her bent cigarette.

"He's spendin' a lot o' time goin' to the movies in the middle o' the night."

•

The Hart kidnapping looked sensible to Ma. A stint of hard work would be good for boys still dazed from the brief brush with tempting Viola Goetz. A kidnapping was a challenge to Ma's natural generalship and talent for logistics, her fondness for clockwork timing. Roadmaps and notebooks were spread on the Florentine extendable dining-room table, Sears Roebuck doilies to one side.

$100,000 was the reasonable ransom.

A neat white clapboard two-story house in a pleasant section of Bensenville, Illinois, twenty miles west of Chicago, was available for the detention of the victim. For a fee.

A long black 1931 Chrysler 8 sedan, white sidewalls and trunk in back, a really fine-looking car, would be used. Its speed and size were practical but its very aristocratic look might turn away possible police interest out on the highway. Ma understood the value of appearances.

An opaque hood over Hart's head and shoulders would be replaced after dark with goggles lined with cotton so that he would not see the kidnappers or the route they took.

Dock sighed with satisfaction as the meeting was adjourned.

"Hart owns a brewery, should be plenty of dough around," he said.

"There had better be. All this costs a whole lot o' money," Sawyer said.

Ma sat back, her heavy features impassive, puffing a cigarette, candy wrappers scattered around her chair.

"This man Hart is evil, providing drink fer the childern of God," she said. "When ye hit such a man, yore doin' the work of the Lord."

She reached in and loosened her corset.

"And as the Good Book says, 'The ransom of a man's life are his riches', Proverbs, ex-eye-eye, four."

"Amen," said Sawyer.

•

Noon, Friday, June 15, a hot cloudy day in St. Paul, Gardner Hart, the tall millionaire bachelor set out on foot from the family brewery for the family mansion where his mother had lunch waiting. Black clouds had been forming all day. If he walked fast, he could beat the rain.

He was half a block from home, well in sight of the double chimneys, Gothic dormers, fat brick tower and ornate weather vane of the three-storied family fortress when the man stepped out on the sidewalk, smiling, hand extended.

"Mr. Hart?"

Hart paused (the man must be an employee), and Alvin Karpis spun him around and Fred Barker shoved him into the back of the long black Chrysler, Dock threw the hood over his head and the prize was theirs. As they bounced away down the street, Karpis raised Hart's hood and Fred shoved the papers across the seat.

"Sign all four," he said. "Sign the papers or I'll bust your fingers."

They stopped in Como Park (sentimental memories of helpful Anton Kuhlberg) to drop Karpis and Fred at the Goetz family Ford. The Chicago supergangster and Romney Daley, swinging his brand-new blackjack, took their places in the Chrysler. Karpis doubled back to the apartment command post to begin the telephoning.

With Hart on the floor in back, attended by Goetz and Romney Daley, Dock drove the white side-walled Chrysler Imperial Eight off through the sweltering afternoon to Bensenville.

•

Far away in Bensenville, Ma read her Bible through the long nervous day, buoyed by an occasional nougat creme and, at midnight, when the Chrysler swung into the driveway of the innocent-looking white clapboard house and braked to a stop beside the back stoop, she took goggled Gardner Hart by the hand and with Goetz pointing the flashlight and Romney Daley holding the blackjack at the ready, led him up the narrow stairs to the second floor bedroom.

With the goggles off, Hart was a right handsome young man with a strong resemblance to one of her dearest favorites, Ralph Graves, the Hollywood picture star. Ma wondered about a nice warm bath.

Hart, exhausted by twelve hours crouching on the floor, stumbled into the room and fell over the wooden chair onto the bed. Romney laughed. Hart played the game. Blindman's buff, Prisoner's Base, it seemed too much a ritual to be real. The urgency in their voices told him it was real. Particularly the one they called Romney. Strange name for a thug. A borderline case. Hart couldn't help feeling Romney wanted to break his skull with a blackjack.

"Now when I take off the goggles, don't turn around," Goetz said. "Face the wall. Don't try to get a look at any of us or we'll have to bump you off."

Romney liked the way Goetz talked.

"You want to use the can, holler and I'll unlock the door. Keep your eyes on the floor, the can is at the end of the hall. Then come back in here and sit down facing the wall and I'll lock you in again."

At the door, he paused, looking at the millionaire slumped in the chair, rubbing his eyes.

"Don't try to catch a look at us, Hart. It could be a bad mistake for you."

The locks slid into place.

While Dock and Romney gassed up the Chrysler, Ma stood

85

at the peephole watching Hart sprawled on the bed shielding his eyes from the naked overhead bulb. Nice-looking boy. A picture star or a baseball player. Real set of shoulders on him.

"Come on Ma," Dock yawned. "Long trip."

Final instructions to Goetz, a last peek at the wealthy young prisoner sitting alone in the tiny boarded-up bedroom reading a tattered copy of *Colliers Weekly* and Ma went back to St. Paul to supervise negotiations.

They got to the apartment at noon.

Scowling Alvin Karpis met her at the curb, his arms loaded with Kewpie dolls, wall pennants and the framed hand-tinted pictures of Jesse James and Jesus Christ.

"Who done it?" Ma said, her poor old mother's heart pounding, "Who blabbed?"

"Some snot around here," Karpis said, depositing his treasure in the back of the Barker '31 wire wheeled blue Dodge sedan. He waved his arm at the surrounding apartment houses.

"Some crummy neighbors," he said and he and Ma dashed back into the building to load the last of their pitiful belongings.

Fred came downstairs full tilt with his .45 caliber golf bags.

"Sawyer called us," he said as he passed.

"Yeah," said Karpis, ushering Ma into the stripped apartment. "Some funny guy said we was suspicious characters but Sawyer's man got on the phone and held up the investigation. We gotta coupla hours."

"Well, I'm glad t'see Sawyer is good fer somethin'," Ma said, collapsing on a wobbly folding chair. "With what I hafta pay out t'him." Her lucky purse clunked to the floor.

"Lord God," she said, mopping her sweaty face.

"Hey Ma," Karpis yelled from the bathroom. "You wanta save this pile grease? Suppository ointment?"

"Oh yes," she said, blowing her nose. "Oh my yes. 'Specially now. I surely do."

•

Karpis wriggled into the drugstore phone booth and called the intermediary Martin Gray, Hart's brewery sales manager, with the news.

"A hundred thousand, that's a lot of money," Gray said, chuckling gamely. Some of Mr. Hart's young friends, big sense of humor.

"We're not kiddin'," Karpis said.

Gray laughed.

"OK, OK," he said. "I got a lot of work to do. Who is this?"

"Listen, you sonofabitch!" Karpis yelled. "You get that fuckin' money and you have it where I told ya or I'll kill Hart and you too!" He slammed down the phone. The receiver danced on its cord.

The druggist glanced over. Young punks, no respect for property.

Frowning, Gray called the mansion.

Mr. Hart was not home. It was not a joke after all.

●

The new apartment was smaller and more expensive. Ma's earthly possessions were left packed in the car. They would live out of suitcases until the Hart kidnap money was paid and they could see their way clear to live like other people without the implacable cops sneaking up on them every fifteen minutes.

Harry Sawyer graciously agreed to handle incoming calls and alert Ma when something important came through. For a fee.

The three Barkers dozed and Karpis slept against the door, .45 in his right hand.

It had been a long, busy day. Too much had happened. Cross country travel, another unpleasant eviction, phone calls to a wise guy. They had an important kidnapping to consummate. The hell with the other apartment. Ma was confused. Hard to tell where they were anymore. Which town. Which apartment. Which day.

She jerked awake out of a snoring nightmare.

"The phone, git the phone!"

Dock had the receiver to his ear.

"Yeah?"

Fred and Karpis struggled awake. Ma studied little Dock's face. Pomaded hair standing on end, he slumped over the phone rubbing his eyes.

87

"Yeah, who's this? Verne? Well fer crissake, howya bin, Verne? No kiddin'?"

"Who is it?" Ma hissed.

Dock cupped his hand over the mouthpiece.

"It's Verne Miller in Kay Cee," he said. "A big one, huh, Verne?"

Ma was furious.

"Verne *Miller?* What the hell's *he* want, callin' up? Tell 'im to git off the line, we got a big call comin' through."

Dock closed his eyes.

"Nah, Verne, it's Ma. She says hello."

"What's he *want?*" Ma yelled. "Is he after a *job?* Tell him we're full up."

Dock turned away, cradling the receiver on his shoulder as he tried to light a cigarette.

"No kiddin' . . . yeah. They did? Jesus, that's against the *law*, ain't it? Hah! That's a laugh, Verne. That's too bad . . . yeah."

Ma clawed at Dock's arm.

"What the hell does he *want?* Git him off the line!"

Dock yawned.

"He wants to know if Alvin and Freddie kin come down an' help him out in Kay Cee. Bring the machine guns."

"Tell him no an' hang up."

"Can't do it Verne . . . Nah, we're all tied up right now. Yeah." His cigarette hung on his lip.

"Hang up on him!" Ma yelled.

"Well thanks anyway . . . Verne. Yeah, lotsa luck Verne . . . you know we would if we could Verne . . . so long, Verne."

He clacked the receiver in the fork and sat with both hands clutching the telephone.

"What's that bonehead want?" Ma said.

Dock shook his head.

"The Federals kidnapped Jelly Nash! They're takin' him back to Leavenworth an' they're comin' through Kay Cee on the train an' ole Verne figgers him an' two good boys with choppers could cut Jelly loose from the cops when they cross to the parkin' lot. He wanted Karpis and Freddie."

Ma stood up, scratching under her beefy arms.

"He did, huh? He's got some nerve tyin' up our phone when we got important business on it."

•

At nine-thirty, Karpis sent a note to Gray's house by cabdriver. With Dock and Freddie, he followed the cab in the Barker family Chrysler and the boys were impressed by the swarm of detectives in Gray's neighborhood.

"The family told the cops," he said.

"We can wait," Dock said.

•

The night dragged on. Karpis went out in the morning to call Hart's go-between again. Fred slept and Dock played solitaire while Ma tried to change the needle in her Victrola for a little "Sunny Side." She thrust the extra-loud-tone steel needle deep into her thumb, pulled it out and sat back to rest. Life was too complicated.

"It ain't the needle," Fred said. "It's the mainspring is busted."

"It's the needle," Ma said. "Don't tell me what it is."

"It's the mainspring."

"Shut yore ridgerunner mouth!" she yelled.

Karpis came back with doughnuts and coffee. He unrolled the scare-headlined early extra edition and tossed it on the floor.

"Get a load o' *this!*" he said. "Lookit that crap! Kansas City Massacree! Verne Miller really screwed up! They killed four cops but *Nash* got killed!"

Ma took a fresh doughnut and passed the sack to Freddie.

Dock studied the first page.

"This don't look so good, y'know? Droppin' people all over the sidewalk . . . I'm damn glad we didn't go *down* there."

"Kidnappin' is a lot easier an' it pays better," Ma said, chewing.

Dock shook his head.

"I thought Verne Miller was smarter than that. He ain't worth a damn now."

"Mother knows best," Ma said.

"I coulda pulled it off right," Freddie said.

Karpis snorted.

"Don't kid yourself."

"Don't try to tell me nothing, Alvin," Freddie said.

Ma smiled at her boys.

"I have taught thee in the ways of wisdom: I have led thee in right paths."

"What about Hart? What the hell is the family up to?" Dock said, tossing the saga of Jelly Nash aside.

"Still foolin' around," Karpis said. "That guy Gray thinks he's a real comedian."

Dock said nothing. Ma began a third doughnut and Freddie dragged into the bathroom.

Karpis stood by the window watching a man down the block watering his lawn. An ice truck pulled up and stopped in the street below. The iceman lugged a chunk to a house and the kids gathered free ice splinters on the tailgate. Karpis yawned and stretched. Nothing to do today except listen to the Barkers eat doughnuts. Bank robberies were more interesting. Less complicated.

•

Ma's idea was to make all the moves under cover of night so they waited.

Fred began to pace.

"Are we gonna git the dough or not?" he said.

"Keep yore shirt on," Ma said.

"I'll fix the phonygraf mainspring."

"Don't yew dare touch that machine!"

Fred was beginning to itch. A simple matter to get in the Chrysler, drive back there to Bensenville and throw 50 rounds of .45 caliber into Hart and teach these rich kids a lesson.

Ma was patient.

Late in the afternoon, Karpis went to a different drugstore, Ma's penciled instructions in his hand. He called the go-between and Gray was very serious. Karpis read from his list and arranged for the money to be dropped that night out north of White Bear

Lake on Route 61, with elaborate identifications, specific recognition signals with headlights. Agreed.

At 10:30, Karpis, Dock and Fred using the big Chrysler and a Ford Victoria raced past the go-between's coupe several times and then at last Dock flashed the headlights, Gray did his part and a briefcase was flung out onto the road. The sound of his coupe died away in the night.

Karpis, cradling the Thompson gun, stepped gingerly out on the dark highway and picked up the case.

A hundred thousand bucks is heavy, he thought, hefting the bag into the car and they took off for St. Paul by way of back roads.

The whole thing had been more or less a breeze.

•

Ma was sitting up, wearing her Chinese shantung lounging pajamas when they tumbled into the apartment and locked the door.

Karpis twisted the knob and pulled. The door was locked.

"It looks OK," Dock said, staring at the unbelievable stacks of bills spread over the rug.

"I told that smart sonofabitch it better not be marked," Karpis said.

"Where the hell is the rest of the cake?" Fred called from the kitchenette.

"I et it," Ma said, lighting a cigarette.

"Jesus Christ," Fred said.

"Blas-phemous," Ma said.

"How do we get rid o' this?" Karpis said, flipping a stack of tens. "Serial numbers."

"Sawyer has a couple of guys can go on a tour," Dock said. "They cut across five or six states spending the big ones and spreading the dough around. It ain't hard. It takes time but it's better'n selling it fer 40 cents on the dollar."

Karpis sat crosslegged arranging the money.

"It's a lot of dough," he said and rubbed his neck. "Christ, I'm tired as hell."

"I wasn't this beat on the bank jobs," Dock said, opening the fake French doors. He pulled on the wall-bed and down it came releasing an avalanche of pillows, pennants, Kewpies, souvenir fans and bathrobes, teddy bears and hot water bottles. An enema bag uncoiled its hose like a slim red cobra.

"Ahhh . . ." Dock said and fell into a chair.

•

Sometime during the night, Ma floated out to the living room and switched on the reading lamp. Staring at the spread out stacks of bills, she seated herself in the armchair, a sad terrible look on her battered face and settled down to look at the money.

All of it, acres of it, all real, all in the room and the door locked. She could barely breathe. It was fake, the color was wrong, anyone could see that, some bastard had tricked them with a cheapshit counterfeit job.

She shook her head.

It was all real. A hundred thousand bucks, cash money, no Yankee paper promises, a hundred thousand dollars, all of it right here.

Granted, they took 240,000 from Concordia, but more than half of it was fancy bank crap, securities, questionable stuff maybe not worth a damn after negotiations. This was different. Real honest-to-God money.

And what an easy way to pick it up. No gunfire. No trigger-happy bank guards, just one well-behaved target to overpower and the dough is yours. Smart.

She wiped her eyes. Her Pa would be proud of her.

"Hey Ma, turn-off that goddam light," Freddie said.

She sat motionless in the chair, still entranced by the sight of the green packets spread across the rug. The sky lightened to a dirty gray and she fell asleep.

•

Viola Goetz, her spectacular naked body covered here and there by a transparent negligee, sprawled on her red velvet chaise lounge, smoking, watching Fred Barker across the room, perched on the edge of the chair like a big-nosed bird about to take flight.

The electric fan roared on in the heat.

"What the hell you lookin' at?" he said. His new hat hopped from one hand to the other.

"You're a wild one, Freddie," Viola said, flipping the cigarette through the open bathroom door. "You're a real wild one."

Fred grunted and stood up. Five visits in a row and no ass. Did she think he just came around with free gin so he could sit and watch her drink it?

"Fred," Viola sat up, lazily swinging her long legs around in front of her.

He saw it all right. He wasn't blind. Maybe she needed a belt right in the teeth. Jezebel. Harlot. She shifted the loose garment around her shoulders. Her nipples were dark rose. He bit his tongue.

"Put somethin' over yourself," he mumbled. "You oughta be ashamed." Cans hanging out like that. Look not upon the nakedness of thy neighbor's wife . . .

She laughed.

"Don't come by tomorrow," she said.

"I will if I feel like it."

"Don't."

"Don't try to tell me."

"I am telling you. You know Freddie, Mr. Goetz may be a dumb cluck but he didn't get that machine-gun reputation for nothing. He might just blow your head off. All the way off."

He glared at her, his new hat sitting his head at a wrong angle.

"There's a rule in this building," she said. "No pets, no children." She licked her lips. "So don't come around anymore." She pulled the negligee around herself. "Find yourself a little pal to play with."

He stood in the hall waiting for the elevator, slapping his twelve-dollar gloves against the potted palm and he thought he heard laughter from the Goetz apartment. That crummy broad was always listening to the radio.

●

At this point, at a small social gathering at Harry Sawyer's apartment, Fatwitted appeared. Freddie couldn't believe it the first time he saw her. Every starlet beachball-holding, pool-splashing, swimsuit-posing, lace stepins-clasping, wide-eyed, cute-mouthed *Film Fun* photo of Toby Wing that he ever salivated over walked up to him and said hello.

Fatwitted's platinum dazzling blonde hair, her soaring bosom, her long perfect legs, her soft violet eyes and full red lips were straight out of his favorite magazine and his most secret orgiastic fantasies.

For once, the pop-eyed terror from the Ozarks was speechless and by the time he regained his voice, he had learned her name, Gladys Hobart, her nickname, and that she had graduated from an exclusive southern girl's school, had operated a comptometer briefly, and (here she giggled deliciously) even been a "madam" in a "brothel."

"Only, only just to help out a dear girl friend you see, only to help on the phone with the bookings, honey, never working in the rooms or anything."

A soft giggle.

She batted her mascaraed lashes and made a note of his $200 suit. The great Fred Barker. Kid Millions.

"I mean, honey, I just *couldn't* do anything of that nature," she murmured. "Evah."

Freddie was sure she couldn't. Positive.

He was therefore a bit surprised, when, taking her home from the evening, he followed her into her apartment and had her on the floor as the door clicked shut behind them. She also did something else that stunned the unsophisticated country boy to the soles of his campus-style two-toned cordovans. He considered it briefly and decided he loved it.

An educational and thoroughly exhausting night followed.

He decided she wasn't really evil, she just loved him so deeply she couldn't help herself. She explained this at some length and then did it again to prove it.

Four days later, when her unfeeling landlady demanded the rent, Freddie paid it.

Ma would love Fatwitted. She was a real down-home country gal but had been to the finest private school in Savannah. Real hightoned. Pretty too. Beautiful. Ma always had an eye for beauty.

•

For her meeting with Ma, Fatwitted wore a shimmering blue silk crepe dress drawn tightly across her buttocks and chest, trimmed with georgette and lace, demure long sleeves and the hem cut just a little higher than usual and she was careful to slide her skirt up over her knees when she sat so Ma could see how truly beautiful her long, silk-stockinged legs were. Real pure silk lace mesh. As she nestled her bottom onto the couch, Fred caught a flash of angelic white thigh above dark stocking that shook his bony knees.

Massive Ma sat rigidly in her button-back velour chair with the Queen Anne legs, bobbling a cigarette between her teeth.

"You got a real name?"

"Gladys. They call me 'Fatwitted' 'cause I'm so smart." She smiled, a wide smile with perfect white teeth. Ma's iron tooth throbbed.

"I reckon yore jest about the smartest, all right," Ma said.

"I graduated from a very exclusive girl's school," Fatwitted said, arching her back like a cat.

"I'll bet it was exclusive," Ma said. "Bars on the windows and guards on the towers."

Fatwitted placed a long white finger against her full soft cheek and frowned slightly.

"What was your school, Mrs. Barker?"

"I didn't go to no school at all, honey," Ma said, grinding her cigarette into the rug. "What I got I got all by myself. An' I didn't get it layin' on my back, neither. I earned everything I own by usin' my brains."

Fatwitted giggled.

"Well, Ma, some got it an' some haven't."

"You got it all right, honey. More than enough."

•

Weekly bathtime. Ma sloshed soapy water over Fred's scrawny back, her thick-fingered, blocky hand shoving the sudsy cloth like a pile driver. Fred sat leaning forward, eyes closed, whistling "Getting To Be a Habit With Me."

"Freddie," Ma grunted. "That Gladys has got to go."

"Fatwitted? What's the matter, Ma?" He grabbed the rim to keep from getting pushed through the end of the tub.

"Fatwitted. That's some name fer a gal. Jest pure trash." She blew her beaky nose in a towel. "I'd never thought I'd see the day, Freddie. I'm disappointed in you, I truly am."

Fred whistled on, dreaming of Fatwitted and secret vice.

"Freddie, I seen her downtown t'day with a black haired feller."

"Fats?"

"That's right. Struttin' along beside him like a female rooster. 'A whistlin' gal an' a crowin' hen, they both will come to a no-good end'."

"She wasn't downtown today."

"She was so."

"She wasn't because I was with her."

Ma pressed her cracked thin lips and wet the rag.

"Here, I'll soap yore leg," Ma said.

He straightened up in the steamy suds.

"I kin do my leg, Ma."

"You never did before, Freddie."

"Well, I can now."

Ma persisted.

Fred lay back, his eyes closed, fingers gripping the rim of the tub so he wouldn't slide down under the gray soapy water.

After a while, he stole a glance at Ma. Hell's fire, if it was a boy's own Ma, it couldn't be wrong.

Ma smiled.

•

For a small consideration, Harry Sawyer told Ma about the Swift & Co. payroll. On August 30, two messengers from the Stockyards National Bank would pick up $30,000 at a railroad car in South St. Paul. For a small consideration, Sawyer threw in a good man familiar with the subject, Charlie Winchester.

Ma marked a street map with heavy black pencil. Concord Street, Gladstone Street Bridge, Point Douglas Road. A different county, at least fox a couple of sheriffs. Thirty grand.

Some ready cash was needed to fill in the awkward time until all the Hart ransom money had been cleared. From time to time, Goetz gave Ma a ransom progress report and usually stayed to thrill the boys with a few yarns of the Golden Age of the Big Gangs. Goetz had just finished report #24 and Ma was squirming in hope that he would leave soon. Perhaps if he didn't, she might step on his foot. Poor old Arthur. Loverboy. A. V. Dunlop would always have a place in her heart.

As regularly as coffee or tea, sang Freddie. Hogging the mirror again, the fool kid had discovered his hair. He combed as he sang. *Ever kiss, ever hug, seems to act just like a drug,/ yore gittin' to be a habit with me.* He parted his matted black hair in the center of his skull, staring like a big-nosed, beady-eyed madman at his shirt-and-tie image.

Ma chewed her lip. Fred had broken with his Ozark beginnings and gone completely St. Paul.

"Cut out that dumb song!" Ma yelled. "I'm tryin' to think!"

" 'At's a good song, Ma." Fred continued, *I cain't break away, I must have yew ever day,/ as regular as coffee or tea.*

"Stop that dirty singin'," Ma said. "It's time yew went t'church again. Plenty o' singin' to be done in church."

He pulled on his jacket, smoothing the swagger peaked lapels, admiring the Hollywood cushion shoulders. Twenty-two inch trouser bottoms, wide overlapping waistband buttoned with three buttons! Nifty slash pockets with button-down flaps. RED HOT! The speediest suit ever designed for a red-blooded fellow! Absolutely the last word and we don't mean maybe! Campus style!

Fred had nearly slugged the pansy tailor (the goof had run his thumb up the tape from Fred's ankle to Fred's balls, pretending to measure his leg) but Goetz had prevailed and the suit had been made after all. Red hot, thought Fred. Goetz himself never looked this classy.

"Gotta take ole Fatwitted out to the Hollyhocks," Fred said. "Put on the dog a little."

"She's an awfully pretty girl," Goetz said. "Really beautiful. I guess it's poetic of me but you know what she has? A look of what they call 'injured innocence'."

Ma snorted.

"It's those enormous eyes, maybe," he went on. "Perpetual surprise. Injured innocence."

"She's a looker, all right," Fred said.

Goetz grinned.

"Why don't you just marry the gal, Fred? There's a lot of advantages. Keeps a man home nights."

Ma brought her fist down on a chocolate cream.

"Now you think yore Dorothy Dix," she yelled. "Advice to the lovesick!"

"The boy's gotta cut the so-called apron strings some day, Kate."

"Why don't you butt outa my bizness, Goetz?" she rasped. "Who asked you anyhow?"

Goetz shrugged.

"Only tryin' to help, Kate."

"Well, *stop* tryin'," Ma roared.

Fred followed Goetz out the door.

"So long Ma, don't wait up."

"Don't be late gittin' in."

"I'm never late gettin' in," he laughed. The door slammed.

"I don't know what's got ahold o' that boy." Ma folded the street map. "But I got a pretty good idea."

•

Roy Purcell and Raymond Thurston, Stockyards Bank messengers, signed the ledger, $30,000, swung the heavy gray cloth bag into the back of the truck and started back to the bank. A Wednesday afternoon in August; the hottest part of the summer. Roy Purcell's mind was on the cool, sparkling lakes up north, drowsing in a boat, when the big, heavy blue Plymouth cut him off. A fender clanged with a frightening noise. He slammed on the brakes, sweating in the heat and swerved against the empty curb in front of the South St. Paul Post Office. There was a stinging sharp smell of hot exhaust. The money bag slid across the back of the truck.

The first shots had an extra loud harsh unreal sound, painfully loud and Purcell's belly turned to mush. He saw the cop running. There was a sense of white hot metal flying through the air. Raymond Thurston had his hands up, scraping the roof of the cab when the two men boiled out across the curb, a big man wearing a dark blue suit; odd, a heavy winter suit on the 30th of August, and a short insane-looking man with a weird suit out of a Valentino movie and the first cop got it with a great smearing red slop of flying blood and gristle which splashed the iron mailbox and his shoes fell off as his torso hit the sidewalk with a sickening smack.

Everyone seemed to be yelling at once as three pairs of hands fought for the gray bag in the back; Roy Purcell trying to give them the bag, the two men socking Purcell's extended fingers with gun muzzles until he howled and the second cop catching a deafening burst of submachine gun fire in the legs and sitting down hard and screaming.

The gray bag was lifted into the air and the two dandies dashed across the red slippery sidewalk to the big Plymouth, doors banged shut, the sedan leaped forward with a roar, and a man energetically smashed out the back window with a tommy gun and red fire flashed all over the muzzle and Purcell scrunched down to the floorboards of his truck and chipped two teeth on the gearshift rod as the windshield glass rained all around him.

He and Thurston crouched there, soaked with sweat for a terrible time until the screaming out on the quiet sidewalk brought them up again.

There was no other sound at all from the dozen motionless people staring at the wreckage of two policemen scattered across the curb next to the crumpled messenger truck. Purcell smelled gasoline and crawled out, his hand pressed to his bleeding mouth.

He wondered dully why the tommy-gunner in the sedan

hadn't rolled down his window instead of smashing it open to poke the gun through.

•

Fred Barker, in the rear of the Plymouth, tommy gun flaming, sprayed the street with machine-gun fire, shattering store windows for two blocks. Bystanders ran screaming or flattened out where they were. He laughed. His control was much better, Dock said. Brass all over the back seat like shiny peanut shells. Clean that shit out when we're outa town, not around here, everybody watching.

"Roll the windows down, I can't stand the smell o' that crap."

"You belong in some other business."

Fred noticed a powder burn on his new suit.

Karpis had a new toy. When the two patrolmen, Joe Dusik and Vernon Bates went down under Freddie's fire, Alvin had grabbed a brand new tommy gun on the dead run.

"Red Grange," Fred said.

"Better," Alvin said.

•

Freddie took the beautiful Fatwitted out for a drive after supper in his new Shadow Blue Chrysler Imperial Custom Eight. A long low exciting car, the engine cowling half its length. Wire wheels, white side-walls, convertible top, rumble seat, floating power, free wheeling. Real leather upholstery, ideal for flipping a platinum blonde on her back. Or her head for that matter. The night was heavy and hot, crickets blasting away back in the heavy bushes around the porches. At the corner, the kid was yelling with an extra urgency. He wore a cap and knickers and held the extra over his head as he faced the traffic at the intersection. Fred stepped on the brakes.

"Extry get yer Pioneer Press!" The kid came up to the car. "Extry, Gangland strikes in payroll holdup, policeman dead! EXTRA! Payroll holdup!"

Fred nudged Fatwitted.

"Gimme a paper, kid."

"Sure," the boy fumbled in his greasy cloth apron for change.

"Keep it," Fred said, throwing the roadster into low.

"Thanks, mister."

Fred stopped again and leaned out the window.

"Gimme all them papers."

The boy bumped against the car.

"Gee whiz, you gonna read 'em all? They're all the same."

"I know, dummie. Gimme the lot."

He flipped the boy a ten-dollar bill.

"Keep it," he said.

"Gee, Freddie," Fatwitted said.

The boy gave a shout and raced away into the dark.

"Gee, you sure are big-hearted," Fatwitted said.

"Yeah, I know."

Fred felt a warm glow as they drove away under the street lights, Fatwitted reading aloud of his skill and daring with the submachine gun.

Later they parked off East Road and she slid down and did that thing again.

•

Her head was too small, perched on top of that great long neck, her eyes were too big and sick and the brown discolorations below were balanced by the thin sad penciled brows above. A long, thick nose was no help at all to the uncertain smile on her small hard lipped mouth.

Romney Daley flashed his big jawed scoutleader grin as he intoduced her to Ma.

"Enid Darrow, Mrs. Barker. The papers call ole Enid 'The Kissin' Bandit', don't they, Enid?"

"Yeah, ain't that a cute one?" The voice was Cookson Hills, red-clay Oklahoma. "The Kissin' Bandit. I got a whole scrap-book I saved up."

Ma busied herself rearranging the souvenir trophies along the mantel.

" 'The Kissin' Bandit.' I swear we're gettin' more amateurs than we had in Tulsa."

Romney chuckled.

"Ever time she rob some sap, she'd give 'im a great big ole kiss! Ain't that right, Enid?"

Enid giggled nervously.

"Well, most of 'em. If they was cute enough I would."

Ma placed the plaster Siamese twins (TWIN CITIES) next to the TULSA sombrero ashtray.

"How much you take in a year?"

Enid blinked her great purple eyes.

"Gee Ma, I dunno. I never keep track."

"Doesn't sound like much, honey."

"Oh it was enough. Mostly fer laughs anyway. You shoulda seen the look on their faces! I like to bust a gut at some of 'em."

Ma clicked her teeth. Romney grinned earnestly.

"Ain't she a riot, Ma?"

"Oh she's a riot," Ma said. "She surely is a riot. She's a double barrel riot. 'The Kissin' Bandit'! Great God . . ."

Romney corked Enid on her skinny arm.

"Ma, I knew you an' Enid would hit it off right away!"

Her souvenir tableau realigned, Ma turned to Enid.

"I tell ye, honey, when *we* git through workin' on somebody we leave 'em somethin' to remember us by an' it ain't a great big *kiss* either."

Enid Darrow nodded solemnly.

Ma paused at the giant floral wreath on the sideboard. She flicked the dead evergreens with her thick finger.

"This looks about right. Send it to that dead copper."

She turned and smiled, her new bridgework glistening.

"It'll show that I forgive him fer attackin' my son."

She straightened the ribbon.

"There's some things a woman understands that a man can't."

She twisted the dead lawyer's ring on her little finger.

"Alvin," she called. "Stick a card on it sayin' 'Good Luck' or somethin' real thoughtful and sweet."

She brushed past Romney and his girl.

"*Kissin'* bandit . . . kiss my ass."

•

The next day, Harry Sawyer told Ma to leave St. Paul. He could control police investigation only so far and then some responsibility had to shift to the Barkers.

"One cop is dead, one is paralyzed for life. Killing people doesn't go down well around here. I can't protect you on that kind of stuff. You know that kid o' yours is trigger-happy."

"Don't you start anything against my boys."

"I won't argue about it. You gotta leave town."

"The cops attacked Freddie! They started in to kill the boy! He's jest a baby and them bastards won't leave him alone."

Sawyer lit a cigar and dropped the wrapper on the floor.

"You got an hour or so. You better get goin'," he said and left, a wisp of El Perfecto turning slowly in the still air.

Ma began the roundup. Chipped plaster Kewpies, the pot-bellied bear from Kansas City, pennants, pillows and pictures. Snapshots of the boys, frowning at the camera in the noonday sun, ragged overalls and patched knickers, caps shading their tough young faces. The Brownie camera Dock stole from a drugstore back years ago. Right handsome photographs. Tears of sentiment and rage welled up in Ma's puffy eyes.

Karpis silently carried the guns down to the car in golf bags. As they sweated down the stairs with the heavy stuff, Fred tried twice to start an argument and gave it up. Alvin wasn't talking today.

Karpis wondered if other gangs moved as often as the Barkers. Freddie seemed more interested in drilling holes in the opposition than in getting away with the money.

•

CHICAGOLAND, QUEEN OF THE MIDWEST: the red letters flowed across a fat bright green silk pillow fringed with buckskin.

Ma placed it in the center of her crowd of Kewpies, pennants and fans in the new apartment.

Chicago was a big city, close enough to St. Paul and still far enough. Big enough to get lost in while the latest St. Paul outrage cooled.

In the great Barker exodus from St. Paul, Freddie decided Fat-witted, his own true love, should accompany the refugees to Chicago. Ma, seeing Fatwitted as a potential witness against them, agreed.

As a means of eliminating Fatwitted's separate dwelling expenses, Freddie decided she should move into the Barkers' new larger quarters in Chicago, the Edgemont Arms. Ma disagreed violently but Dock convinced her that until the hot Hart kidnapping money could be exchanged, austerity would have to prevail.

In the Barker mob, heavy with overhead, there were serious financial problems. Too many of the gang newcomers weren't bringing in money. Namely, the girls. The big city mobsters all had women and the women all had talent for spending money. $20,000 from a bank was a decent take for four country boys living under one roof, but a drop in the bucket for clothes, nightclubs and 8-cylinder wirewheeled cars for free-loading northern girls.

Slowly but surely, Ma could feel her grip on the gang lessening. Nobody listened. Nobody listened to anything. In the rush for more money, jobs were pulled without adequate planning, without Ma. Instead of a prudent thousand mile round trip, a bank in the next town or the next block might be the target.

Police were less cooperative.

Armor plating was installed by a friend of Goetz from the old Chicago days.

"Fine lotta good that tin is gonna do if ye gotta fight off a hunderd cops, ye dumbbells," Ma said.

Freddie grinned and kicked the steel side.

"We got smoke hanger-nades too," he said. "Just like the goddam U.S. Army."

"Don't swear, Freddie," Ma said and waddled over to the elevator, leaving him alone in the parking garage with his armored roadster.

•

The boys went into action immediately.

Yellow smoke boiled over the narrow crowded street in thick choking clouds blotting out both armored cars as the gang made their getaway. Somebody rang an alarm and two fire engines howled down the street from opposite ends and locked bumpers in the opaque fog.

Foul yellow phosphorus hung in layers. Two payroll messengers had been jumped, several official bags taken from their truck.

The gray-haired police sergeant stood coughing in the smoke, a wet handkerchief to his red face, shaking his head at the destruction. A light pickup truck lay on its side.

Machine-gun fire had broken windows, chipped brick and plaster and punctured radiators. Blood spattered across the concrete steps where the patrolman fell. When the sergeant saw the face, he was sick against the side of the truck. He had never until then seen what a machine gun did to a human being.

They were Depression cops. The sergeant provided his own weapon, a 1916 Colt revolver, and bought his own ammunition. The patrol car, a 1928 Ford, was provided by the city, gasoline paid for by the boys at the precinct house. Times were hard, budgets were low. The murdered officer made $20 a week.

Wiping his mouth on his handkerchief, the gray-haired sergeant walked slowly back to the squad car. He shook his head again.

Smoke was a new wrinkle in gang getaways. Next thing, airplanes. Death rays, men from Mars. Ming the Merciless.

The gang had expected to heist a payroll. The bags they stole contained regular mail.

•

"You dumb punks!"

Ma kicked savagely at the machine gun recoil spring which twanged into the side of her Venetian carved chair and Karpis sighed.

"Don't do that Ma," he said. "I need all them parts to put the chopper back together again."

In BVD undershirt, light gray bellbottoms, white leather belt and two-tone shoes, he crawled on his hands and knees, feeling for the long slim spring.

A Thompson submachine gun lay in scattered parts on a pillow slip in the center of the rug, guarded by a blonde named Connie and a brunette named Florence.

"If you squirts knew what ye was about, ye wouldn't have so damn much trouble," Ma said. "Lissen to me, now and again. Stop actin' as if ye know it all."

"Yeah," Karpis said, beginning the reassembly of the gun. "Where the hell is the actuator?" he yelled.

"What's that mean, honey?" Connie the blonde said.

"Shut up," Karpis said.

Connie shrugged, tapping the buffer rod idly against her left breast, glowing pink in a lacy white bra.

"Put on some clothes, damn it," Ma said.

"It's too hot," Connie said. "Anyway, Alvin would just pull 'em off, soon as he wants it again." Karpis grinned.

Ma snarled incoherently and fell heavily into her favorite velour club chair. A spring popped. The bead fringe jiggled on the fat sculptured table lamp.

In the humid heat, Ma wore her Beatrice Lillie silk beach pajamas, a source of cruel delight to the young girls in the gang. When Ma had tried to reach a top shelf for chocolates, the jacket split. The flash of pulpy white flesh naturally caught the eye of the girls.

"Elephant meat," whispered Connie.

Ma marked Connie for the Soldiers and Pioneers Cemetery. Different country.

Connie rarely appeared in more than bra and lace-trimmed pants whether out of laziness or satanic practicality, Ma never knew. Hatred flickered very close to ignition around the girls.

Florence the brunette was something else again. Her usual costume was a short satin dressing gown and, as Ma learned at a glance, nothing else. The two girls spent all their time as close to Alvin as possible.

Slanty-eyed Billie Gunther was of more immediate concern to Ma.

Billie, a smart, striking girl with glossy black hair, had caught little Dock's eye and, having stunned him, moved in to live with him. Talks with Dock had only one result; Ma was angrier and more frustrated than before. Appeals to common decency, common sense or religious faith brought only yawns. Dock was infatuated with the olive-skinned girl with the dark sloe eyes.

Financial hardship was shrugged aside. Dock had now lost his mind too.

"We'll hit another payroll," Dock said. "In a burg this size, there's plenty of chances. Make a fair payday."

Billie smiled across the room at Ma and Ma clicked her teeth.

Karpis rammed home the rear trigger grip and slid the frame forward in its guide in the receiver. He slid the wooden stock into place and it locked and the submachine gun was assembled again.

"There, by God. I got 'er back again," he said.

"Ain't you something," Fred said.

"You oughta try it," Karpis said. "Be a good idea if you knew somethin' more than just which end the bullets come out of."

"I got more important things to do." Fred closed his pop eyes.

"D'you know how to reload the drum fer instance?"

"Sure."

"Let's see ya load one."

"Whaddya talkin' about? Lemme alone, Karpis. This is my day off fer crissake."

"Butthead," Karpis said. "You don't even know how to throw it on single shot."

"What I need single shots fer? I jest blast 'em and that's that."

"You tell 'em, Freddie," Ma said. "Oh boy."

Karpis flicked the lever to single, then back to full automatic. Telling Fred anything was like talking to a tree.

Fatwitted ambled in from the bedroom and spilled over a chair with such abandon that Ma had to look away. Platinum-blonde Fatwitted wore the uniform of the day, bra and pants of an exotic, lacy, film-starlet-magazine kind that made Ma's fillings hurt. Freddie had been felled like an ox at first sight.

Billie dumped a mailbag on the carpet.

Ma sneered.

"Are you gals goin' to church with me tomorra?"

Fatwitted grinned, full lips cherry red.

"Are you kiddin', honey?"

Ma pulled herself to her feet, silk pajamas wrinkled and damp in the heat. She reached down behind and daintily tugged the cloth from the crack of her massive rump.

"Those are her pajamas and she's stuck with 'em," whispered Fatwitted. Billie was convulsed.

"What's funny?" Ma said.

"Laughin' at the jokes in *Ballyhoo*," Billie said.

"What's that?"

"It's a candy bar, Ma."

"Oh." She belched. "You ain't goin' to church, then?"

"Enn oh," said Billie. "That spells 'no.'"

Ma pouted.

For on the scaffold I must pay / for gambling on the Sabbath Day, she sang.

"Got any other hot news, Ma?" Fatwitted fanned herself with the TULSA fan.

"Put that down," Ma said.

"Sure," Fatwitted said and dropped it on the floor.

Karpis dumped another cascade of mail on the rug and shook out the gray official bag.

"Bunch o' no good mail, fer crissake. Worthless."

"So what?" Fred said.

"So we wasted time fer nothin', that's what!" Alvin said.

"Waste o' time! Time is money! Ole businessman Karpis, always on the ball," Fred jeered.

"Shut your trap, stupid," Karpis said.

"Don't tell me to shut up, boy," Fred said, sitting up.

"Maybe I'll shut it for ya," Karpis said.

"Some o' these letters are pretty funny! Lissen to this . . ." Fatwitted said, leaning dangerously low over the piles of letters.

"Cut that out," Connie said. "Don't you know readin' other people's mail is a goddam felony?"

"You're just sore 'cause you don't know how to read," Fatwitted said.

"Ah shut up."

"Make me, you two dollar jerk."

"Both of ya shut up, er I'll bust yer goddam legs off!" Fred said.

"Calm down, Fred," Karpis said.

"Don't tell me to calm down," Fred said.

Ma placed her beefy hands over her puffy eyes.

There was a piercing scream from the bathroom.

"BY A WATERFALL, I'M CALLING YOU-WHO-WHO-WHOO!!!"

"Lord God, my head is gonna split!" Ma cried.

"WE CAN SHARE ITALLL. . . . BENEATH A SEE-LEEN OF BALOO!"

Dock looked up from his paper.

"WE'LL SPEND A HEVUNNLEE DAY!"

"What's the matter, Ma?"

"HERE WARE THE FLICKAREEN WADDERS SPLAY!"

"That Ray-Mon-Nah is in there singin' again."

Dock grinned.

"Yeah. She's a pretty good ole gal."

"I tell ye, that gal's voice could break *windows*."

Ma searched the end table for something to eat.

"I don't know why I don't go live in Florida with the rich folks."

She took an apple from the bowl and bit into it. In a burst of indignation and wax chips she threw the artificial apple at the fireplace.

"More goddam funny Yankee jokes," she said.

The girls smiled to themselves.

Ma turned to Dock and punched at his newspaper.

"Don't do that, Ma. That makes my eyes jump."

"There's too many *people* with us, Dock."

"There ain't too many, Ma."

"The hell there ain't, we're all jammed up with 'em!"

"Ma, when we work with a bunch this size, it's better to keep 'em all together where we can keep watch on 'em."

"That's jest it, Dock. They's too many *of* 'em."

"The more the merrier, Ma."

"Thirteen is too many, an' it's plain unlucky."

"How's it unlucky?"

"You use that armor-plate in the cars and smoke hanger-nades and you kill a cop and end up with five bags o' mail! Not even any *dough!* You think that ain't unlucky?"

"That's just a accident, Ma."

"When you kill a cop, you make the rest of 'em pissed off at ye. You got every cop in Chicaga lookin' fer ye."

"I reckon so, Ma." He straightened his paper.

Four-inch black headlines listed the dead and injured, calling for civic revenge. A retouched photograph of the policeman's widow and children. When is my Daddy coming home?

Ma smacked the paper with her fingers.

"Look at that, I knew it was unlucky!"

Dock rubbed his eyes.

Billie seated herself on the arm of Dock's chair, her slim arm around his shoulder, the curve of her breast against his cheek.

"Aw, fer Pete's sake, Ma," she said. "Stop yellin' at him. Lay off 'im, why don'cha?"

Dock straightened up, whitefaced, and cuffed Billie smartly across the face.

"Don't you talk to my Ma like that," he said.

Ma smiled horribly, iron teeth and wax chips.

"Dock, yore jest the best ole son any mother could ask for."

Dock was trembling with rage.

"Don't you worry, Ma. I'll see she gits some manners."

"That's right, Dock," Ma crooned.

Billie stood near the door, rubbing her cheek.

"Dock," she said. "You're in fer a long dry spell."

•

Miniature golf would get the boy out in the fresh air and a mother could guide him gently away from sins of the flesh. Ma wore tennis shoes, ankle socks, pleated skirt, a middie jumper, a spinachy-green sash around her head and a green sun visor just like Helen Wills.

Freddie wore his old golf costume still streaked with Kansas City mud.

The weather-stained greens were littered with cigarette butts, matchbooks and candy wrappers. First hole was a Dutch wind-mill, a cast-iron Negro with his mouth open was the third hole, number five was a tiny lighthouse. Object, hit ball through base of lighthouse into drainpipe avoiding curved tin guard rails or ball will reappear in foot of water in tiny cement pond.

Ma dug in with her new tennis shoes and swung.

"That counts one stroke when ya miss," Fred said.

"You know hoors are unfaithful, don't ye?" Ma said.

"What's hoors got to do with me?"

Ma hit the ball down the plank, through the barn, out across the wrinkled fairway against the backstop and into the cigarette butts.

"You know Fatwitted is a hoor?"

"Ah, that's jest talk."

The ball scuttled uphill, wobbled in warped fairway, struck the wooden backstop and disappeared.

"It ain't jest talk, it's a plain fact. She runs a hoor-house, she's a hoor."

"Ah, you know how gossip is."

The ball smacked off the blue wooden deflector, struck the yellow wooden Mickey Mouse, dropped down the red tile chute, fell out next to the cup and rolled to a stop against a half-finished candy bar.

"Freddie, you ain't accusin' yer own mother of bein' a *gossip*, are ye?"

"No, Ma, gee whiz. I never said a thing like that."

"Well I should hope not." She sank the putt. "I win, you owe me."

A large milky condom draped over the red guard rail.

"Must be lettin' coons use the course," Ma muttered.

•

Fred pulled toward the inside door and Fatwitted flipped off the apartment hall light. Three in the morning.

"Come on Freddie. We don't have to go in the house."

"Jesus, Fats . . ."

They clung together in the dark vestibule.

"Do it Fred," she hissed in his ear.

"I can't."

"Why not? Sure you can." She buried her tongue in his mouth, then pressed her face to his ear.

"Do it standing up," she whispered.

"How?"

"Hold still, I'll show ya."

She did.

•

BOOK
TWO

□□

In the soft orange glow of Ma's bead-fringed lamps, the Barker gang passed a quiet September evening at home. The girls filed and enameled their nails, marcelled their hair and yawned, waiting for Ma to go to bed so the merry-go-round could start. Ma, frizzy hair fiery from fresh henna, sat bright-eyed and alert, humming "Keep On The Sunny Side," chomping caramels from a new sampler.

Estelle Williams, 22, was Alvin Karpis' new friend. They sat in a shadowy far corner of the living room and redheaded Estelle ran her fingers over Alvin's skinny neck and giggled. A satin robe trimmed with ostrich feathers and mules just like the gun molls wore in the movies.

Dock Barker, the gang intellectual, read the *Chicago Tribune*. Pages of crap about the N.R.A. Goofy initials being stuck on everything. C.C.C., A.A.A., T.V.A., F.C.A., P.W.A., H.O.L.C. Alphabet soup. Sally Rand at the Chicago Century of Progress World's Fair. Tickling her tits with ostrich feathers. How'd you like to biff that? He turned to the sports pages.

"Levinsky's a bum," he said. "Sharkey'll murder 'im."

"Betcha fifty," Fred said.

"You still owe me from the Smellin' fight."

"Anybody bet on that sauerkraut don't deserve no money."

Dock slammed down his paper.

"He was the heavyweight champeen."

"He got it by grabbin' his balls," Fred said.

"Sharkey hit 'im in the balls. That's a foul," Dock said.

"The hell Sharkey did. Sharkey hit 'im on the chin and he sat down and grabbed his balls!" Fred yelled.

"Watch your language, there's ladies present," Fatwitted said.

"Yeah? Where?" Karpis said.

"All right, Karpis!" Fred yelled. "Step outside!"

"Attaboy, Fred!" yelled Ma.

"Shut up and sit down," Dock said, gold-headed stick tapping against his palm.

Fred flopped on the rug next to Ma's overstuffed chair.

"Tell about Fort Smith," he said. Ma smiled beatifically.

"When Cherokee Bill was hung," she said, "he was asked at the end if he had any last words. 'Hell no,' he says, 'I come here to die, not to make a speech.' He was covered up with soil to keep th' buzzards from cheatin' th' worms. Ole Hangin' Jedge Parker took to drinkin'. He went to the bottle oftener an' stayed longer. Ugly as home-made sin."

Freddie sighed.

"Tell about Grandma," he said.

Ramona and Billie yawned with extravagant boredom.

Ma lit a cigarette, spilling sparks over her barrel belly.

"Grandma loved kissin', wrasslin' and boiled cabbage; hated hot weather, tight clothes and circuit riders. Believed in the remission of sins. Things're different today. Gals ain't near as pretty, fer one thing."

"Fatwitted is a good looker, though," Freddie said.

"*Fatwitted!*" Ma snorted a shower of sparks and smoke. "That squatty old lard-stand of a gal? You know, that gal looks fat enough to *kill!*"

"Ole Ma's a card." Karpis grinned as he sighted the tommy gun. He swung it around, "POW! POW! POP! POP!" until it was aimed at friendly young Estelle. He dragged the muzzle across her smooth bodice and the satin robe parted. Sure enough, there were two round white breasts. Still there from last night. Smiling demurely, Estelle closed the robe and with her soft white hand she pushed the blueblack barrel aside.

"Leave that thing here and bring the other one," she said sweetly as she led him out of the room.

Ma had the vision of an eagle.

"Damn if we ain't runnin' a regular crib here," she said.

"Now Ma, don't git exercised now," Dock said behind his paper. "We ain't all that hightoned."

She turned on him.

"How long's it been since you went to church?"

He rattled the pages. Sally Rand's knockers. Ooooh. Um umm.

"I don't remember, Ma."

"Well, you oughta think about it boy."

"Come on now Ma, this ain't Tulsa."

"No, Dock, it sure ain't and that's one thing *wrong* with it."

"Come on Ma, I'm tryin' to read the paper." Sally Rand.

"You'd be better off readin' the Bible."

"Yeah."

Ma found the packet of fiber needles, pressed one into the battered playing arm, cranked furiously and placed her thick old record of "Keep On The Sunny Side" on her Victrola.

Ramona and Billie stood up. Ramona yawned. Billie blinked sleepily and winked at Dock who cleared his throat as he studied Miss Rand's leg.

"Damn chippies," Ma muttered.

Goetz, the well-known legend, looked up from his card game. He was due to go back to his own apartment any hour.

"Gee, Kate, you shouldn't be so rough on the gals."

"Don't call me Kate," Ma snarled. "Kate . . ."

Ramona and Billie, the Duncan Sisters, linked arms and softly sang, "*K-K-K-Katie*" as they exited.

Ma sank her steel fingers into the overstuffed mohair.

"I heard that."

•

The Florida palms stand silent in the mist at Lake Weir. Through the blueblack gloom three FBI agents crawl slowly up behind a thick hedge bordering a lawn. Submachine guns slanting in the murky light.

The Negro, Lennie, crouching behind the hedge with the FBI, points out a white two-story cottage gleaming faintly off in the mist beyond the palms.

"That's the place," he whispers.

"You're sure, now?" Lafferty says.

"Hell Mister, I work there."

A sheriff claps a hand on the Negro's arm.

"OK boy, you stay right here with us."

The Negro shrugs as he squats down.

"I sure hope I don't git *blamed* for this," he mutters. He feels around his overalls. Left his goddam tobacco home. Ask to borrow some from Mr. Charlie and get hung to a tree.

The cottage is ghostly and still, back of the palms.

An agent leans on his submachine gun, gazing into the drifting mist.

"So that's where the Barkers are holed up."

"Karpis is most likely with 'em. He's one tough son of a bitch."

"Look at that goddam fog."

Extra drums of ammunition laid out.

"We'll have to wait for the fog to settle. You can't see a damn thing in it."

"Cain't see from here to there."

"One thing sure with fog this bad, they're probably not going anyplace. We'll wait for things to clear off a bit."

A sheriff is impatient with the college-boy cops.

"The hell with it, let's move in an' git 'em."

"Anybody makes a dumb move like goin' after 'em in all this fog will have to answer to me personally. That's all they need to make an easy getaway."

"Hell, we could go in there an' take 'em right now."

"I'm in charge here. Any more lip and I'll take your gun away."

The sheriff moves off in the gloom, muttering about know-it-all Yankees.

"We gotta wait for the fog to settle, we'd be shootin' into one another. Harvey's gonna have twenty people over behind the place."

"What caliber you think is best for this kind of work?"

"Thirty ought six. Penetrating power is OK, maybe .45 is safer."

".45. When I hit 'em, I don't want 'em getting up again."

"Tear gas?"

"Charlie's got the stuff in the truck."

"I'll never wear one 'o these damn vests again. Forty-five pounds, they feel like a ton. I can't breathe."

"You know, I'd hate to shoot a woman."

"Not this woman, you wouldn't."

"I can hit the house from here, easy as pie. How many people in there, you s'pose?"

"Prob'ly several. They always got a crowd around."

•

Someone in the Chicago crowd had spilled a drink across Ma's new CHICAGOLAND, QUEEN OF THE MIDWEST pillow. Ma wanted to know where Dock kept his .45. Dock pushed through a mob of dancers and yelled at Ma over the good-natured Christmas uproar in the apartment. A lampshade was removed from one of Ma's imported floor lamps. She lumbered through the celebrants to grab the vandal.

Freddie waved a sprig of mistletoe.

"Gimme a kiss," he said.

"First get a new face," Viola Goetz said.

She poured most of her new drink into her full-lipped mouth.

Fatwitted climbed on Ma's mahogany table in a furious Charleston and Barry Cameron, newest Barker thug, a Kansas City sophisticate with a sense of fun, shined the light on her flashing knees.

"Wow, you can see your reflection in the table top!" she yelled.

"No pants," said evil Goetz.

Toasts were lifted to Prohibition.

Eddie Green from St. Paul clapped an arm around Dock.

"Ain't I always been a right pal to you?"

Goetz told a Capone joke.

"I thought that would hand you a laugh," he howled, spilling his drink on Ma's carpet. "A real hardboiled egg, that's him. That's he."

Freddie had more cough medicine for his throat and told Cameron Fatwitted never wore pants.

"You oughta know," Cameron said.

"You and what army?" Freddie said.

"Tell it to Sweeney," Cameron said.

"Oh yeah?" Freddie said.

Cameron thought a while.

"Yeah," he said.

"Says you," Fred replied.

Billie, Fatwitted, Ramona and Goetz commandeered Ma's new piano.

Five feet two, eyes of blue/ can she, can she, can she woo/ rolldown hose, turned up nose/ peppy? yes, she's one of those.

Ma leaned against the sideboard and grimly watched Freddie and Fatwitted wolfing down the smorgasboard from the delicatessen in the block.

"We was better off hittin' country banks down around home," Ma said. "I don't see what's so all fired wonderful about sittin' around Chicagah with ever cent tied up in ransom money ye can't spend."

Fatwitted grinned, her pretty mouth full.

"Good chow, Ma, have some chow."

"Chew with yore mouth shut!" Ma roared.

"Ah, blow it," Fatwitted murmured.

"What?"

"I said, I know it."

"You . . ."

Fatwitted sucked her beautiful teeth, patted her chest and grinned.

"Good chow, Ma. For once it ain't that southern fried pig meat."

Ma blinked her bulging moist brown eyes.

"Fat*witted*, maybe we don't need you *around*."

"Yeah?" She placed her hand on Freddie's lap. "Ast Freddie, Ma. He needs me around."

"We'll see."

"Don't bet on nothin', Ma."

Fatwitted selected a thick breadstick and she and Freddie giggled at a private joke.

Freddie's Christmas-present golf clubs were dumped on the rug.

Romney Daley swung the driver and whacked a plaster divot from the ceiling.

"Fore!" he howled.

"Keep them ridiculous clubs out in the garage!" Ma roared, "They don't belong in the house!"

"Can't do that, Ma." Daley grinned. "Somebody might steal 'em. We're having a crime wave."

"Have a drink, Ma." Roscoe Gibbons clapped Ma on her spongy back.

"Not on yore life," she said. "That Canada whiskey burns my gums."

"Right off the *boat*, Ma."

"Yeah. Right off the bottom."

Gibbons' red face lit up.

"Hey Ma, yer a *real card!* Hey, Felix, you hear what *Ma* said?"

He stumbled off to find Felix.

Ramona Levrette, former Thrush of the Ozark Network in Joplin, had agreed to sing. She removed her bra so she could get her chest into it.

"How about the 'Isle of Capri'?" Fatwitted cried.

Goetz, at the keys, riffled a few U. of Illinois frat house runs and patted Ramona's bottom.

"Sure honey, either that or 'Love In Bloom.' "

Ramona placed her drink on the piano top. She jiggled her bosom.

" 'Isle of Capri,' " she cried.

" 'Getting To Be A Habit With Me,' " Fatwitted called.

"Bulloney!" yelled Ma.

"Hold it down, willya Ma," Goetz called. "Ramona is gonna sing the 'Isle of Capri.' "

"Does she have to?" Ma said.

Goetz wheedled.

"Come on now Ma, the piano cost dough. OK, Ramona . . ."

"Can't she sing an American song?" Ma yelled.

Goetz paused.

"Wait a minute, start over, Ramona honey."

"I don't like them modern songs!" Ma howled.

"We heard your church records enough, Ma, give us a break."

"I'd *like* to give you a break," Ma said, struggling to her feet.

"Come on now Ma, be a sport," Goetz said. "OK, Ramona, honey . . . *'twas on the Isle of Capri* . . ."

In one of the bedrooms, Freddie found Viola Goetz. Viola had gone into the gin over her depth. She lay now drowned, her superb legs far apart. Fred locked the door and got even with haughty, imperious, beautiful Viola. When he finished, he placed the sprig of mistletoe where Viola couldn't possibly miss it.

Karpis' old girl, Connie, gave a free holiday performance of her celebrated strip routine from the Gayety. The top of Ma's mahogany table was now crossed and recrossed with spike heel tracks, a varnished skating rink.

Ma chewed her thin lips.

"Dock, let's git the sluts outa here so's we kin go over the plan."

"Now Ma, cut out that talk."

"All right then, take these *ladies* upstairs so's you kin git yore mind on the work."

"Ma, why don't we wait and go over the plan tomorrow?"

"Tomorrow you'll be somewheres else with these bims."

"Ma, we're havin' a little party. Let's make it some other time."

"I tell ye, Dock, it's spin the bottle day an' night around here."

Dark-haired Billie, wearing a low-necked velvet evening gown, stood just beyond Ma's beefy shoulders.

"Gotta relax once in a while, Ma," Dock said.

"You got so you relax six months at a time. It didn't usta be like this."

Billie chose that moment to retrieve something from the floor. As she slowly straightened up, her beautiful dark sloe-eyes met Dock's.

"No Ma, it didn't usta be like this," he said.

Ma followed his glance and sloe-eyed Billie met her with a hard little smile.

Goetz pounded the piano. "Hey, Ramona, sing 'Headin' For The Last Roundup'!"

Ramona, Billie and Fatwitted sang, grinning at Ma.

Ma glared and opened her Bible.

•

Christmas wreckage was cleared away by two hired Negro maids. Ma listened to her sacred music and read The Book until they finished. Dock had a hangover and Ma lectured him on demon rum.

"Be not among winebibbers; among riotous eaters of flesh; for the drunkard and the glutton shall come to poverty; and drowsiness shall clothe a man with rags!"

Freddie had a severe headache from his cough medicine and from being hounded by the police. Ma sat watching her genuine fire scene lamp, marveling at the realistic flames which rippled through the burning forest.

"Come on Fatwits, movie time," said Fred, new double-breasted overcoat, gray fedora, spats.

Ma turned off the forest fire.

"Where ya goin?"

"To the picture show, Ma." His mad bulging eyes sparkled and he flicked the four-inch brim of his campus-style hat.

"What movie?" Ma said.

"I wanta see that one *The Public Enemy*, that one where the guy blows the crap outa them guys with a Tommy gun."

Posing at the Florentine mirror, Dock tilted his British derby and twirled his gold-headed stick.

"That's *Scarface*," he said.

"The hell it is!" Fred said. "That's *The Public Enemy*."

"Where you gittin' the money?" Ma wanted to know.

"I got some."

"Where'd you git it?"

"Ah knock it off, Ma." Fred moved toward the door. "Come on Fats, take the damn chow *with* ya. Eat it on the way."

"Bye Mama," Fatwitted waved the chicken leg.

"Freddie, you better *lissen* to me!" Ma said.

"Ah get off my neck, willya Ma?" Freddie squeezed through the door.

"Yeah, Ma," said Fatwitted.

Ma leaned out into the hall.

"Who's gonna think for ya, you *dumb cluck?*" she yelled.

Nobody listened anymore. Not since the place was overrun by buck-naked girls.

"I *tell* you, Dock," she said and stopped.

Dock wasn't listening either. He stood profile to the mirror and ran his fingers over his Hollywood Screen Star rolled lapels, the very latest California style, guaranteed to make the fair sex sit up and take notice. Or lie flat and take adulterous pleasure with innocent boys, thought Ma, chewing a Walnetto.

That two-fer-a-nickel chippie. . . .

•

Out from under the whirling cardboard disks flashing 15¢, the movie marquee with the broken lightbulbs, removable letters (DISH NITE, BANK NITE, TRIPLE FEATURE 15¢, ICE-COOLED AIR, CHARLES BICKFORD, TALLULAH BANKHEAD, "THUNDER BELOW"), Ma and young Freddie moved into the freezing windy night past the well-dressed unemployed jerks on the corner selling apples, to the parking lot and Freddie's white side-walled roadster.

"Dirty minded show," said Ma.

"Umm," Freddie said.

"Freddie, ef you git married with that Fatwitted hoor I'll rip yore hide off by my ownself."

"Don't fret, Ma." He scuffed an empty cigarette pack along the sidewalk. "Maybe I won't get married to her after all. Why buy a cow when milk is so cheap?"

•

Ma tossed her purple cloche hat into the closet, slammed her sealskin coat on a hanger and kicked the machine guns in the golf bag. A dull pain spread through her fat toe. Freddie, the all-American collegiate kid, passed in a trance, headed for the back bedroom, his two-tone campus shoes slithering down the hall.

"*I used to think your love was something that I/ could take or leave alone . . .*" High nasal Ozark whine.

Ma rummaged noisily through the cherry creme delights in the silver bowl.

"*I must have you for my own,*" cried Freddie in the distance.

"Nothin' but trouble since that Fatwitted har-lot showed up around here," Ma mumbled. She fell into the club chair and opened her Bible. Red letter edition. (Words of Jesus in red.) Divinity Circuit binding with thumb index. For Ma's powerful thumb.

FOR A WHORE IS A DEEP DITCH; AND A STRANGE WOMAN
IS A NARROW PIT.   Proverbs, XXIII, 27.

•

Fatwitted sat nude before the cream enameled Louis XIV dressing table absorbed in her triple image as she gently moved a comb through her platinum hair.

You got me in your clutches and I can't get free, she crooned. *You're gettin' to be a habit with me.*

She turned to the left and admired the fullness of her breasts, the delicate pinks, the luminous sensual velvety skin.

Every kiss/ every hug/ seems to act just like a drug . . .
Live somewhere nice with Freddie. Away from Mom.

She swiveled slowly around and inspected herself from a different angle. She stretched her smooth golden arms over her head, noting the lift of her exquisite breasts. Away from Mom, a good apartment. Maybe in Florida. Too bad Ma didn't seem to like her. Maybe it was her private school education that annoyed Ma. She crossed and uncrossed her long beautiful legs. Smooth sleek muscles, slim perfect ankles.

SHE ALSO LIETH IN WAIT AS FOR A PREY, AND INCREASETH
THE TRANSGRESSORS AMONG MEN.

Freddie contemplated the gentle swell of her pale pink bottom from the door, then he crossed the room and kissed her warmly along the long sensual line of her throat. She turned on the satin cushion and her arms encircled his waist. He had a brief glimpse of her voluptuous writhings in three mirrors at once. The stag show at Luna Park. The bench creaked under their weight.

•

Ma slammed the wet sponge across Freddie's back and a ring of suds spattered the bathroom. Freddie hunched forward and grabbed his ankles. Foam splashed his bony acned shoulders.

"Washed in the blood of the lamb. Pure-ee-fied," said Ma. "Fatwitted was dancin' with a Eyetalian-lookin' feller at The Oriental last night."

"No she wasn't. She was with me."

"Oh. Musta been some gal resembled Fatwitted. Purty gal, lotsa fellers pokin' 'round."

"Ummm," said Fred.

"No wonder yore so highstrung," Ma said, "always worried about that gal. No wonder ye wind up shootin cops an' all."

Freddie mumbled in a low monotone.

"The jerk was shootin' at me. What was I suppose to do? Sit there an' take it?"

"Freddie, you done the *right thing*," Ma said. "It plain wasn't your fault."

"You said a true word there, Ma."

Ma sloshed the sponge up his knobby spine.

"Just like Yankees, raisin' all that hell when it's only money."

"It was him or me, Ma."

"You couldn't help it, Freddie. It's just not good, shootin' policemen. It draws attention to ye."

"Not my fault, Ma."

"I know that, Freddie. Oh I know that for sure. You just needed yore ole Ma. You need somebody knows how to figure these things out fer ye."

She dragged the sponge through the water and squeezed it over his skull. She chuckled.

"Ye know somethin'? When yore head gits wet, it looks jest like a cocoanut! Pore Freddie."

Freddie blinked the soapy tears.

"I'm a lucky boy, Ma."

Ma slid her thick arm around his waist and buried the sponge between his legs.

The door clicked open and Fatwitted nearly fell into the tub.

"OOOOOOPS!" she shrieked. "Ex-*cuse me!*"

"We'll be finished in a minute, honey," Ma said, not looking up.

"Maybe we need another bathroom!" Fatwitted said, and edged out past Ma's massive rump.

She flopped on the couch next to Billie and lit a cigarette.

"She spends more damn time in the can with those boys."

Billie nodded behind her *Photoplay*.

"When they were small, they only had two beds. The kid that swiped the best stuff that day got to sleep in the other bed with Ma."

Dock held his .45 up to the lamp and blew through the barrel.

"She's just bein' a good mother. Nicest mother a boy could ask for," he said.

"That's one way to put it," Fatwitted said.

•

The apartment house was dark. Street lamps cast soft orange pools of light half a block apart.

Freddie parked the Chrysler and Fatwitted slid over on him.

"Take it easy," he whispered. "Ma might see us from the winda."

"I'll show ya somethin' nutty," she murmured.

"Yeah? What?"

They thrashed around, the roadster rocking slightly on its springs.

He giggled. "What the hell you doing?" She laughed a low muffled laugh. Her fingers danced like needles on his flesh in the dark. He was aware of her lips.

Fred moaned and hoped Ma was not standing at the French windows on the fourth floor.

Fatwitted applied more and more pressure and Freddie felt the entire world rise up and explode.

Sweat glistening on his brow, he lay back on the seat, eyes closed, mouth open.

"Jesus," he breathed.

Fatwitted laughed.

"I bet your Ma never did that for ya," she said.

Ma pulled her furs around her and moved away from the tree. She was shaking with fury and a breathless, dizzy kind of excitement.

•

SOUTH ST. PAUL DANCE MARATHON CHAMPIONSHIP, red letters splashed on canvas draped across the front of the brick armory.

The St. Paul crowd screamed with excitement and the band struck up "Has Anyone Seen My Gal?" doubletiming it and people climbed up on chairs to see the scramble out on the floor. TWENTY-SEVENTH DAY! SPECIAL ACTION SPRINTS! 2 FALLS AND THEY'RE OUT! CONTINUOUS DANCING 'TIL THE FINISH!

Ma strode up the wooden steps shoving through the knots of spectators crowding the aisle and down to the first row at the edge of the dance floor. The audience roared as a girl contestant slid to one knee and the bald fatman referee waved her out of the marathon.

Harry Sawyer chewed his cigar and banged his fat fist on the railing. Ma pounded him with her purse.

"SAWYER!" Ma bellowed.

Sawyer lost his cigar.

"What? Fer crissake, Kate! Fer the love o' Jesus, what you doin' back in town? The boys with ya?"

"No they ain't. I'm here about somethin' important. I want to git a snotty young gal shipped off to Mexico."

"Huh?"

"I want to git a certain gal shipped to Mexico."

Harry turned to face Ma with a tolerant smile.

"Kate, you been seein' them movies again."

"Come on Sawyer, you can fix it."

"Mexico? I can't fix that, Kate. That's another country."

"All right, then," Ma said. "Suppose she gits arrested on a prostitute rap."

"She'd be out again in ten minutes. The bulls and the reform people have a tough time with that one. You can't make the charge *stick* here. The town ain't set *up* that way."

"Suppose you got her a job down in Steubenville."

Sawyer laughed.

"Impossible, Kate. They got more'n they can use now. The depression's hit them, too."

He glanced at the staggering dance teams out on the floor.

"Sawyer, listen to me! I'm talkin' to you!"

He waved her away impatiently.

"Sure, Kate, wait a minute, I got a fiver ridin' on that stumblebum out in the middle. Number 10. She's gonna fall on her face. If she goes inside o' six minutes, I collect."

"Yeah, well pay attention to me a minute. There must be *somethin'* you can do."

"What ye wanta git rid of her for?"

A rocking explosion of noise from the crowd.

"Never mind! I want the smart aleck outa commission!"

Two scarecrows stumbled against another team and all four clawed at each other in their sleep. The audience roared. Sawyer stood up to watch the marathon.

"Kate, you better think o' somethin' else," he said. "Why not bump her off?"

"She ain't worth the ammynition!" Ma yelled in exasperation and shoved her way back through the screaming jumping mob, up the aisle and out.

Sawyer struggled up out of his seat, cigar ash spilling down his damp shirt as he churned his stubby arms at the slow-motion teams plodding in place out on the floor.

"Come on! Come on, you chiseler!" he yelled. "Her knee touched the deck!"

•

"*Let us greet with a song of hope each day/ Though the moment be cloudy or fair/ Let us trust in our Savior awa-a-ay,*"

Ma rasped. *"Who'll keep us ever one in his care!"*

She belched patiently.

Weekly laundry time in the Spanish Morocco bathroom sink.

A gentle tap on her elephant-wrinkled elbow and there stood Fatwitted, platinum blonde angel in gossamer pants and bra.

"Would you mind scrubbing these out for me?" she smiled. "I don't want to ruin my hands. Freddie likes them nice and soft, if you know what I mean." She winked.

"I never knew you wore underwear," Ma said, staring into the soapy water.

Fatwitted giggled softly.

"I didn't, but I saw you peekin' the other day and I thought I'd better start." She wiggled her young bottom as she left.

Ma made a noise deep in her throat. Then she strangled Fatwitted's panties and dropped the limp corpse into the toilet. The roar of the rushing waters was music to her smouldering ears.

"Her shroud's in the house and some of the next grass will grow on her grave," Ma said, wringing out the last of her own spacious bloomers.

Finished, she emerged with an armload of her damp finery and bumped bellies with Dock, hurrying in.

"Excuse me, Ma, can't wait," he said and locked the door.

"Nature in the raw is seldom mild," said Fatwitted.

"Whaddya mean by that crack?" Ma said.

"That's what it says here in the magazine," Fatwitted said. "Right here in this cigarette ad."

"No young lady smokes," said Ma, marching to her bedroom.

Ma was in a hurry to get back to *Bomba The Jungle Boy*, a birthday present from Dock the reader. Seventy-five cents from Sears. Ma was almost to the part where Bomba. . . .

Dock shuffled out of the bathroom, suspenders dragging, carrying his *Chicago Tribune*. Roosevelt recognizes USSR. Red Heebs to run riot in Christian America, cries priest. Dust storms in South Dakota. Let the farmers get guns and stick up banks. Only saps work.

"The toilet is jammed up," he said. "It won't flush."

"What happened?" Fatwitted said. "Did Ma finally take a crap?"

"That reminds me of a joke," Goetz said. "Seems these two little Jewish boys were treading water in hell . . ."

"Anyway the can is stuck," Dock said.

"Tell the landlord," Billie said.

"He's in Florida."

Billie yawned.

"Then throw it out the window. In Chicago, who'd know the difference?"

•

"Fred, we're goin' to California. Just you an' me. Not Ma. Just us, Freddie." Fatwitted slid her active white hands over Freddie, convincing him.

"Sure, Fats," he mumbled, studying his tattoo. "Pretty soon now."

"Pretty soon nothin'! Right now. You can do all right by yourself, Fred honey, you don't need your mother or your brother always tellin' you what you should oughta do. Alvin Karpis and Loretta got their own apartment, when're you gonna bust out?"

Freddie scratched his round head, egg-eyes blinking.

"Karpis is nuts," he said. "He shouldn't a got married. Anyway, Ma has some idea about goin' down to Hot Springs, maybe." Karpis' recent marriage to eighteen-year-old Loretta Donovan still rankled. Alvin had somehow committed treason, moving out on the gang, living his own life. Fred rubbed his nose.

"I guess I oughta stick around and go with Ma to see she gits settled OK."

Fatwitted turned her wide innocent eyes on poor Fred.

"Let Dock do it. Let him see after her."

Fred sat up in bed.

"I dunno. She's my Ma. After all, Fats, I owe her somethin'."

"Ahhhh," said Fatwitted at the French window, hands on her smooth white hips, staring down at Chicago.

131

Fred stuck a cigarette in his petulant mouth.

"Gee whiz, Fats, wait a week. Maybe we could take off."

"A week? Hell, I could wait a month, an en-tire God damn year, you'd still be afraid to get off your ass. I'll go myself. You don't like me."

Fred stuck a small torch to the cigarette.

"Nah, wait a minute, Fats, don't do nothin' crazy now." He grimaced in the smoke. He coughed. "Lemme ask Ma when she's goin' to Hot Springs."

Listening in the hall, Ma shuddered. Now everybody was getting married. Fatwitted would have to be eased out ahead of time.

•

Fatwitted finished her soft curving brows and began the mascara. She contemplated her beautiful self as she moistened the black slab.

"Gladys."

Ma stood right behind her.

Fatwitted jumped, her full white breasts jiggling.

"My God," she choked.

"Excuse me, Gladys," Ma grinned. "I never meant to scare ye like that. Never."

Fatwitted blinked and caught her breath.

"Gladys, I was wonderin' ef you could do me a kind of a personal favor."

"Sure," Fatwitted said. "Sure Ma. What's up?"

"Well, the other day I was suppose to git a new .38 off ole Earl Dudley, you know the boy, that talkative one always hangs around at the Casino Club?"

Fatwitted nodded. Earl Lee Dudley. The dumbest guy in Chicago. In Illinois. In the U S of A.

"Well, hell's fire, Gladys. I'm dogged ef I didn't go an' fergit to take that gun off ole Earl when he was here and now he's over across town at the Erie Hotel an' he's got the damn gun with him."

Fatwitted watched Ma as she stuttered along, rubbing her thick arm with one beefy hand.

"I was wonderin'," Ma said. "I shore do hate to ask you an' all, but I jest wondered ef you could go over there this afternoon and pick up that old gun from Earl."

"Why, sure, I guess I could," Fatwitted said. She cupped her exquisite white breasts into a lacy bra and reached around and hooked it.

"Freddie could run me over in the roadster."

"Freddie is out to Bensenville an' he won't be back in time," Ma said. "That's why I asked you. I wouldn't want to bother ye, otherwise."

Fatwitted glanced at Ma in the mirror.

"Why sure, Mrs. Barker. I'd be glad to go," she said, smiling.

"Well bless ye, Gladys," Ma said, grinning with her iron tooth. "I'll be glad to pay fer a cab fer ye."

"No, no mam, nothing doing," Fatwitted said. "I'd be happy to go. Glad I can be of help to you." She smiled again, drawing on a shiny white satin blouse.

Ma stood grinning humbly, tears misting her puffy brown eyes. Little Gladys was indeed the most beautiful girl she'd ever seen. The look of injured innocence.

The fragile line of that delicate nose.

•

Twenty minutes after Fatwitted left, a vision in a few hundred dollars worth of new clothes, Freddie arrived.

"Where's Fats?" he said, flopping into an armchair.

"Gladys?" Ma said. "Why she ain't been here since early this morning. I thought she was with you, Fred."

"She ain't been with me. Goddamit I told her to be here when I got back. Christ!"

He tossed an empty cigarette package at the fireplace and missed by two yards.

"Is anything wrong?" Ma said.

"Christ, how do I know? That bitch was suppose to be here, that's all."

He lit a fresh cigarette and drew the smoke deep into his lungs. His eyes bulged and his skin had a sick oily look.

"I hope there ain't nothing wrong between you two," Ma said.

"Huh? Whaddya mean? Whatya talkin' about? What's wrong?" He squinted in his smoke.

"Oh nothin', Fred. I shouldn't said anything at all. I jest wondered."

"What? Wondered what? What did you wonder?" Fred sat straight in his chair.

"Well, it's jest that, well, Hell's Fire, son I shouldn't stick my old nose in, it's none o' my business, I suppose . . ."

"What the hell're you gettin' at?" Fred yelled. "What is all this crap?"

"Fred, it's fer yer own good. I reckon at last I gotta tell ye a few things."

"Go on," said Fred, puffing furiously, dragging again on the cigarette.

"I been worried about you and Gladys fer sech a long time, Freddie, it like to broke my old heart."

Fred watched her, expressionless.

"Fred," Ma said. "You ain't exactly handsome."

Smoke curled down from his nostrils.

"Well, Fred, any girl would take up with a feller looked like you, might very well take up with other men, too. Once these northern gals git to spreadin' their limbs apart they don't know when to stop. That's God's own truth, Freddie."

Fred flicked his ashes. His eyes had a flat, sad look.

"They ain't like southern wimmin, Freddie. Up here's a lot of foreign blood around."

"She's from Savannah," Freddie said. "Georgia."

"Freddie, it truly tears at my pore mother's heart to see you get lied to that way. I asked a few people who knew her before, Freddie, an' she's jest plain northern trash. She made all that other up. She was born at Duluth, Minnesota."

Freddie said nothing.

"She's the kinda gal lives around with coons," Ma said.

"What?"

"Freddie, honey, where d'ye think she learned all them strange things she knows? No God-fearin' white lady would even *know* them terrible things."

Fred sat very still. How in hell did Ma know about that?

"She's a right generous little gal, Freddie. I b'lieve she couldn't help offerin' herself to a rooster like ole Earl. He'd keep on after it and she jest might not be able to resist lettin' him do it."

"Earl? Earl Dudley? That two bit sap?" Fred was out of his chair.

"I tried to reason with her, Freddie. The Good Lord knows I did. It's jest satanic lust unbridled."

"Earl Dudley," Fred said. "That sonofabitch is got a room over to the Erie Hotel! Ain't that right?"

"I believe that's so," Ma said. "I tried to reason with that little gal, I surely did."

"Jesus!" said Fred. He tore open the closet door and rummaged through his golf bag. The brass knuckles gleamed as he slid them into his coat.

"I always did suspec' ole Earl o' havin' a bit o' nigger blood in him," said Ma. "It ain't jest his fingernails, he's got that funny look, Freddie, it's somethin' a woman jest knows in her very bones."

"I'll be back later," Fred said, grabbing his hat.

"I tried to reason with her, Freddie," Ma said, tears in her eyes. "I tried to save you from bein' made a fool of."

She caught Freddie at the door and hugged him to her massive chest, crushing his bony shoulders with her heavy arms.

In his ear she whispered, "Hit her a good lick fer me."

•

After midnight, hatless, face flushed, weary Fred slammed into the apartment and tossed his brass-weighted jacket into the closet.

Ma woke in her chair.

"She won't pull nothin' like that again," he said.

Ma lumbered to the kitchen after him.

"What'd she say, Freddie?"

"Oh, she tried to gimme a lotta crap about she wasn't doing nothin'." Fred yanked the cabinet open and found his cough medicine.

Ma pursed her thin lips.

"Such is the way of an adulterous woman; she eateth, and wipeth her mouth, and saith, 'I have done no wickedness'."

Fred waved his red-knuckled hand. His eyes were wet.

"I didn't waste time listenin'. She never fooled me."

"How dumb did she think you was, Freddie?"

"The bum . . . imagine . . . Earl Dudley!" he sobbed. "Baby Lord Jesus . . . layin' around with *that* jerk."

"You're right, Freddie."

"I busted her up . . . I really busted her up!"

"You done the decent manly Christian thing," Ma said, "I run you a bath, there's a lotta hot water."

•

The Great Depression had reached Harry Sawyer. Payoffs were not coming through the way they should. Mobsters came to town, they broke the rules with a local heist, more often than not shot somebody and were forced to leave. There went his protection fee. Rent. Rent on cars, weapons, girls, torpedoes. His overhead continued, Depression or not. Two-way cops had to be paid anyway or they would come see Harry and break his legs. He shuddered. Times had changed. Everybody was out for a fast buck these days. No professionalism. Nobody wanted to take time to build a solidly based career anymore.

The Barkers had looked promising for a time. Good material, lack of big-time experience yes, but the stuff was there. A sound reputation in Missouri, Oklahoma and Kansas. Eager, looking for a rung up on the ladder . . . And yet. . . .

Sawyer blew a perfect ring at the ceiling of his office and sighed. His stomach was worse. Sharp stabbing pains right below the old belly button. Unbearable, hard to breathe when they struck. They usually struck after a session with Ma Barker. Christ preserve us. God save us from harridans like Ma. Carrie Nation, Joan of Arc, Attila the Hun.

Bisodol, Pepsin Charcoal, Digestettes. Spirits of Peppermint,

Bell-Ans, Diapepsin Compound. Nothing helped. Stay away from Ma Barker. That might help.

Still, good jobs were possible. The Hart kidnapping was a good piece of work. Smooth, nobody killed, good pay. Everyone happy. The payroll heists were out. Bulls were getting too sharp, too quick with the guns. Some police were actually equipped with tommy guns. That took the edge off a bit. Bank guards were actually hired to stand around all day with guns waiting to take a shot at holdup men.

Now the Hart job . . . Wait a goddam minute. Hart, Hart, who was the other guy? Same type, tall, good looking . . .

Bowman! Edmund J. Bowman, Northstar State Bank. President.

Sawyer folded his fat hands, puffed the stub of his White Owl.

Bowman, of course. If Hart the brewer was good for a hundred thousand, Bowman the banker should be good for two. Two hundred thousand bucks. A veritable empire of money seemed to spread across his desk. A green continent.

Goetz, Karpis, Barry Cameron, Beaver, Roscoe Gibbons. Byram Roland and the Barker kids. Dock and Fred. Keep old Ma out of it. Save Sawyer's stomach lining. A good, sound idea.

Sawyer decided he deserved a shot. Bottle of Old Panther-Piss in the desk drawer. Call Goetz, call the Barkers tomorrow night when the rates were less.

Use the same house in Bensenville, same team on the eight-hour drive to Illinois . . .

Two hundred thousand. His share could pull Sawyer out of a lot of holes he was in.

The bourbon slid down his throat like fire. Yes sir.

He might go see the stag show upstairs at the country club tonight. Two colored broads from Chi. Natural sense of rhythm.

●

THE WAGES OF SIN; SCARLET WOMEN AND SATAN'S WORK.

White theatre marquee letters on the little glass-cased sign on the church lawn.

Cloche hat pulled down over her puffy eyes, fox furs twisted around her jowly neck, Ma stood on the stone steps of the

Shiloh-Zion First Love Baptist Church talking to the pretty young preacher, son Freddie a sullen captive at her side. He dug his bruised hands deep into his new polo coat, savoring his Sunday morning headache.

"This is your son, Missus Blackburn! Oh, I knew it! Versed in the ways of the Lord. A beautiful young man indeed." He rubbed his moist hands together. "Such lovely clothes."

Fred pressed his arm against the shoulder holster under the polo coat.

Ma took the preacher by the elbow.

"Reverend, it was jest bewdiful!" she said. "I did admire the part about the fallen woman and the evils of drinkin', ye know, like it says, 'Wine is a mocker, strong drink is raging; and whosoever is deceived thereby is not wise.' "

"Missus Blackburn," he cried. "I wish we had a thousand more like you! 'Be not among winebibbers; among riotous eaters of flesh . . .' "

" 'For the drunkard and the glutton shall come to poverty;' " cried Ma. " 'And drowsiness shall clothe a man with rags.' "

" 'And a word fitly spoken is like apples of gold in pictures of silver,' " the preacher said.

Ma clapped her pudgy hands.

"Oh, Reverend, you said a true word there."

•

The scrub cloth moved with a firm easy motion across Dock's slippery white shoulders. Ma's voice was low and gentle as she paused to wring suds from the cloth and slapped it onto the rim of the tub.

She appealed to Dock on the diversity and rottenness of the changing group.

"Great God, we got a speakeasy drunkard, a golf teacher, a shoplifter, a bootlegger. We even got a dago with us. Too many damn wimmin an' too many foreigners. To think we usta have such nice times together."

Dock toweled himself and Ma sat on his bed inspecting her heavy water-wrinkled hands.

"Poor Freddie, you seen the terrible trouble he almost got

into, if it hadn't bin fer his Bible study made him see the light from above."

Dock stood at his mirror carefully combing his slick black hair back in approximation of Chester Morris.

"Take that cigarette outa yore mouth. No wonder yer so puny," Ma said.

"Ahhh," Dock said.

"Who so committeth adultery with a woman lacketh understanding; he that doeth it destroyeth his own soul." Ma sighed. Dock had two photographs of Billie in his mirror. Ma would tear up one of them tonight. See if he missed it.

Dock, fully dressed, sat at the phone in the hallway off the living room, tapping his fingers along the brim of his derby.

"Yeah, Ma hold it a minute. I'm tryin'a talk on the goddam phone."

"Don't *swear* so much, Dock. And take that sorry hat off while you're on the phone."

"What? Shutup, willya Ma?"

Ma waddled into the living room, slumped into the Arabian-mosque patterned velour club chair and opened a copy of *Liberty* magazine.

Barry Cameron sprawled across the davenport, his face buried in *Figure Studies For The Serious Artist*, green rotogravured photographs, his rising fly infuriating Ma.

As Dock droned away into the phone, Ma flipped the pages of *Liberty* impatiently.

" 'Is *Roo*-sevelt a *Fass*isst?' . . . hightone *crap!*"

She sailed the magazine across the room with a rush of paper and exhaled a soft raspberry.

Dock stood next to the fire-scene lamp, rubbing his chin and fumbling for a cigarette.

"Old Harry Sawyer on the phone, he's got a real soft touch."

"Sawyer! That plumb clarified damn fool? Old Helpless? Now I've heard just about everything."

Gathering like cats sensing a battle, Billie and Ramona watched from the kitchen. Billie gently rotated a silver cocktail shaker of gin and ice.

Dock placed his derby on the table and stuck a cigarette between his lips.

"Ma, it sounds like Sawyer's got a real good idea."

Ma's eyes bulged, cruel little lights dancing back in the brown depths.

"Oh, it's *Sawyer* now? *Sawyer's* got a real good idea, has he? Well you jest go right along and let that sorry fool make your plans for ye and see jest where it gets ya."

Dock shrugged and flicked the match on his thumbnail. There was a small burst of flame.

"Don't get sore, Ma. We gotta go up to St. Paul."

"So, we gotta go up to St. Paul and jest leave me here! Jest cut me clear out of it, is that it?"

Dock blinked as the smoke rolled into his eyes.

"Wait a minute," he said.

"Wait a minute!" Ma yelled. "All my work and scrimpin' and savin' and laborin' over you boys is jest fer nothin', huh? You're jest throwin' me out like nothin', is that it?" Ma was choking, her face was red. "And despise not thy mother when she is old, Dock! That's what The Book says!"

"There she goes," said Billie, unconsciously synchronizing her bosom with the shaker.

"You shut yore fuckin' mouth, you harlot!" Ma roared.

"Oh Mama, your language!" Billie said.

"I'm blushing!" Ramona said.

Ma turned to Dock.

"I have taught thee in the ways of wisdom; I have led thee in right paths."

At the far wall, Ramona sang, *"Keep on the sunny side, always on the sunny side . . ."* She threw bumps and grinds and Barry Cameron put aside his art studies to keep time.

". . . Sunny (bump) *side of life"* (bump bump). Billie joined her, rhumba counterpoint with cocktail shaker ice.

In a private little competition, Billie raised her skirt, Ramona raised hers. Billie raised hers higher. Above the dark mesh stockings, her thighs were full and white.

140

Ma shrugged her hippo shoulders.

"Well, I reckon you boys don't need yore ole Ma. Not with all this poontang around." She waved her stubby arm at the grinning girls.

"You got it all figgered, aincha Dock? Jest listen to yore bright city friends. All right, you dumb peckerhead. Go on over to St. Paul and your Mr. Sawyer. I don't care!"

She swung at the fire scene lamp and it went over with a crash.

"I'm gonna stay in Chicagah and live by my ownself!" she screamed. "I got money! I tell you one thing fer *sure*, Dock Barker. I'm not agoin' to hang around and watch you roll on the floor with the *hawgs!*"

"Oink! Oink!" Ramona said.

Ma crunched through the fire scene lamp fragments.

"Have a drink, Ma," said Billie.

"Don't you call me Ma, you mattress-back bum!" Ma roared.

"Oh ho! Ma's been listening at the door! Naughty!" said Billie.

"Hey, get Ma!" said Cameron. "What's frostin' her?"

Ramona bounced on the bed in the other room.

"Shut up an' come in here," she called.

Cameron rose from the couch to obey.

"Why, *hon*ey!" Ramona cried. "You're all *read*y, aintcha?"

Dock spat tobacco shreds and chopped at the smoke in his face. He squinted at Ma.

"Where ya goin', Mother?"

"I'm goin' to my own damn apartment an' shut the damn door an' lock it! That's where I'm goin'."

" 'Headin' for the Last Roundup!' " A laugh and a creak of bedsprings from the open door.

Dock tossed his cigarette in the fireplace.

"Gee Ma, you ain't sore, are ya?"

Ma tore the closet door open and yanked savagely at her coat.

"Me? Sore? Why would I be *sore*? Huh? No, Dock, I'm *happy!* See my *teeth*? *See* 'em?" A stab of cold air hit her iron tooth. "I'm *smilin*', you ignerant Ozark *clodhopper!*"

She dug her powerful arm into the silk lining.

"I tell ye, Dock, you ain't got sense enough to run in the house if it was rainin' dead cats!"

Derby in hand, Dock followed Ma into the apartment hall.

She glared at him as she fought to stuff her other arm in its sleeve.

"Goddam it, Dock. I jest do hate to see a right good outfit I put together get tore down by a bunch of lickered-up chippies an' smartass big city punks with dumb ideas! *Look* at all those jerks millin' around in there. We start out with a gang, we ended up with a *zoo!*"

She stomped off down the hall, stopping at the head of the stairs. She turned for a long hard look at crestfallen Dock.

"The trouble with you!" she yelled.

Dock blinked, aware of neighbors leaning against their doors.

"You think you know it all!" Ma roared and, shaking her furious head, she clumped down the carpeted stairs.

"So long, Ma," Dock said.

He shrugged. He twirled the derby on his forefinger and caught it. As he turned back toward his apartment, he scratched his rump.

A wave of girlish laughter from the broads.

Where did he leave that pack of fish-skins?

Back in the apartment he might have to screw his way through a wall of human flesh.

•

In his office over the Green Lantern Saloon on Wabasha Street, Harry Sawyer looked over the assembled troops. Fred and Dock had responded with alacrity that was satisfying to a man with Sawyer's natural talent for command. Alvin Karpis sat working on a fingernail. A good man. Goetz, smiling as always, another new suit.

Sawyer wondered if he should walk to a blackboard and use a pointer. He decided to do this one sitting down.

"First, I was gonna hit the bank itself," he announced. "Then I figgered why not snatch the president?" He looked around. "Good, huh?"

Karpis was unimpressed.

"I thought this was gonna be a bank job," Dock said.

"What's wrong with hittin' the bank?" Karpis said. "It takes too goddam long anyway to convert the ransom dough. We need cash, not a lotta goddam crap we can't use."

"Take it easy," Sawyer said. "There's ten times the loot here if you don't get panicky."

"Screw it," Dock said. "Karpis is right. It takes too long to clear the dough. An' look what happened to the boys who snatched Urschel. Christ, they throw the building at ya now fer kidnappin'. They think everybody is killin' the Lindbergh baby."

Sawyer watched them through the drifting blue haze.

"I don't like another kidnap," Fred said.

Sawyer's patience evaporated.

"OK, OK," he said. "Maybe I shoulda known better. Maybe you birds ain't the ones I had in mind fer this. If you're afraid of it, I'll get another bunch."

He rocked gently back in his varnished swivel chair.

"Two hundred grand is good money," he said. "Maybe it's beyond you boys. I didn't realize you'd get shaky. Maybe you haven't got it any more. It's understandable. Guys run out of nerve. I sure never figured you guys fer yellow but what the hell, that's your business."

Freddie glared, popeyes staring. His bony hands trembled. Karpis sat quietly, watching Sawyer. Dock gently tapped his stick on the desk.

"Go easy on the finish there, Dock," Sawyer said. "I just had the damn thing revarnished."

Dock rapped the edge an unmistakably sharp one. He stared at Sawyer, his dark eyes showing white as if he were startled at something just past Sawyer's shoulder.

Sawyer shuddered. All the Barkers were nuts. That goddam hypnotic stare just like the old lady. Belly pain.

"Well, what about it boys?" he said.

No one spoke.

"Scared," Sawyer said.

"Nobody's scared," Dock said. "It's a crappy idea. It's half-assed." He banged his stick on Sawyer's floor. "I'd like to see what Ma thinks about it."

"Your mother!" Sawyer blew up. "Jesus Christ! Can't you guys do anything without your old lady?"

"Shut up!" Fred yelled, getting up.

"Sit down," Karpis said, forcing him back in his chair.

"I'll cold-cock the bastard!" Fred yelled.

"Don't call me a bastard, now!" Sawyer cried, just as hyper-thyroid as anyone else.

"Everybody shut up," Karpis said.

Sawyer lit a fresh cigar, swore and threw it against the far wall.

Karpis got to his feet. Everybody was dippy.

"OK," he said. "We'll take the job."

"Well," said Sawyer. "I just thought it was funny that grown men couldn't decide something without running to Mother."

"OK," Dock said. "No more o' that crap."

Sawyer shrugged.

"Keep yer wisecracks to yerself," Freddie said.

Goetz blew his nose.

"I guess we'll hit Bowman, huh fellows?" he said.

"Just keep yer wisecracks to yerself," Freddie said.

"S'matter Fred?" Goetz said. "You nervous about some-thing?"

"Ole Fred is kinda itchy," Sawyer laughed. "He ain't shot no-body for two whole weeks."

•

Hal Nolan agreed to help his friend Charlie catch the Peeping Tom who had been upsetting Charlie's wife. She had an unbeliev-able figure and it was almost to be expected that some neighbor-hood nut would sooner or later start hanging from the telephone pole near her window or climbing along the second story ledge of the hardware store or snaking up a tree in freezing darkness to get a closer look at bedtime. She had sensed the monster out there for the last four nights running and now it was up to Char-lie to defend his home and all its treasures.

Charlie told his friend Hal Nolan when they checked in for work at Northside Express the next day and they decided that after quitting time that night, together with Herbie, who was a weight lifter, they would check out the neighborhood thoroughly.

Still wearing their uniforms and caps from the job, they cruised slowly down the street, then the alley, checking the hardware store, watching for the slightest suspicious movement around the fences by Charlie's back windows.

A car, a sleek Chrysler Imperial roadster, turned into the alley and they fell in behind it.

Fred Barker drove east through the dirty slush, gunning the roadster along the dark alley. These birds following him day after day were getting to be a real pain in the ass. Sometimes five guys, sometimes three. Once, he swore to Christ, a plainclothes dick on a bicycle.

He might be going out of his skull, that goddam sonofabitch foreigner Harry Sawyer. Fatwitted, that filthy perverty lowdown hoor, that rotten naked bitch French twotimer bastard.

They were behind him again, no, by God, a different bunch, a cheesy two-door sedan, a cop car this time! Christ! He speeded up and slammed on the brakes.

A guy in a uniform and visored cap jumped out of the sedan.

Two fucking cops, by Christ, three of the snotty bastards hounding his ass from morning 'til night, he picked up the tommy on the seat beside him and the volley of steel-jacketed .45 caliber bullets lifted Hal Nolan backward and sent him dancing through the air to rack over a line of garbage cans, frozen garbage hitting slush and the bullets hit the other guy the miserable cop and his legs wobbled and he fell sideways into a drift of dirty snow, his hat rolling on its rim as Freddie slammed the roadster around, brown slush flying, accelerator to the floor and he tried to run over the hat as he raced up the alley and made a shrieking turn at the avenue.

Hal Nolan moaned as he lay face down in freezing dirty slush, blood pumping out of his torn legs in frightening regular spurts.

The puffy bloody holes burned like numbing fire and he began to cry.

●

In the warm cheery corner of Ma's apartment next to the Tulsa fan, the potbellied Kansas City bear, souvenir pennants and photos of the boys, the ornate walnut-finish console (with genuine veneer front panel enhanced by Tamo-wood overlays top and bottom) a veritable cathedral of an eight-tube superheterodyne radio concluded Eddie Cantor's Sunday program and Ma switched to the news.

". . . In St. Paul, believed to have been fired by a machine gun in the possession of the man who then turned his car around and drove away at top speed."

"Great God, there they go!" yelled Ma. "Already fucked up like a Chinese fire drill! *Mis*ter Sawyer an' his big ideas!"

●

"I shoulda known better!" Sawyer yelled. "Two guys! Two guys in a goddam alley!"

Karpis and the Barker boys lounged around the office, listening idly to old fatgut Harry and his newest policy review.

"The whole thing is off!" Sawyer roared. "Off! I wouldn't touch it with a ten-foot pole! Do you know what's happening?"

Karpis yawned.

"Do you?" Sawyer screamed. "The coppers are grabbing everybody in St. Paul, that's what! They're searching every house I own in the goddam town!"

"Too bad," said Dock.

Freddie struck a match on Sawyer's desk.

"Don't do that, please," Sawyer said. He buried his face in his hands.

"I tried to tell you birds," he said. "No more o' this shooting people! Did anybody listen? Huh?"

"What's on your mind?" Karpis said. "What the hell is the meeting for?"

"The thing is off!" Sawyer cried. "The Bowman snatch is off 'til this dies down! Christ!" He slapped his forehead. "Who done this? Huh?"

"Who knows?" Dock said. "Some outa town punk."

"We can't go through with the Bowman job," Sawyer mumbled. "We'll hafta wait now. This does it, by God, this sure as hell does it."

Karpis shook his head. The boys were on their feet moving toward the door.

"I'm gonna sell apples," Sawyer said. "That makes sense. My God, you guys go at this like you're butcherin' hogs!"

"We're gonna go ahead and hit Bowman anyhow," Karpis said. "We need the dough. We come up here from Chicago to pick up some cash, we ain't gonna sit around waitin' fer you to stop peein' yer pants. Make up yer mind to it. We're gonna hit him tomorrow morning."

At the door, Alvin paused to run his hand down Sawyer's tweed lapel.

"That's a cheap suit, Sawyer," he said. "You oughta look around and git yerself some halfway decent suits." He flicked a match at the frantic boss.

"Maybe with rubber pants," he said.

•

On Wednesday at 8:30 A.M. a cold crisp clear morning with snow on the ground, Edmund J. Bowman, president of the Northstar State Bank drove his daughter to school, dropping her at Goodrich and Lexington and started for his office.

He was watched from a black Ford Victoria at the curb.

"Get a load o' that Lincoln," said Alvin Karpis. "Payday." He swung the Ford out behind Bowman.

Freddie grinned and got the pistol ready.

"Try not to shoot anybody this time," Cameron said from the back seat.

Fred told him to shut up.

Karpis tail-gated Bowman a block to the stop sign and then Fred leaped from the Ford, eyes bulging, yanked open Bowman's right hand door and shoved the pistol at him.

"Don't move, buddy, or I'll let you have it," he said.

Edmund J. Bowman looked at Fred, then immediately shoved

into low gear and a second car, a long black Chrysler Imperial 8 slid across his bow and stopped. Trapped.

Bowman threw open his door and got one leg out when Freddie, lunging across the front seat, brought the gun down across his skull.

Karpis ran from the parked Ford with Cameron and they slammed the door hard on Bowman's ankle to quash any further initiative, then dragged him into the back seat. Fred started Bowman's Lincoln. Dock, at the wheel of the Chrysler, slammed into reverse and got out of his way.

With Fred in the lead, the two cars roared off for Lexington Bridge, south out of town. Edmund J. Bowman, between Karpis and Cameron, now wore taped goggles. He sprawled in a daze, cold air stabbing his torn scalp, blood dribbling down his collar. That man who hit him with the gun had looked insane.

Well past the city limits, where St. Paul police jurisdiction ended, into Dakota County, beyond St. Paul sheriff's jurisdiction, both cars pulled off next to a snowy field, the big Chrysler covering the Bowman car from the highway.

Dock, in derby and pearl gray overcoat, hurried across the crisp snow with a handful of papers, the dapper little business manager.

"Bowman," he whispered. "You're kidnapped."

The big man sighed and nodded his bloody head.

"Sign these papers," Dock whispered. "Who do ya want fer intermediary?"

Bowman tried to think.

"Calvin Leeds. He's a contractor in town," he said.

Fred yawned, leaning his head on the wheel, humming to himself. Cold sonofabitch of a day. Two hundred grand in the back seat. He blew his breath on the windshield and wrote F-U- with his finger. Nice car.

Dock took Bowman's watch and wallet for identification and Karpis secured the goggles on Bowman's bleeding head with a long strip of adhesive tape. Then he and Campbell pulled and carried the groggy, blindfolded banker over to the Chrysler and shoved him into the back seat and slammed the door.

Bowman's left ankle was throbbing with pain sharpened by the January cold; blood oozed down his neck from the chop on the scalp. Perhaps these lunatics wouldn't hold him for ransom after all, just gradually beat him to death. That first damn fool looked capable of it. Eyes like headlamps. The Depression was bringing the weird ones out from under the rocks.

In June, the boys had transported Hart; now in January, the big Chrysler Imperial headed again for Bensenville and the frame house in the respectable neighborhood.

Hart had been bagged six months before, almost to the day.

A milk run, thought Dock. Two snatches a year and we'll live like millionaires.

They cut across South St. Paul.

Karpis stared out the window.

This one was supposed to be a bank job before fatgut Sawyer fell back on the kidnap idea. Sawyer seemed to be stuck on a giant payday on each job. Jelly Nash used to say smaller ones didn't attract all that police attention. Out the window, off to the left, lay the stockyards by the river, the South St. Paul Post Office, scene of the messenger robbery. Karpis wondered if they ever got that sidewalk washed off. Those were the days.

●

". . . Edmund Bowman, president of the Northstar State Bank of St. Paul, heir to the Great Prairie Railroad fortune, whose bloodstained limousine was found by police, is presumed kidnapped and feared to be a victim of . . ."

Ma's thick fingers twisted the volume knob and the sound died.

"Fred an' his little temper," Ma chuckled. Just a baby. Baby Fred. A right sweet-natured boy most of the time. Blood stained limousine.

Amos and Andy time! In panic, Ma flicked on the massive radio.

". . . and as we join the boys, they are . . ."

"I'se regusted!" cackled Ma. "Aahwah!" She tore open a fresh carton of glazed doughnuts.

●

149

Easing herself into the beauty parlor chair, the fat lady grinned at the white-smocked operator.

"I want a henna application," said cultured Mrs. Claypool, formerly Ma Barker.

The operator smiled and shook the apron out and fastened it around Ma's hippo neck. Ma smiled to herself.

Get pretty red hair and some Sunday grab that young preacher right out of his pants.

The girl worked the red-brown mess into Ma's stringy hair, packing it like mud around her simian skull.

"It's terrible the way those gangs get away with killing and robbing and kidnapping like that," she said, patting Ma's head.

"It's jest awful," Ma said. "No one is safe."

"It's going on all over the country. Nobody seems to care anymore. There's no morals at all these days."

She slapped the red mud around Ma's head, slap slap slap until Ma began to get angry.

"There's too little churchgoin'," Ma snarled. "Too much drinkin' an' layin' around with loose women."

The girl carefully worked a gob into Ma's egg-like eye.

"It's dreadful . . . Do you have any children?"

"Three lovely boys." Ma grinned with pain. This hoor was trying to blind her.

"What line o' work are they in?" the girl crooned, slapping and patting.

"The insurance business. Good church men, no bad habits."

"I sure can see why, Mrs. Claypool. With a mother like you I'm sure they are wonderful men." She cleaned Ma's bulging eye with a towel and Ma smiled.

"I always did my Christian best with 'em. 'Withold not correction from the child; for if thou beatest him with the rod, he shall not die. Thou shalt beat him with the rod, and shalt deliver his soul from hell.' Twenty-three, thirteen and fourteen."

The girl shook her head in wonder.

"It's a darn shame those men that kidnapped Mr. Bowman didn't have a mother like you. They wouldn't have turned out bad, I bet."

A five-dollar tip for the hoor. She recognized quality folks.

•

The room was on the second story rear of that same lovely home in the nice neighborhood. Bensenville, Illinois. Karpis and Fred had been spared the place on the Hart kidnapping but this time, under the Sawyer-knows-best plan, they had guard duty. Bowman was in the tiny bedroom, the boys quartered in the large room next to it. A 1930 calendar tacked to the gray-green plaster wall, a rolltop desk with a drawer missing, a gooseneck lamp and five wooden chairs. Old newspapers scattered over the uneven plank floor. Two cots with flat greasy mattresses. Harry Sawyer and his unbeatable connections.

"Can't expect the Palmer House, boys, not in your line of work," he said.

"You're in this too," Fred said.

"Different capacity," said Sawyer. He smiled. "You guys are hired hands this time. Just keep it calm, boys, and I'll handle everything. You don't have to know any more than what I tell you."

Fred was nervous at living in the house with the victim. A bank job was a different thing, move in and out fast and blast anybody who gets in the way and be done with it. Sitting around with the guy like he's an old buddy gave Fred the creeps.

He watched through the peephole as Bowman ate the cheese sandwich and drank the pint of milk. Rich guy manners. Born to dough, no wonder he's good-looking. Bowman smiled at something and Fred turned away. Rich smartass, I ought to let him have it right now. Double-breasted suit, $25 shoes.

Fred doublechecked the locks on the door and walked back down the hall. When would they pay the dough? This thing could drag on forever. He decided to load the spare drums for the Thompson.

Why not collect the dough and kill the guy? Eliminate the witness?

With a feeble grinding noise, the phone rang. Fred caught it, listened and slammed it back in the fork.

"Wrong number. That makes five today." He looked at his brother.

Dock stood at the ten-cent store mirror over the washbasin, testing different angles on the bowler hat. The little fairy with his derby.

Fred smacked his hands together.

"Put that crummy hat away or I'll take it and that fairy walkin' stick an' I'll shove 'em up yer ass sideways."

Dock turned to his taller, ferret-faced kid brother. The old story. "Don't talk to me like that, banjo-eyes, or I'll bust your head open for ya. Don't try to crap me like you crap these other boys because I know ya. Jest siddown and shut up."

"Don't call me banjo-eyes," Fred said. He leaned against the window frame, watching the soft fall of soot settling on the rooftops of Bensenville.

"We never shoulda lissened to that jerk Sawyer," he mused. "He's got this deal so screwed up we'll never git out of it. I never seen a mess like this."

Karpis flipped his cigarette butt at the wall. With the Barker boys it was a lot of talk. More noise and less paydays. When do we get on the ball?

Goetz entered. Old nervous Goetz with his seven dollar shirts and his hands shaking all the time. Seven dollar shirts and he sweats today like a W.P.A. ditchdigger.

Goetz rambled on. His bear-greased hair was mussed. Booze welts across his handsome face.

Thumb hooked in his shoulder holster, Karpis studied the big-time professional from the Golden Age of Crime. The old Capone torpedo was falling apart.

"That lamebrain Harvey whatsisname didn't pick up the money," Goetz said. "Howd'ya like that? The sap lost his nerve three blocks from the dough!" Goetz was out of breath.

He looked around the dreary room, mouth open, waiting for either applause or a burst of gunfire from the boys.

He mopped his face.

"Sawyer is fed up," he announced.

Fred spun around. "*Sawyer* is fed up! Jesus! Whaddya think *we* are? Lissen, Goetz, one more goddam crap-up . . ."

"OK, Freddie, now calm down a little. I don't like it any better'n you do, fella." He tried a smile. Good guy. They ignored him.

"We shoulda gone an' talked to Ma," Freddie said.

"Probably right." Dock tapped the stick on the floor. "We never got this loused up before."

"Well anyhow, it's too late now," Goetz said. "We're in the soup. Harry Sawyer wants to call it off."

"What?"

"Call it off. He wants to call the whole deal off."

Dock's stick became a club. "And what about the dough?"

"Just forget the money." Goetz licked his dry lips. "We can't collect it. Just call the whole job off."

"Sawyer is out of his goddam mind!" Karpis said. "After the work we went to?"

"Well, it's a mess and Sawyer knows it. He says it's safer to just let Bowman go and forget about the money."

"Let him go, hell!" Fred said. "So he can put the finger on us? D'you know this is a federal rap and they *kill* ya for it?"

"Yeah, sure, I guess so."

"You guess so. Well, I tell ya what *I'm* gonna do. I'm gonna kill that bastard *Bowman!* I'm not gonna let that bird point me out to no cops."

"Calm down, Fred," Dock said.

"Calm down, nothin. I told ya we shoulda talked to Ma about this. Now these blockheads are gonna turn that boy loose with no dough comin' and he'll lead the cops right to us. I'm gonna kill him."

"Fred, you ain't gonna kill nobody."

Fred looked at his brother. Mama's favorite ass-kisser.

Karpis leaned against the radiator, his arms folded, chewing a match.

"That's right, Fred," Karpis said.

Old Alvin the Eagle Scout. Fred bit his lip.

"You're with *him*, huh?"

Karpis spat the matchstick on the floor.

"We'll go have a talk with Ma," Dock said. "She knows how to work these deals."

"I dunno . . ." Goetz said.

"She did OK with the Hart job," Karpis said. "We'll go talk to her." Anything to get out of this looney bin.

Fred stood with his back to them, staring out the window, watching the thick black smoke from a brick chimney, gray sky, tops of winter trees.

"Nobody's killin' Bowman," Dock said. "I give him my word on it."

"Goetz and I will go down to Chi and talk to Ma," Karpis said. "You stay here and keep an eye on Bowman." He indicated Fred, whose back was still to them. "Keep an eye on the boy."

•

CHICAGOLAND, QUEEN OF THE MIDWEST.

Ma dragged her stubby fingers across the raised letters on the green silk buckskin-fringed pillow.

The fancy doorbell rang. Bing bong bang, fairy music. Out to the foyer she waddled, flapping along in her silk and rayon robe with brocaded tea rose design, ruffled cuffs and fluffy bow tie at the side. A 190-pound Kewpie doll with lovely orange hair.

She peered through the tiny speakeasy window in the door, screamed, then slid the bolt and pulled it open.

"Well! As I live and breathe! Alvin Karpis!" She saw Goetz. "And ole Sgt. York!"

Goetz, double-breasted John Gilbert overcoat and executive bellbottoms, swept off his pearl fedora.

"Good to see you, Missus Barker."

"Missus Barker! Real manners an' everything! Not 'Kate' today, is it? *Missus* Barker."

Alvin Karpis stood expressionless, hat in hand.

"Well, come on in Alvin," she said. "Don't stand out there lookin' foolish."

They sat on the edge of Ma's Florentine living-room couch,

Goetz with a tight smile as he contemplated his fingers and cleared his throat.

Ma giggled.

"I swear, Goetz, you're lookin' as humble as a dead nigger." She fingered her nose.

"What's the matter with yore face, Goetz? Too much booze, huh? Goin' to the bottle oftener an' stayin' longer!"

Goetz grinned sheepishly and tried to find a point in the room on which to fix his gaze. Kewpies, TULSA fan, Kansas City souvenir bear. Fred Barker at fourteen. Herman (God took our dear son to his rest) and Dock (Your devoted boy).

"How you bin, Ma?" Karpis said.

"Oh fine. Yes sir. Fine."

"We got a little trouble, Ma."

"Oh you said a true word there, Alvin. Oh yes. Yes indeed."

Ma leaned forward, grinning, her jowls quivering slightly in the light of the beaded lamp. Her dark eyes glittered.

"You got trouble, right enough. Oh my yes."

She snickered.

Karpis took a breath.

"This deal ain't laid out right, Ma," he said.

Ma sat back in her chair, chin resting on chins. She smiled a sad little smile, oozing compassion.

"You laid out the Hart job pretty good," Karpis said.

"Oh yes," Ma said. "That was a smart job. Back then."

"Well," Karpis shrugged. "We're stuck."

Ma nodded.

"Ye got yoreself in a mess. That's too bad, boys."

"We could use some help, Missus Barker," Goetz said.

"I bet you could," Ma said.

"We'll cut you in on it," Karpis said.

"Sure, a good piece of it," Goetz said.

Ma grinned, cracked lips clamped shut. She tugged at the bow knot on her robe. Tea-rose brocade.

"Oh," she said. "A *piece* of it. Well. Ain't that nice." She scratched her fat arm through the brocade.

"Wait a minute," she said. "It's time fer Amos 'n Andy. I always listen to them two. It's my favorite story."

She switched on the walnut-finish 8-tube superheterodyne cathedral. It crackled. She peered at Goetz.

"Do you like Amos 'n Andy, Goetz?" she said.

"Sure. Oh surely. Never miss 'em," he said. "My favorite likewise."

"Shhh," Ma said, pressing her heavy face to the ornate speaker.

•

Bensenville was quiet.

"Sawyer," Fred said, pouring himself a new one. "You fucked this whole deal up."

"Now hold on there," Sawyer said, pitching his voice into the lower register, fingering the trouser crease along his broad thigh.

"All by yourself," Fred said. "All by yourself, you fatbelly bastard."

"Now come on, now, Barker," Sawyer boomed. "Let's keep this businesslike."

"Ah ya both shut up," Dock said, whacking the table edge with his stick.

"Boy oh boy," Fred said, solemnly swallowing bourbon.

"Who's got the watch?" Dock said, "Beaver?"

"Yeah, the cement-head. Willie the Beaver. He can tell ole Bowman all our names an' addresses."

"I'll look in at 'em." Dock jumped up. "Beaver may be makin' a deal fer all we know."

"Honor among thieves," said Sawyer primly.

"Shut yer crappy mouth, Sawyer," Fred rolled his crazy eyes.

"Don't get excited Fred," Sawyer said, sweating. "Stay calm, please."

"Don't tell me 'don't get excited,' " Fred's mouth dribbled at the corners. The beginnings of foam, thought Sawyer.

"Calm down, please." He waved Fred away weakly, grinding his cigar between his teeth. "We should let Bowman go. This job is all outa whack."

"We oughta blast you, you peckerhead. If we'd a talked to Ma in the first place we wouldn't be crapped up."

"Yeah, yeah," Sawyer sat the chair like he was riding a horse. "Mebbe. May be."

He sighed, lifting his tortured belly and gently lowered it again. Pain burned his left side. German appendicitis.

Dock walked into the room and fell into a chair.

"Beaver is in there with him. Bowman is facin' the wall. I wonder if his eyes are OK. He sits in the goddam dark all the time."

"Who cares?" Freddie said.

"Well Christ, Fred. I'd hate to see a guy go blind."

"Ah fer the love o' shit, shut up about it. He's got enough dough to buy new ones."

"That ain't the point," Dock said.

"Fuck it."

"Well boys." Sawyer stood up. "I guess I'll go downtown."

"Sit down, Sawyer, you ain't goin' anyplace."

Sawyer paused, watching Dock. The employees were getting restless.

"You stay where I can see ya 'til we get the dough."

Little Dock was showing white around his eyes again.

Sawyer slumped back onto his hard wooden chair. Another twist of pain in the left gut. Of all the hoods in America, he had to get wound up with the mad dogs.

The thing was, they were supposed to be working for him. He had relied on his superior intelligence to control them. That had been his worst mistake.

So, a beautiful business lay shot in the ass. A nice little empire, farm in the country, place in town, expensive neighborhood, nice car, payoffs from a thousand guys and he had to meet the Barker family. Disaster.

There *was* something about these wild-eyed idiots and their spooky fat old lady.

Who did kill Arthur Dunlop?

•

Karpis stood in Ma's Chicago apartment trying not to show his anger. The old biddy had some good ideas, a lot of experience. Better to put up with a certain amount of crap than to blow the whole thing right now.

Ma sat like a satisfied toad on her overstuffed velour throne. She was eating doughnuts and brown gravy.

Goetz tried not to watch.

"Nobody ever listens to me," she grinned, chins glistening. "I'm jest a dumb ole woman."

"Oh now, Mrs. Barker," Goetz cut in. "I've always thought you were the best brains in the business."

She snorted. Gravy bubbled.

"You wouldn't kid me," she said.

She placed her napkin on the moist remains of her meal and stretched her chubby arms. Her bulging eyes sparkled.

"I know where you boys dogged it up," she said. "Aside from lettin' Sawyer say anything to start with."

They listened.

"I'll come in fer a equal share," she said.

Karpis nodded. Goetz had his schoolboy notebook out.

"First, the money.

"Two hundred thousand. It's a fair price. 'The wicked shall be a ransom for the righteous.' Ex-ex-eye, 18. Eighty-four thousand in fives, one hundred sixteen thousand in tens. Unmarked. The serial numbers will prob'ly be sent to the Federal cops, that's too bad. We can still git Ingstrom to take the dough to Havana and sell. There's ways."

Karpis nodded.

Ma sucked her tooth.

"Yore trouble is yore pickup. I got a better way worked out. Do it like this. Get in touch with yer Bowman man. Leeds. Tell him to git the ransom money ready, divided out the way we say. When he's got it, he takes it to a spot in St. Paul where you got a car of yer own parked, key in it. Mark this car some way ahead o' time so's he'll know it. He'll leave his own car, drive your car . . . Wait a minute . . . Be sure the car you leave him is a small car, a coupe. A sedan an' he's liable to git funny and load it up with cops er guns er somethin'. A coupe then. Safer."

She belched and spread out her gas station maps.

"He drives the coupe out the state highway to Farmington."

Ma consulted the maps.

"There he waits fer the bus to Rochester. Git the schedule. Around 9 er 10 at night. When the bus leaves Farmington, he falls in behind it. This way we know when he's comin'."

Ma tapped the thick black pencil on the map.

"Now when he gits five miles from Zumbrota here, he sees four red lights beside the road. Git yorese'f red flashlights. Red bulbs. Any hardware store. He turns off the main road an' follows this side road, drivin' *slow*.

"Now here's where you come on in yore own automobile. Follow him. Flash your headlights five times at him.

"He stops and sets the money beside the road, then takes off."

Ma placed her pencil on the map and folded her hands.

"That's all. It's simple. You got the dough."

She smiled, iron tooth and wattles.

"When ye come to take Bowman back to St. Paul, yer gonna be carryin' this bird in the car. Four hundred miles. Ye can't stop in gas stations. Stash the gas in cans along the highway. You gas up that way."

She sighed.

"You got all that?" she asked Goetz.

"I think so, Mrs. Barker. Lemme be sure now."

He read his notes back to her.

Karpis pulled on his heavy coat. It sounded right. Not a lot of dumbbell guesswork and last-minute ideas like Sawyer. Ma knew her stuff all right.

"Two hundred thousand is a nice piece o' change," Ma said. 'He that oppresseth the poor to increase his riches, and he that giveth to the rich, shall surely come to want.' That's why the bankers must suffer, boys. Share the wealth."

Karpis got Goetz out of his chair and into his coat.

"One other thing," Ma said. "The Federals have your finger-prints, they got Dock's and they got Freddie's from the pen. Everybody wear gloves. Why help the bastards out by leavin' prints around?"

"Yeah," Karpis said. "Gloves."

"Aincha go' stay fer Amos 'n Andy?" Ma said.

Karpis threw on his muffler.

159

"No, thanks, Ma. We gotta move out. It's a good long drive back an' I wanta get started as fast as possible. Every minute we wait the cops get closer."

Ma nodded, flipping the radio switch. Tubes hummed.

Goetz put on his hat, then quickly took it off for the grand farewell.

"Take it easy on the road," Ma said. "They's a lotta ice. We don't want nothin' goin' wrong now, do we?" She winked horribly.

The two men backed out into the hall, grinning goodbye.

"You could stay over, Alvin," Ma said.

"Thanks Ma, that's nice of ya," Karpis said, fading away down the carpet to the elevator.

•

Everything then went according to Ma's plan. The money was paid, Bowman was freed, the press cried out for mad dogs brought to justice, club-women letter-writers demanded torture for the kidnappers. And the FBI went to work and reconstructed the crime with considerable help from the boys.

As Ma had specified, there were no stops at any gas stations and they had worn gloves. Stopped for refueling near a farm in Wisconsin, Dock decided he had earned a cigarette. He did not blow up all the gas cans, themselves and Bowman but he removed a glove to strike the match. One perfect fingerprint, Arthur (Dock) Barker, Oklahoma State Penitentiary. Car theft, Tulsa, Oklahoma, 1918, escaped; recaptured, Joplin, Mo. 1920, Arrested Muskogee, Oklahoma, 1921, bank robbery suspect, Discharged after six months jail, 1921, convicted murder of Thomas J. Sherill, watchman, Tulsa Hospital—given life; paroled Oklahoma State Penitentiary Sept. 10, 1932. Here he is again. Hello old friend.

They left behind four empty gas cans and a funnel.

They had got the flashlights Ma called for, flashed the signal to Leeds and then left all four lights on the ground at the contact point outside Zumbrota, little dreaming anyone, much less the cops would ever pick them up. And find out they had been bought in St. Paul, not even Chicago, and that the salesgirl would recognize Alvin Karpis from a mug-shot as the purchaser.

The boys hadn't done too well. But, after all, Ma couldn't be everywhere at once.

Desperate for cash, the gang selected a money changer in Chicago instead of Cuba and within days he was arrested.

Freddie got more and more nervous.

•

Sunday, March 4, Clarence Webber, cement salesman, went out in his decrepit old Plymouth to buy the papers. Bring home the funnies, Daddy. A chance to get out of the house and away from the income tax forms. How do you pay income tax when you haven't sold any cement since 1930?

In your dreams whatever they be, dream a little dream of me . . . he sang. The clutch was sticking again. His glasses steamed.

The traffic light turned red and he coasted to a stop.

Instantly another car smashed into him from behind. His rear-view mirror was knocked out of line but he didn't need it. Two flat burning eyes fixed on him and an absolute lunatic wearing a polo coat thrust his oily big-nosed face in his window.

"What in the goddam hell you think yore doin', boy?" the monster screamed. A southerner. Out of town. A tourist.

"You ran into me," Clarence Webber said.

"Fuck that, you four-eyed sonofabitch!" the apparition yelled. "Don't lip off at me!"

Clarence reacted badly to provocation.

"Get your hand off my car," he said.

"Gitcher ass outa there!" shrieked the maniac. "Step out here and git what's comin' to ye!"

The sour odor of whiskey was unmistakable. Bring home the funnies, Daddy, says the kid and here you sit with a drunken cracker spraying you with spit.

Other drivers cut around the tiny real-life drama, laughing and honking.

"Hire a hall." "Get a room." "Kiss him again, he's still breathing," in falsetto.

The lush reached in and tried to seize Clarence by the throat. His hand was clammy and cold.

Clarence Webber shifted into low and stepped hard on the gas.

There was a sickening thump as Dracula's elbow was struck by the rear post of Webber's window and then Webber was free, high-tailing it along Glenwood Avenue for home.

What a morning. His heart was banging against his ribs. He hadn't had a dumb thing like that happen since junior high school. He wiped his handkerchief across his forehead. His glasses were steamed. Sour taste.

Then he saw them following.

He pushed down on the pedal, skinning two cars and causing a third to lock its brakes as he shot through traffic. Enough of this damn nonsense. Didn't anybody have any sense of humor anymore? After all, the guy had hit *him*, hadn't he?

He sweated as he pushed the old Plymouth around corners, through stoplights and up side streets and the Chrysler stayed just behind all the way. The man was an impressive driver. Clarence felt the old dread. Maybe the man wasn't just a drunk. Maybe he was crazy. And what about the others in that car with him? Couldn't they talk the jerk out of it or were they crazy too?

Out along France Avenue, past Cedar Lake, they sped, Clarence Webber's Plymouth weaving desperately across the tree-lined highway, the long black Chrysler roaring along in its wake.

No cops out today.

He pulled around his corner on two wheels and with a scream of brakes, racked to a stop in front of his white frame house. He had a vague impression of a small white face at the window, Daddy did you get the funnies, and he was out of the car with the Sunday papers insanely jammed under his arm and he was running across his small front yard for the porch.

The loudest noise in the world exploded all over him then. Something plucked at the shoulder of his coat, a swarm of sharp ripping fireballs plowed through his back and the last thing he saw was the face of his son at the bay window and then the tommy gun slugs tore his head to pieces and his body scrambled onto the porch and fell apart against the front door.

The funnies scattered in slow crumpling shapes across the dead grass.

Fred Barker climbed back in the big Chrysler, awkwardly trying to hide the submachine gun under his polo coat.

"What you got there, boy?" Roscoe Gibbons yelled. "That don't look like a gun to me, that looks like somethin' else!"

The others screamed with laughter.

"Let's git the heck outa here," Freddie said, suddenly embarrassed, trading the Tommy for the Old Grandad on the seat. Brown gurgly liquid sloshing around in the quart bottle.

"Never took no shit off no one, particularly no Yankee sonofabitch," he said. "That's the truth."

"Did you get the look on that boy's face?" Gibbons cried as they swung out into traffic. "Pure rabbit!"

Fred giggled.

That was pretty fair shooting back there. One squeeze, single burst. OK.

Too bad ole Karpis didn't see that one. Take him down a peg er two.

Bigshot Karpis married up with that little broad in Chicago, thought Fred, hoors are all alike.

He drained the bottle and thrust his tongue into the neck.

•

The press of St. Paul reacted to Freddie's latest escapade with its usual lack of understanding. Sawyer ducked out of town. Back to Chicago went the boys. No spending money. Two hundred thousand dollars worth of ransom but negotiable cash was needed right now. Not all the Hart money had yet been cleared and they were stuck with another ton of green paper to get rid of.

"My pore baby, what they tryin' to do to ye?" Ma asked, holding Freddie's ugly face in her thick-fingered hands.

"Cut it out, Ma," said Fred, lowering his bloodshot eyes. "A bird in a car got snotty with me, that's all."

Dock tossed his coat in a corner.

"The blockhead can't keep his dumb finger off the trigger, that's all," he said.

"Fred never took no guff off nobody," Ma beamed. "Did ye kill 'im, Fred?"

Fred blushed.

"Bonehead," said Dock from the couch.

"All right, Dock, put 'em up," said Fred, assuming his Jack Sharkey stance.

"Sock him Fred!" yelled Ma.

"Aah shuddup," Dock said, covering his face with the *Tribune*. Karpis set Fred's suitcase in the hallway and lit a cigarette.

"This is serious stuff, Ma," he said.

"I'm so proud o' Fred," Ma said.

"I mean the fingerprint. The word is all over that Dock is on the Federal wanted list."

"Don't you fret, now." Ma placed a beefy hand on Karpis' arm. "I got a real good doctor lined up fer all you boys."

•

The office was on the ground floor, dirty white tile, mustard yellow walls. The smell of ether, alcohol and urine was so strong as to be almost visible.

Dr. McCoy, former convict, abortionist, former surgeon, currently the 1934 indoor drinking champion of Chicago. A thin, cadaverous-looking yellow-skinned wreck whose red-blonde hair had turned to faded straw in the booze-fires.

"It's the face and the fingers, doctor," said Ma.

"Not much anesthetic," the doctor mumbled.

"No operation," said Fred, sitting up on the greasy operating table.

"It won't hurt all that much," the doctor giggled. His operating room discipline went as far as a brisk rolling up of his sleeves. His little kit of shiny stabbers were in about the same shape he was. Washed in alcohol.

"Buck up, be a man," Ma said.

"That's right, son," McCoy snickered. He tried to pick his nose and missed. "Be a man."

"Shut up an' do the work," Fred said. "I ain't payin' you fer advice."

"You boys go traipsin' around leavin' fingerprints, ye might as well have the doctor take 'em off yore fingers," said Ma. "Ye ain't got enough sense to wear gloves."

McCoy dug into Fred's eyebrow and Fred screamed.

"How about a shot of booze for this fellow?" McCoy said, leaning against the table.

"My son don't drink," Ma said.

McCoy bloodied the other side of Fred's face.

"Turn the other cheek," he said and laughed. "Turn the other cheek."

"That's from The Good Book!" Ma cried. "Oh I jest knew you was the doctor fer my boys!"

"You sonofabitch," Fred said. Karpis held Fred's hands down.

"Get some newspaper for the floor, please," McCoy said. "We in the profession have standards."

Ma spread the *Chicago Tribune* under the table. Red drops spattered noisily across the reports of the Mason City, Iowa bank robbery while McCoy gouged his scalpel into the side of Fred's nose. Fred puffed and blew under the torture, blood flooding his nose and throat. A large greasy crimson bubble formed at his nostril.

"Cut it out you stupid prick!" he shouted, sitting up. Blood streamed down his chest from his soggy red face.

Little Freddie wouldn't be so attractive to girls now, thought Ma. Hoors.

Affluent Dr. McCoy had a small radio in his abattoir.

She switched on Amos 'n' Andy.

"OK, OK," McCoy said, stumbling over to the sink. He peeled off his blood-flecked shirt and took a long swig of Old Grandad.

"You know what the hell you're doin'?" Karpis said.

"I'm a doctor, am I not?" McCoy steadied himself against the sink.

Fred shuddered with pain and groaned again.

"Hush up son, I'm tryin' to lissen to the nigger show," Ma said.

•

He reached out and rearranged Ma's CHICAGOLAND, QUEEN OF THE MIDWEST pillow and placed the plaster Siamese twins to the left of the carved pine Missouri mule. He tapped his cigarette ash in the fireplace and whistled softly to himself as he waited. Medium height, stocky build, narrow high-domed head, brown hair. His suit was a dark pin stripe, an expensive one.

From the back, he was an ordinary-looking man.

"Hey, Johnnie!" Fred Barker said, coming into the room.

The man turned quickly, his shoulders tensed and then he stopped as he recognized Fred. If from the back he was ordinary, his foxy narrow face was famous. The cleft chin, the hard mouth, the ski nose, the lined cheeks.

His eyes were extraordinary. Slanted, narrow, sleepy, oriental, completely calculating.

John Dillinger.

Ma trotted forward, smiling girlishly, her fox furs flopping, square-heeled black oxfords clumping on the carpet, her big square-fingered hand thrust out.

"Hello, Johnnie," she said. "Please to meet ye. Heard a lot about ye."

Dillinger watched her, the sleepy brown eyes unchanging.

"Don't believe all of it," he said.

Ma flopped into her club chair.

"How's things with you boys? Busy?"

He shrugged.

"Oh I can't complain. Make a little, drop a little. It evens out."

Ma put a cigarette between her teeth.

"I heard ye hit Mason City fer a few thousand."

"Yeah, a few."

She struck a match.

"Them seeds out in Iowa got any money?"

"Some. You have to know how to get at it."

Ma inhaled, coughed smoke and sparks over her mountainous bosom.

"What ye in Chi fer?"

"I thought I'd look in on this guy McCoy," he said. "The doctor."

"Yeah, we know 'im," Ma beamed. Fred sneered.

Dillinger turned his fingers over.

"I thought I'd maybe change the face a little, fix the prints."

Ma giggled.

"Change the face, huh? Maybe with your face, John, it's a good idea."

Dillinger gazed calmly at Ma, his face expressionless, stuck a cigarette in his narrow mouth, struck a match, touched the tip, pulled on the smoke and grinned faintly.

"They told me you were a card, Ma," he said.

•

The winds of March sighed along darkened Cermak Road, nudging a soiled, wrinkled sheet of newspaper. Mud-spattered headlines. Depression, the coldest winter in years, the N.R.A. was folding up.

Goetz, the Arrow-collar hero of the Great War, sat in his warm, friendly favorite bar. An attentive audience of minor thugs listened. The hour was late and there had been twenty scotches since noon for Al Capone's most trusted marksman. Goetz was a natural talker, a narrator with total recall and he was more than willing to discuss recent and somewhat little-known events. He placed his manicured hand on the shoulder of the sleepy pug on the next stool.

"Louie, I said to Eddie Bowman, you know, Mr. Edmund J. Bowman, well that's what I always called him, Eddie, I said, 'Eddie would you ever have believed I was a fraternity man? I mean, just to look at me?' And you know what he said? Old Eddie, he said, 'Goetz, I'd have known you were university people anytime.' Anytime! Isn't that something? He could tell. Eddie could tell I was above average, right off. He and I used to have some real talks, let me tell you. He's a college man just like I am you see, and he told me when he met me that I was obviously real class. That's just what he said, real class. Isn't that nice?"

Two men slid off their stools and quietly left, turning up the collars of their black overcoats. Louie noticed something moving in the big mirror back of the bottles. Somebody had entered the bar.

"I thought it was nice," Goetz said. "I don't usually talk about myself much but then you gotta admit that it's not every day you kidnap a multi-millionaire and sit around three weeks chewing the fat with him, either!"

Back in the gloomy depths of the mirror, Louie thought he recognized a familiar face. Who was that guy? He seemed to be watching Goetz.

Louie sighed.

It was Fred Barker. Alvin Karpis was with him.

"No sir," said Goetz. "Mister Edmund J. *Bowman*, and he and I sat there out in Bensenville having some real bull sessions just like the old days at the frat house! None o' the other boys could hold up their end o' the discussion when old Eddie and I started in. The Barker boys never went past fourth grade and that Karpis fella, well, I don't know whether he went to school at all. $200,000 ransom and divvied it up right there in my own apartment! Isn't that something, Louie?"

Louie couldn't keep his eyes off the mirror. Fred Barker and Karpis were joined by a shorter man.

"Louie, you're not listening," Goetz said.

"Oh, sure," Louie said. "Sure I am."

"It's not the hour, it's the company, huh, Louie?" Goetz laughed and whacked the bar.

Louie shot a frightened glance at Fred Barker (closer now) and back to Goetz. Goetz turned. He gulped. Then he managed a crosseyed smile.

"Well Karpis! Fred! Goddamit, Dock! The whole bunch. How about a drink, fellas? Ah, bartender . . ."

He snapped his fingers and they slid wetly, no sound.

"I never could do that right."

Karpis and the brothers watched him. Louie got up and left.

"Could you, Karpis? I mean, you know, snap your fingers?"

Alvin Karpis gazed sadly at Goetz. He shook his head.

"I never tried," he said.

"Well, what're ya drinkin'?"

"I dunno, Goetz, you tell me."

Goetz thought hard. Something was bothering the boys. Old Freddie with all those red scars across his ugly face.

168

Little Dock sat watching Goetz calmly, derby at a slight angle.

"Uh, Dock," Goetz began, as the drinks were placed on the bar. "Dock," he lowered his voice. "I hope you won't take this personally, boy, but you know, a gentleman never wears his hat at table. Or bar, either . . . you know . . . Dock?"

Dock stubbed his cigarette and dropped it on the floor. His small handsome face was sad.

"I know, Goetz. There's a lot I got to learn."

There was another skincrawling silence. Goetz lifted his drink and willed his hand not to shake.

"Only tryin' to help, Dock," he said. "Happy days, boys."

He gulped the whiskey.

Nobody moved.

Dock lifted his drink and looked at Goetz.

"Here's to silence," he said.

•

Karpis handed the shotgun to Fred and shut the closet door.

"Goetz is sittin' in a bar shootin' his dumb face off," Fred said.

Ma smiled and cranked her Victrola.

"Old Sgt. York has got to go," Fred said. "Blastin' Germans is one thing but we don't need any loudmouth war heroes around here. He jest can't seem to keep his big trap shut."

"Doncha want some fried chicken?" Ma said.

"No time, Ma. Dock is down there now, watchin' the door. If we hurry we can catch him."

Ma nodded, her wattles wobbling. Her orange marcelled hair fit her head like a rippled skull cap.

"I warned ye about that smart aleck. Nobody ever listens to me. I'm only yer old ma!"

Fred slipped the shotgun inside his overcoat and Karpis held the door.

"If you boys had any guts, you woulda shot him long ago!" Ma called after them.

•

Alvin Karpis coasted the big Chrysler to a stop in the dark blur between street lights half a block from the bar and Freddie leaned over the seat from the back, the shotgun glinting in the faint yellow glow from the lamp.

"Put that sonofabitch on the floor," Karpis said.

"Whatsamatter, Alvin, you nervous?" Freddie said, giggling. "Ain't you never seen a guy git his head blowed off before?"

"Put that fucker on the floor before somebody sees it or you won't blow *no*body's head off."

Fred grinned and lit a cigarette.

Down the deserted street opposite the bar, the short man in the double-breasted gray topcoat stopped, raised one arm and lowered it.

"That's Dock," Fred said. "The sonofabitch is in there, OK."

"You want me go in the wrong side o' the street, do ya?"

"Yeah, hold it to the last minute and skim over that side and slow down. I wanta lean it on him."

"There ain't much traffic," Karpis said.

"This late there never is."

Up the street, Dock hugged himself, stamping his feet on the sidewalk next the Bar & Grill.

"Colder'n a welldigger's ass in Maine," Karpis said.

"I ain't gonna roll down the window 'til I have to," said Fred, touching the fresh scars on his cheeks. He would kill Dr. Mc-Coy sometime, too. For fun.

Through the misted window of the Bar, Dock could see Goetz, shoulders hunched, arm waving, regaling his pals with yet another saga of Gangland's Golden Age. Goetz was eating a turkey sandwich at the bar, washing it down with scotch.

IF THINE ENEMY BE HUNGRY, GIVE HIM BREAD TO EAT;
AND IF HE BE THIRSTY GIVE HIM WATER TO DRINK.

The lines ran through Dock's mind.

Goetz finished his meal with a great flourish, wiped his lips with elaborate care, shook hands with his loyal audience and slid into his fur-collared cheviot coat from the hook near the door.

FOR THOU SHALT HEAP COALS OF FIRE UPON HIS HEAD
AND THE LORD SHALL REWARD THEE.

"Amen," said Dock.

No cars in sight, he raised his arm twice to the dark Chrysler down the street.

The door clicked beside him, and he cut around the corner as Goetz lurched out, buttoning the fur against the cold. Goetz, eyes watering in the wind, looked up and down the street for a cab and then he saw one approaching slowly, a large cab at that, or was it just difficult to make out in the dark? It had a passenger; the passenger was rolling down the back window. The guy probably told the driver to stop for him.

My lucky day.

The cab swung over to his side of the street to make a depression-style illegal pickup and well-dressed Fred Goetz, handsome war hero, former lifeguard, ace gunner for Mr. Capone, born story-teller, university frat president, and loving consort of beautiful Viola, took a deafening double load of shot full in the face.

•

Dock was tired. He placed the golfbag containing the shotgun in the hall closet. He leaned against the kitchen sink and splashed cold water over his head.

"Well?" Ma said.

"Yeah," he mumbled, rubbing his pale handsome face with a dish towel.

"Hah!" Ma said, clapping her fat hands together. "I never did like that Yankee. What kind o' name is Goetz anyway? Is that a Jew name?"

"No, he was Catholic."

"The worst kind," Ma said.

•

Gray-and-white Fred Goetz smiled in the soft amber light.

Fred Goetz smiled in his tennis sweater, leaning forward, one foot up on a bench, elbow on knee, his other thumb hooked in the pocket of his plusfours. The photograph was framed with crepe.

Black-haired Viola sat alone in the darkened apartment, buttoned up to the throat, drunk and formal in the hardbacked chair, prayer book in her lap. Half hidden among the cigarettes, flowers and handkerchiefs on the dusty end table was her kitchen glass of gin. The faint rustle of the city came from beyond the drawn shades on the locked windows

She sipped from the glass and the tears began again.

Her dark eyes glistened in the brownish light. A moist highlight on her nose, glitter of wet cheeks, her long beautiful legs oddly muscular in black net stockings. Black lace for mourning.

Ma Barker, cloche hat and fur coat, a vengeful woodchuck, glided soundlessly over to the windows and both shades whipped up with a noise like pistol shots. Waves of dust sparkled in the long slanting shafts of cold sunlight.

"Git some light in here, Viola," Ma said.

Viola swung her head around unsteadily.

"Please . . . Mrs. Barker . . ."

"Viola, you got $75,000 around here somewheres."

Viola tried to clear her throat.

"Mrs. Barker, I'm in mourning."

"Yeah, I know, but I want that money," Ma smiled.

She moved lightly around the room, cloche hat and beaver, straightening the small framed pictures, running her leather-gloved finger along the mantel.

Viola stared at the rug, her head wobbling slightly as she spoke.

"I don't know anything about any money, Mrs. Barker. I'm too upset to talk about money. Poor ol' Goetz, he was such a sweet-natured, wonderful . . ."

Ma slapped the mantel.

"The money, the money."

Viola spread her hands.

"Mrs. Barker, with Goetz gone, I'm all alone. I need a couple dollars." A sharp smell of gin.

Ma was right behind her chair.

"I want it all, honey."

"Let me have a little. A thousand dollars."

"No. All of it."

"Let me just have Goetz' share."

"Goetz is dead. He's *got* no share." Ma pulled up a chair. "Look at it like this, Viola, honey. A nice lookin' gal like you, you can git another man. That don't pose a problem." Ma lit a cigarette and slowly exhaled the smoke.

"However, Viola, if someone was to chop up yore face it might not be so easy. Think about it, dear. Seventy-five ain't so much if it means lookin' like Lon Chaney. Don't ye jest know it?"

Viola took a large sip of gin and it spilled down her chin. She blinked her mascaraed eyes. Her glass was nearly empty.

"That money belongs to us anyhow, honey," Ma said softly. "It's rightly our own. Think it over, Viola. The boys get awful riled ef they think somebody is tryin' to cheat their ole Ma outa somethin'. Little Freddie is liable to do somethin' *crazy* to ye an' I don't believe I could *stop* him, either."

Viola closed her swollen eyes. Her head fell forward. Ma leaned on the arm of Viola's chair.

"You know Viola, one time down home, Freddie he caught a Cherokee gal cheatin' on him an' he cut all her fingers off with a butcher cleaver. Oh she *yelled!* It was jest a *terrible terrible* sight . . . I felt so *sorry* fer that little gal . . ." Ma paused. "*You* don't have too many *friends*, honey."

Viola set the gin glass on the table with an unsteady double bump. A lipstick-smeared thick tumbler from the five and dime.

"All right, Mrs. Barker. I'll get you the money. It's in the closet." She frowned sleepily. "Under the floor."

Ma smiled a cast-iron smile. " 'A gift in secret pacifieth anger; and a reward in the bosom, strong wrath.' Viola, honey, I just *knew* you'd see the light."

•

The morning light in Florida is brightening in the eastern sky. Against the dark palms, purple-gray clouds are breaking up and the ground mist is disappearing.

A Florida sheriff wipes moisture from his rifle barrel with a bandanna.

"Sun's comin' up," he says. "Get ready, we're gonna move."

Chief Agent John Lafferty removes his new gray fedora and places it carefully on a porch for safekeeping. He loosens his tie, hefts his armored vest and shrugs his arms, an effort to make the forty-five pounds rest easier.

At the parked Ford, an agent takes aim with his submachine gun then reaches out and wipes the dew from his front sight.

Lafferty moves at a crouch to a position across the street from the Barker cottage. His second in command has just made it back through yards and driveways with the word that everyone is in place, ready to go. The house is blocked on all sides, roads are sealed. The local lawmen will take their cue from the FBI agents. Firepower assembled is impressive. Rifles, pistols and submachine guns are trained on the Barker house. Mist evaporating, the buildings stand out sharply against the colorless sky.

Lafferty studies the front of the cottage, the dark windows.

The Barker gang has about run out of time.

•

Ma's imported $23 Black Forest cuckoo clock struck the wire gong four times, the bird jerked out over the pine cones and the cuckoo sounded back in the mysterious works. Fred had broken off the bird's head.

In the blazing Chicago heat, the apartment was an inferno.

Down in the hot streets kids were yelling "Extra" like Christ was back in town. Shot down in an alley by the Biograph movie theatre. Thrilling gun battle. Tiny Melvin Purvis, Ace G-Man. Feds shoot it out with desperado. Celebrating the biggest catch since Jesse James was laid out on a slab, the corpse-buffs filing past as they did for Valentino. In Ma's apartment, electric fans buzzed at the windows. The heavy scorching air was motionless. Ma groaned, her sweat-splotched silk-rayon dressing gown stuck to her gorilla's body as she crouched over the ink-smeared extra edition. She chewed on a frozen Milky Way swallowing valiantly on the cold sugary chunks.

Photographs of the alley, thick dotted line down to the "X" where the body came to a stop.

174

Little Dock, bedraggled in his undershirt and damp gray bell-bottoms, studied the front page over Freddie's sticky shoulder.

"They musta shot ole John in the back," he said.

"Betrayed by a *woman* in red!" Ma screeched, choking on Milky Way. "I *knew* it! What'd I *tell* you boys? They'll do it ever *time!*"

"I don't like that Federal agent stuff," Dock said. "They move around like they own the country."

"A woman told the cops!" Ma cried. "A woman!" She licked the chocolate from her fingers.

"The Federals are gettin' to be a pain in the ass," said Fred, flicking sweat from his pimply upper lip.

"John Dillinger," Dock said. "Jesus, this is bad news. When they shoot him down everybody's in trouble."

"A woman!" Ma yelled. "A woman done the whole entire thing!"

Dock studied his mangled fingertips and pulled on his shirt.

"Somebody's always talkin' it up," Dock mused. "Just can't keep their mouth shut. Few more drinks and they can't shut up."

"It was a woman," Ma insisted.

"It ain't just wimmin, Ma, lotta stool-pigeons around."

"Yessir, the woman in red." Ma was sure.

Dock took something heavy from the airless closet and got his fancy summer straw.

"Come on, Fred."

Fred pulled himself to his feet, stuffing in his sweaty shirt tail, slung his wrinkled jacket over his arm, stuck his greasy Panama on his round head.

"Poor ole Johnnie," Ma crooned. "A woman done the whole entire thing."

•

"That whole bunch!" Dr. McCoy crowed. He pawed his dead straw hair out of his eyes and wiped his red face. The drinkers in the downtown hotel bar listened. "The Barker boys, Alvin Karpis, all of 'em. I got 'em right where I want 'em now."

Back near the glass doors, Dock straightened his tie and nudged Fred.

"Too many people are talking," he said. "We want to wind up dead, like Johnnie Dillinger? Too many stool pigeons. Making deals . . . talking to cops."

A FALSE WITNESS SHALL PERISH.

●

In the bar at the yacht club that night, McCoy continued.

"Right in the palm o' my hand!" he yelled. Members of the Lake Property Boat Owners Association listened. "I fixed their eyebrows, I touched up their prints, I took off warts, I gave 'em brand new faces!"

"Doctor, you got too big of a mouth." Freddie moved in, "You're as bad as poor ole Goetz."

"Don't touch me."

"You get likkered up," Fred murmured, "an' you start tellin' the people all about Bowman an' us."

"Watch your step now, you dumb hood."

"Doctor, you just talked yerself into a boat ride."

McCoy snatched up his glass to throw the drink at Fred and his glass was empty.

"Don't you dare get tough with me, sonny boy!" he cried. "I got enough on *you* to hang your smart Ozark *ass*."

Dock laughed and shook his head.

"Hell, don't we know it. That's why yer gettin' a new overcoat." Fred laughed. "Solid see-ment overcoat, doctor!"

Club members snickered.

"Take yer goddam hands *off* me you crummy little punk!"

Club members shook their heads and turned away. Roughnecks always clowning.

"Shouldn't oughta said that, McCoy," Dock said. "You never learn."

"Talk, talk, talk," Freddie said.

"Bring the bum's hat," Dock said.

"That's my new hat!" McCoy screamed.

Out on the dock, McCoy caught his foot in a large iron ring sunk into the planking. Freddie kicked the foot loose and McCoy cried out.

"Come on now, doctor," Fred said. "That don't hurt. Buck

up. Be a man." He chuckled at his own wit and began slapping
the doctor with his free hand as they dragged him over the rough
boards, a monotonous, mechanical cuffing that eventually stung
his palm and he quit.

"Where's your other cheek, doctor?" Fred laughed.

The doctor struggled like a wounded animal as the boys hus-
tled him along the decking past the boat house to the Chris-Craft.

"He's plastered," Dock said to a clubman relieving himself off
the pier.

The man wore a navy blazer, white ducks and wide brimmed
boater.

"Whoopee!" he said and giggled.

He shook it off and threw them a smart salute as they climbed
aboard with their squirming cargo.

"All ashore that's going ashore!" the man yelled.

"Let's take that prick-head too," Fred said.

"Shove off," said Dock.

"Aye aye sir!" yelled the dockside drunk.

"Get him on the way back," Freddie said.

Cutting through the water, the Chris-Craft roared out onto
the lake, smashing waves into fine stinging spray as Dock held
a steady course away from the clubhouse.

"Put the doctor in the *barrel*," Fred said. "Niagara Falls,
doctor. Over the Niagara Falls in a barrel!"

He wrestled the scrap iron over to the beer barrel on the
deck. McCoy tried to get up and Fred kicked him a hard one in
the groin. Dock stopped the boat. The waves slopped against
the side. Across the water from the clubhouse, they could hear
faint music. *Little Man You've Had A Busy Day*. 1934.

Time to do a return job on the surgeon's head. Dock picked
up the .45, thought momentarily of Freddie and Ma and smashed
the doctor a crunching blow across the face. He saw what he
had done and threw up over the side. Fred laughed. His brother
never could drink beer.

They hauled and shoved the heavy barrel up onto the stern.
Dock groped his way forward and started the engine. A cool
breeze was blowing.

"Ole Doctor McCoy gonna be famous," Fred hollered above the engine roar. "Famous with th' fishes!"

Dr. McCoy, barrel and all, tumbled into the lake with a crash muffled by the noise of the engine as they sped away into the night.

The new straw skimmer bobbed on the oily surface like a flat-bottomed boat, shipping water which gradually darkened the red silk lining.

•

Dock popped the receiver back in the fork and shook his head.

"The cops picked up Harry Sawyer," he said. He took a deep breath. "By Christ, now we're in for it."

"Sawyer!" Fred said, "Jesus! The cops?"

"Different cops. That's what that damn fool gets, leavin' St. Paul."

Ma blinked her piggy eyes.

Dock sat down and slapped his hands together.

"Sawyer's wife and two broads were out boozin' it up and they got in a real beef, yellin' at each other and everything. Somebody called the cops."

"I knew it!" Ma yelled. "I never trusted that idiot. His wife is even worse than he is. Loudmouth! Loudmouth! Now this! All right boys, let's git packed. 'A prudent man forseeth the evil and hideth himself', ex-ex-eye-eye, three."

"Here we go again," Fred said, "Kee-rist."

"The Feds are bound to get in on this," Dock said. "They stick their nose in everything now. I better call Karpis."

"He's holed up with that kid chippy," Ma said. "Why call him?"

"I'll call him," Dock said. "Don't fret about it."

Ma began the litany.

"It's like I told ye. It's wimmin. Wimmin and booze. 'Trust not the woman who partakes of the grape; strong waters shall set loose the tongues of treachery.' Al Spencer got turned in by a woman in nineteen and twenty-three. Al Spencer was hidin' on the Osage reservation an' she went an' blabbed. Turned that pore man in!"

"Come on, Fred," Dock said. "You bring that box fulla junk, I'll take the guns downstairs."

"A woman told 'em where to find him," Ma said. "A big Federal reward on his head because the cops said he robbed the mails when he hit the train. That was a lie. 'All our enemies have opened their mouths against us.' A lamentation."

"We better get a good long ways away," Dock said. "When the Feds get Sawyer to sing, he's gonna start namin' people he don't even know."

Freddie paused in the door with a battered cardboard carton loaded with fourteen tons of drugstore relief.

"Ma, you wanta tote all this medicine? This pile suppository stuff? Huh? For piles?"

"A real lowdown lie," Ma said. "The Federal Gov'ment murdered Al Spencer because he was a pore man . . . 'The pore is hated even of his own neighbor; But the rich hath many friends.' Ex-eye-vee, twenty. The posse come right on the Osage reservation and murdered him. They busted two laws right there."

Dock was back.

"Christ, Fred, ain't you moved this shit outa here yet?"

"Don't rush me. These goddam boxes got nothin' in 'em but doosh-bags and enema rods an' a lotta dumb-ass medicine. There's crap here was bought back in Joplin."

"Throw it away," Dock said. "We're gonna move light fer once."

"Al Spencer had ten thousand in Liberty Bonds on him when they killed him," Ma said. "The posse stole them bonds fer their ownselves and brung his body back to town in a tumbleweed wagon and nailed it up on the post office door as a example. There was talk that they cut off his sex organs, too."

Her brown eyes glittered.

"Harry Sawyer, fer crissake," Fred said. "That bastard starts to talk, we'll be back in the pen before mornin'."

"Pen, hell," Dock said. "We'll get the chair. Kidnappin', buddy."

"I shoulda croaked that bastard when I had the chance," Fred said.

"Al Spencer was a real gentleman," Ma said. "A fine-lookin' little feller. Puny but brave. Al Spencer was brave enough to attack Hell with a bucket o' water."

"I'm gonna see Billie," Dock said. "On my way outa town. I'm gonna tell her goodbye."

"Yeah?" Fred said, "Billie?"

"Too goddam much trouble," Dock said. "She's always hackin' at me. Trouble all the time."

"She's a good-lookin' broad," Fred said. "Coozie. Juicy lookin'."

"All right," said Dock.

"The crimes the law officers committed against us would fill a book," Ma said, hugging her barrel belly.

The phone rang. Dock picked it up, pale, frightened.

"Yeah?"

He listened, then carefully hung it up.

"Romney Daley," he said. "They picked him up in Cleveland. Him an' Enid Darrow."

Ma roared with laughter.

"That *Kissin' Bandit!* I *tole* Romney! You think he'd lissen? Lallygaggin' around with that bird-faced floozy!"

"Ol' Romney," said Fred.

"She prob'ly *told* on him!" Ma yelled. "Told the coppers where he's at!"

"Come on, bring the Kewpie dolls an' let's git," Dock said. "The bulls are prob'ly five minutes from here right now."

"Henry Starr was shot in the back, it's God's truth," Ma said.

"Come on, Ma. You can tell us in the car." They stumbled down the stairs.

•

With Fred at the wheel, the big Chrysler Imperial swung out into traffic. Ma sank into the pillows and blankets and closed her piggy eyes. The time they all piled into the dusty old Nash, leaving Tulsa for St. Paul for the first time. Handsome old Arthur Dunlop sitting in the back, shaking in his boots. The boots she bought for him. The lovely scenic day and night trip through Wisconsin and Kansas after leaving Arthur at the lake. FOR THERE SHALL BE NO REWARD TO THE EVIL MAN; THE CANDLE OF THE WICKED SHALL BE PUT OUT. The scramble from Kansas City when the FBI grabbed poor Wilding and Hatton. Harvey Bailey, one of the best. Old friends, gone now. Piling all the stuff in the back of a car and driving like the wind for the state line. Always on the run, never in one place long enough. Maybe this would be the last move.

Nothing much to show for all that work. A couple of nice pieces of furniture, usually leaving the heavy stuff behind. Console radio lost in Kansas City. All that beautiful beach furniture at White Bear Lake. Brand new speedboat, left to the cops. Nothing to show for it all but a couple of souvenir pillows, some wall pennants. Cute little plaster Kewpies, Siamese twins for Minneapolis and St. Paul. Fatwitted broke the Tulsa sombrero ashtray but then Fatwitted got hers too. Almost everything thrown away this time. Travel light. Just the essential things, small souvenirs, sentimental stuff. Ma felt strangely light and free, everything suddenly behind her. Leaving the bad dream behind, headed back south, back among true friends, away from people like Sawyer and loudmouth Goetz. That creepy Fatwitted.

All her plans had gone sour in two measly years. Northern women, unbridled lust, satanic whores soiling her Christian boys with alcohol and unspeakable evil. Dishonest men like Harry Sawyer, a far cry from the old gangs around Tulsa, men like Al Spencer, Henry Starr, poor old Jelly Nash. All gone now and blabbermouth Sawyer in the hands of the Federal men. GO FROM THE PRESENCE OF A FOOLISH MAN, WHEN THOU PERCEIVEST NOT IN HIM THE LIPS OF KNOWLEDGE. There is a time to stay and a time to get the hell out.

Fred glanced in the rear-view mirror, hunching his skinny shoulders as he wheeled the Chrysler around the smaller cars, Fords and Chevys, the black boxlike sedans of the working saps, down the drab avenues with soot-stained two-story two-family houses, all the same, all grimy, all ugly, all freezing cold. Noisy as hell. Back down home for a little peace and quiet.

"Harry Sawyer, that sonofabitch," he said.

"He's tellin' about jobs ain't even been pulled off yet," Dock said. "Namin' us fer every blessed one of 'em."

"You know, I got a place picked out that might be jest the ticket," Ma said. "A couple months ago, I figgered I'm gettin' too old fer these damn northern winters." She lit a cigarette. "I'm gettin' tired too o' runnin' ever two weeks from the coppers. I'd like t' settle down fer once. Ree-tire." A fragment of paper stuck to her cracked lip.

Fred went between two streetcars, missed a truck and swore.

"Drive me to th' depot," Ma said. "I'm goin' on ahead. I'm gonna ride the train like white folks. I'm damn sick an' tired o' drivin' in auto-*mo*biles."

"OK, Ma," Fred shrugged. "You got dough fer the ticket?"

"I got enough."

"Ma, I'm gonna stop off an' see Billie."

"Oh yes, yes," said Ma.

"I'm gonna say goodbye to her, Ma."

"Oh, Dock, that does touch a mother's heart."

"Yeah," Dock said.

"Is that a bull?" Fred said. "The black one behind the Essex?"

"Nah," Dock said. "I been watchin' him since he got behind us. He looks like somebody's grandpa. He ain't no cop."

"Florida," Ma said.

"You're sure he ain't no cop?" Fred said.

Ma leaned forward.

"Are you two saps go' lissen to me?"

"Sure, Ma," Fred said. "What's on your mind?"

"I got a *place* picked out, ef you give a damn. I was thinkin' it out. You know what I figgered? *Florida!* Who'd ever think to look fer us in Florida?"

•

Standing beside the car, hunched against the freezing wind blowing across the station parking lot, Ma smoothed the roadmap on the hood and wet her black pencil in her thin lips. In the hard autumn sunlight, she looked suddenly very old and tired.

"I never *was* to Florida before. Okla-wa-ha." She laughed. "How's that fer a name?"

She dug a thick black circle around the name on the map.

"Ma, yer still markin' up maps," Dock laughed. "How far is it from the state line?"

Ma grinned. Her puffy eyes were moist from the wind.

"Don't worry about that. No more jobs fer a time. We're jest goin' to rent a nice quiet little place in a high toned neighborhood an' live well."

•

"Careful with that sponge, bonehead," Freddie snarled. "You're gettin' my shoes wet."

In the flickering shade of a palm tree, Florida license plates, six gleaming wire wheels with white sidewalled tires, a spare mounted in the fender on either side of the long, elegant hood, a beautiful wooden dashboard covered with chromed gadgets that delighted Ma, lemon-yellow paint job with red leather upholstery, chrome fittings that sparkled in the Florida sun. A 1930 Packard Sport Phaeton bought for next to nothing from a Miami Beach playboy, a charming two-story cottage rented on exclusive Lake Weir, a speedboat and a real southern colored boy named Lennie to cook, mow the lawn and wash the car.

Ma lay on an ornate chaise lounge under a purple and yellow beach umbrella. She wore tight blue silk beach pajamas and a wide green ribbon for her finger-waved orange hair. She snarled like an old tigress as she tore at the leg of fried chicken, smacking her thin lips with pleasure, then threw the bone across the lawn and fumbled out a cigarette.

"Jest like old times," she belched, holding her cigarette between her teeth. "Now if we can just get Dock and Alvin to come down here without them floozies we could buy all new furniture, a nice living-room set, everything."

Fred stared at his shoes.

Ma belched again and wiped her greasy fingers on the grass.

•

With Ma snoring upstairs through the hot afternoon, Freddie

183

sprawled drunk across the Moorish divan, Tommy gun gripped in his left hand, staring at the rotogravured movie magazine open beside him.

Wampus Baby Stars, startled by the naughty photographer, scampering cuties on glamorous Santa Monica Beach. Swimsuit and thighs, cannonball knockers.

He blinked his swollen eyes.

Nookie-pigs like that an' drive 'em right through the mattress. Evil, scarlet woman, my ass. Holler it up, Ma, the chapter and the verse. What'd Ma ever know about it? Arthur? Arthur V. Dunlop, the dish-washer. Kissing in the back seat of the Essex. Fred shuddered. Old people, smelling sickly sweet, blundering around like evil kids, grabbing old flesh.

He picked up the Tommy and sighted down the barrel at the Kansas City pennant thumbtacked to the yellow and blue wall-paper. Arthur V. Dunlop, the lounge-lizard raper with a big blue hole in his crummy forehead.

•

There was something wrong about the place from the start.

Alvin Karpis stood in the center of Ma's rented Florida living room and lit a cigarette. Fred was stowing away the fishing gear in the garage.

"Come on down and bring whatshername. It's a swell layout. We can go fishin' all day long." A long distance call from crazy Freddie and Karpis had driven down with Loretta, six months pregnant, for a reunion with the old bunch.

"Fishing" meant taking Freddie's speedboat, a flatbottomed wooden tub with a 1924 outboard motor, out on Lake Weir looking for an alligator. With the faithful Tommy gun, his inseparable companion. Karpis wondered if Fred slept with the damn thing. From the looks of him, Fred wasn't sleeping with much else these days.

The best part about fishing for alligators wasn't the Tommy gun. The best part was the live pig towed as bait.

"Why don't you just tie the pig to a tree an' shoot him?" Karpis said.

"Jesus, Alvin, I thought you was a sportsman," Fred said. "I thought you liked fishin'."

Hard to believe, but Fred had changed for the worse. A fairly ugly young guy had gone to pieces in the short months he had been south. Fred's skin seemed to be shrinking on his skull. Broad reddish patches spread over his big nosed leathery face as Golden Wedding gradually replaced his blood. From time to time, he rubbed his endlessly roving eyes, bleary with fear and exhaustion.

There was a sense of doom about the Barkers that never was there before. Maybe it was this dumb Florida hideout.

The first afternoon, Karpis wanted to make a telephone call. Only one phone in Lake Weir, Alvin, it's at the Post Office. Karpis was alarmed at that. Suppose some friend got word the bulls were coming, what did he do, write you a letter?

He looked around the village. Only one road in or out, one telephone. Lake Weir was no hideout, it was a trap.

Ma sat out in the yard knawing on fried chicken all day. Fred was so screwed up about killing that alligator, he'd have shot off all the available ammunition in another week. What if they should happen to need some?

Not all the Bowman ransom money had been exchanged yet. Ma was supremely unworried. Plenty o' time, Alvin, the heat from the cops ain't so bad here, have some chicken.

The coon servant seemed to be laughing all the time. A real freak show in a haunted house.

Ma waddled in, wearing a heavy wool-skirted bathing suit with geraniums embroidered across the belly. Her thighs were twin pillars of blue-white dough. The barrel belly was unbelievable in a bathing suit. Her gargantuan breasts were belted at the waist.

She posed prettily in the beaded doorway, and wiped her hands on her suit.

"Did ye shoot 'im, Fred?" she yelled.

"No, no I never!" he yelled from the bathroom.

"How come ye never shot that alley-gator, Fred? Are ye worth a good goddam er aincha?"

"Knock it off, Ma," Fred said with a mighty flushing and rattling of enema tubes.

"Yew better practice with that Thompson gun more. Cain't hit a bull in the ass," she said, rubbing her massive arms.

"When you figure the rest of the dough will be exchanged?" Karpis said.

"Oh plenty of time." She smiled. "Plenty of time." She fanned herself with the souvenir of Tulsa.

Fred shuffled into the room. A new scar on his cheek.

"I beat th' boy with the .45 again night before last," Ma said. She scratched at her neck with the fan. "It he'ps little Freddie."

She grinned and lit a cigarette.

"I tole that boy to cut his toenails," she said. "One thing I cain't abide, it's sloppy toenails."

Fred giggled, staring at the floor. He stank all the time now, since he took to sleeping in his clothes. Fried chicken stains on his trousers. He shivered as he lit a cigarette.

"What the hell's that?" he said, jumping to his feet. He crossed to the window. "Them bastards next door. They run that goddam car in an' outa that garage twenty-five times a day."

He grinned at Karpis.

"It's a snazzy place here, ain't it?" he said.

•

When Karpis was alone with Loretta, she said, "How long we gonna stay around here, honey?"

"We'll shove off tomorrow," Karpis said. "There ain't any dough."

"This whole place gives me the creeps."

"Yeah," he said.

"There's bottles of cough medicine all over the house," she said. "Half full. I even saw one stuck in a palm tree out on the lawn."

"Yeah. I guess so."

"He keeps sayin' it's the Florida mold that smells. It's him."

Karpis said nothing.

"That boogie cook is laughin' at Fred behind his back," she said.

186

"Don't go gettin' ideas," he said.

"Well, that's how it looked."

"Forget it," he said.

•

Dock arrived that afternoon with sloe-eyed Billie the beautiful brunette and a set of matched luggage with his initials on the side.

"Get that fairy stuff," Fred said.

"How come you brung the gal?" Ma said.

"Don't talk like that to Billie," Dock said.

"I'm your own mother, your own flesh and blood, I suppose it's asking too much to have some respect fer yore own Ma I suppose."

"OK, Ma, cut it out," Dock said.

"You couldn't have common ordinary courtesy not to bring hoors an' bimbos in the house," she said. "You're still smokin' cigarettes, Dock. You'll always be a midget."

Billie yawned.

"Where's the ice?" she said. Karpis showed her the kitchen.

"Jesus, nothing has changed has it?" she said, pouring gin from a flask.

"Things don't look good," Karpis said, staring out the window. A fine view of the lake. But suppose somebody is coming up the road.

The uproar increased from the living room.

"A hoor! A wumman who has sex intercourse in bed with the organ of a man she ain't married to!" yelled Ma.

Billie grinned and swallowed her gin.

•

Dock and Billie left during the night. Chicago was Ma's guess. Her oldest boy (outside of Lloyd in prison) and he ran off with a loose-moraled chippie. Enough to break her stout old mother's heart.

•

Karpis packed their clothes while Loretta rested her large new burden. Time to leave before something bad happens around here. Goddam Florida was a spooky place anyhow. All those nutty palm trees. The Barkers are stuck worse than ever on making giant scores, world championship paydays. Jelly Nash was right. Small steady paydays attract less attention. Don't be the biggest crook in the country or you'll have the government zeroed in on you. Be the third biggest. A series of good steady jobs in the $30,000 price range. A man could certainly live on that. A good fast smooth-working small outfit, no deadwood. Cameron, Roscoe Gibbons. Not the Barker circus.

Fred was at the door.

"Come on Alvin, one last try fer the alligator before ya take off."

"OK, Fred," Karpis slammed the suitcase shut. "Be back in a while, baby," he said to Loretta.

Ma had furnished the Florida living room in Son of the Sheik Moorish. No air stirred the red velvet drapes hung from genuine wrought iron spear rods.

Loretta sat in Ma's new Jacquard Velour Queen Anne armchair with her feet on the matching ottoman. Three months to go. She sighed. No kicking yet this morning from the little stranger inside.

Ma swaggered in from the kitchen resplendent in her wool flower-encrusted bathing suit, a brass number disk gleaming on her left shoulder strap.

"I swiped the tag from the Excelsior Plunge in Chicagah," she beamed. "It kinda dresses up the suit I figger."

Loretta agreed.

"The boys are fishin'," Ma said.

"Alligators," Loretta said.

"Yessiree," said Ma. She wore a platinoid metal link barrette, guaranteed not to tarnish, strung across the back of her skull like a skid chain.

"I thought you was kind to animals, Ma."

"Th' alley-gator ain't a beast, he's a fish. I figger if these rich fools have a fish hung on their settin' room wall, Fred an' me kin have us a alley-gator. It'll look right nice up there."

"Alvin Karpis huntin' alligators, for cryin' out loud," Loretta said. "Who'da thought it."

"You don't understand Alvin. He's jest highstrung."

"Highstrung! What's that mean?"

Ma smiled her patient old woman-of-the-world smile from Ruth Chatterton.

"How old're you, honey?"

"Eighteen, why?"

"Kids—you don't even know the score."

"Oh, I know enough."

"Kids. Punk kids. Look atcha."

"Well, like they say, Ma, a full belly makes a strong back."

"Strong back, weak mind."

"You oughta know, Ma."

Ma ignored the try.

"How you could ever do sech a sorry thing as this to a nice boy like Alvin Karpis, I'll never know," she said.

"It was easy."

"Everything's easy when you're eighteen."

"I guess so." Loretta studied a framed photograph of Freddie (Love to my pal, my mom) on the end table. "Ma, whatever became o' Fatwitted?"

Ma's little eyes glittered in her heavy blank face.

"Fatwitted . . . yeah. I don't know what became o' that little gal. I heard she lost her looks."

She leaned her head against a lace doily on her Guadalajara chair. The palms beyond the window stirred in the breeze.

"That little gal argued like a steady fall o' rain," Ma said.

"Ma, can I ask you something?" Loretta's eyes were baby blue.

"What?"

"Ma, how come you work with the gang?"

"What ye wanta know fer?"

"I just wondered, Mrs. Barker."

"You're fulla questions, aincha?"

Loretta waved her small white hands.

"I guess I'm just nervous, Mrs. Barker. What with a kid and all . . . I don't want to fight with anybody."

Ma studied Loretta, miserable in the heat, pale frightened little face, hands clasped over her mountainous middle. Ma allowed herself a faint smile.

"Well, I tell ye, honey. I'm smarter'n they are. They're good muscle but they can't git outa their own way. They *need* somebody to figger things out fer 'em."

"Yeah. It's odd."

"It is, huh?" Ma's pulse went up again.

"Well, it's just kinda unusual, I guess. *My* ma fer instance, if she was alive, she'd *skin* me if she knew I was goin' around with holdup men. An' I got two sisters both married to gunmen too!"

Ma yawned.

"Ooooooh! Think of that."

"I never knew a mother like you, Mrs. Barker."

Ma turned in her chair and stabbed a thick finger at her.

"Don't go gettin' any ideas, honey, just because I laid out a coupla bank jobs fer the boys. We ain't criminals . . . Not at least like some folks said. That's a lotta damn talk. People always did talk an' gossip all the time about us . . . Even back in Missoura . . . The boys never did *half* the things people said. Dock never killed that watchman and poor Herman was forced to shoot himself by the highway cops; Lloyd never held up no U.S. Mail and Freddie wasn't a thief and I don't believe he killed that nosey sheriff an' even if he did, it wasn't Freddie's fault, he was drove to it by that law man. The coppers kept after Freddie 'til they made him a nervous wreck! He's a sensitive boy an' they keep on pickin' at him, day an' night!"

She was on her feet, across the carpet to the sideboard and the melted chocolate creams.

Loretta lowered her eyes.

"That's a shame, Ma. About Freddie."

Ma tore through empty wrappers, searching out the remaining juicy ones.

"All I ever wanted was to have enough money like everybody else had," she said. "You know, the good book says, 'Men do not despise a thief, if he steal to satisfy his soul when he is hungry'."

"It does?"

"Yep. Right there in the Proverbs. 'My soul was hungry.'"
She crunched down on a satisfying Caramel Supreme.

"It says that in the Bible?"

"It surely does."

The roar of the outboard drifted in from the lake. Loretta sighed again.

"Well, it's a nice place ya got here . . . It's real nice."

"This ain't a good life," Ma said, moving to the windows. "Look what happened to Johnnie Dillinger. He robbed from the rich an' gave to the poor. He did a lotta good you never hear about. He never killed a man in his life. The Federal men shot him down, shot him in the back just like Jesse James was shot. He never had a chance. I might go to live in Mexico but there's too many greasers there. I'm tired o' the coppers bein' after us all the time. It's not fair. The whole entire business has changed. It usta be the cops could chase ye as far as the state line an' no farther. Now the Federal men go anyplace and pay no mind at all to the state lines. They don't obey *that* law at *all*. It's not fair."

"Oh I know. Alvin tells me."

Ma flung the drapes apart with a thrust of her beefy arms.

"I'm tired of doin' all the thinkin' fer everybody an' arguin' with these blockheads who can't be trusted to blow their own nose. I'm gonna retire. I earned it. Jest one er two more big ones and that'll be it. The coppers ain't about to catch up to me anyhow."

She gazed out on the lake, brown and sparkling in the sun.

"In all the places that I lived in, this is the best hideout I ever did find."

•

Alvin Karpis carried Loretta's suitcases out to his maroon Auburn. With any luck he'd be well on the way to Pittsburgh by nightfall. He looked around. One road in, one road out. No back door to the town. No telephone. A perfect trap. Ma the Brain was slipping. Welcome to Ambush Lake. He slid his fingers over the .38 in its holster.

"D'ya like my bathin' suit, Alvin?"

"Yeah, Ma. It's sure somethin', all right."

"It ain't too revealin', is it?"

"Huh? Uh, no, Ma, it's fine."

"I wondered maybe was the skirt too short."

Goodbye to Ma Barker. Say so long to Fred if he ever sobers up. Ma smiled the old familiar smile, a leer exposing her iron tooth. Karpis knew it was goodbye. She was half dead already. Something in her pouchy, haunted eyes.

She placed a cold hand on his arm and her lips were trembling.

"Goodbye Alvin honey," she said. "Hurry on now, er I'll be cryin'."

"So long, Ma," Karpis said and carried his suitcases to the car.

Loretta sat in the front seat, waiting.

"Where do we go now?"

Karpis glanced around. The yard, the boat dock, the lonely sand road. He grimaced.

"North. Atlantic City. I gotta get back to work."

He jazzed the motor and the Auburn rolled forward.

Ma Barker stood on the porch in her crazy old bathing suit with geraniums on the belly, waving goodbye.

•

January cold in Chicago. Freezing wind and a warm girl.

"Chicago!" Billie said, squeezing Dock's arm. "Now we can have some fun without Ma breathin' down my neck."

Dock grinned.

"Ma's the sweetest, dearest mother a boy could have!"

"Dock, you're a comic," Billie said. "You really are!"

He touched his finger along his new Ronald Colman mustache, as yet a faint dark line under his patrician nose.

"How ya like it?"

"It's beautiful!" Billie laughed. She was a very pretty girl. "And I don't have to listen to Ma makin' cracks about it."

He kissed her lips and they swung down the brown steps, arm in arm, a smart young couple out for the evening.

Sloe-eyed Billie was beautiful in furs as dark and soft as her wavy hair, Dock elegant with his pearl gray topcoat and British bowler, gold-tipped stick and spats. The Prince of Wales and his best girl. Obviously. We don't subscribe to Vanity Fair for nothing.

They had reached the corner when the men appeared from behind the parked cars, young, cleancut, well-dressed, earnest.

"You're Dock Barker," one said.

He stopped, paralyzed, and reached under his arm and it wasn't there. He knew they were cops and the initial wash of fear gave way to a slow crazy feeling of relief. This was where it ended. The chase was over. "Never surrender," cried Ma. Little Dock stood there on the sidewalk, surrounded by Federal agents, Billie beside him in tears, and he was too tired to resist.

"This is a hell of a time to be caught without a gun," he mumbled.

Six FBI men took Dock downtown and the others went back into his apartment and began the thorough search.

In the bedroom, one agent found a loaded submachine gun. The serial number said Stockyards Bank payroll job, dead policeman. Another agent unfolded a gas station map and shook it.

"Florida," he said. They studied the map closely.

"Somebody couldn't resist drawing a nice *black circle* around the place."

He pointed.

"*OK-LA-WA-HA*, Florida."

•

"OK-LA-WA-HA." Ma laughs in the dark, cigarette glowing in the Florida bedroom. "Fred honey, ain't that a comical name, though?"

Fred rubs his oily face, his bulging eyes blinking away sleep and early morning despair.

"Yeah, Ma, it's a scream." His stomach lurches dangerously. His undershirt smells of mold. So does the entire bedroom. Time to get up, face life.

"You'd think brother Dock would write us a letter once in a while."

"Maybe he's busy," Fred yawns. Busy banging Billie day and night.

"Jest a letter once in a while."

193

There's a bright and a sunny side too . . . cries the phonograph, guitars twanging away, a warm down-home country sound, church harmony, *Keep on the sunny side, always on the sunny side!*

Fred slumps barefoot on the edge of the cast-iron bed, pulling on his two-tone shoes.

It will help us every day / it will brighten all the way . . .

(I'll go north, I'll find Fatwitted and make it up with her.)

"I'll fix some coffee, Fred, the coon is late again."

"Maybe I'll throw him to ole Joe. Teach 'im a lesson."

•

The fog has gone.

In the gloom of early morning, the lakeside neighborhood is alive with lawmen, dark murky shapes moving among the palms.

There is a last minute check of rifles, machine guns, weapons glinting in the soft light. It will be shotguns and pistols for the Florida men.

Beside the tommy guns and teargas, the FBI has a number of harmless looking long guns, smallish, handsomely designed shotguns. The Winchester .351. The riot gun.

Five quick shots in what appears to be a hunting rifle and is in reality a hand-held cannon. A blasting device.

It fires Double O Buck, a shell containing nine lead pellets each the size of a .38 slug. Bullets, really, that spread apart one inch per forward foot of travel. At twelve feet, you have a group of .38 bullets traveling in a group one foot across, at twenty-four feet the spread is two feet wide, at thirty-six feet (a more realistic range for the Barker job) nine .38 slugs are traveling in a formation three feet across.

Thus you can be hit with nine bullets from one pull of the trigger, wrecking muscle, bone, cartilage, organs, everything. Nine homicidal Dr. McCoys operating on you at once, each using a pneumatic street drill. Scarcely a shotgun, in the familiar sense.

Working the pump, five of these expanding loads can be unleashed in seconds. Quite a weapon.

The Barkers won't know what hit them.

As they wait, everyone feels the tension; conversation is in whispers. Thick palm trees are favored positions. The agents are not optimistic about a parked car stopping bullets. They have seen too many riddled and torn by gunfire. A Florida officer grips his rifle tightly and shuts his eyes. No smoking. An Ocala man stolidly chews tobacco, his gaze fixed on the silent two-story cottage.

Lennie, the Negro cook, crouches on the wet grass with the FBI men. Fred and Ma and Alvin must have been pretty important to get all these men after them. If they actually shoot all these guns at the cottage, Mr. Broadwin is going to be mighty sore about it. Anyhow, we'll see how tough Mister Fred is now.

"Everybody in position, ready to go?" whispers John Lafferty. "Check your equipment. We can *not* have any screwup on this one. That's the *word*."

Agent Lafferty feels almost calm at this moment. Everything has been done that could be done.

This is the most important job of his life.

In July, Inspector Samuel P. Cowley, the top field agent, led the group that got Dillinger. Two months ago, Inspector Cowley caught up to Baby Face Nelson. A vicious gun battle in the open, Nelson is dead and so is Sam Cowley. Hoover has moved Lafferty into Cowley's place as agent in charge of the Special Squad, Chicago.

One week ago, in the other half of the Chicago roundup that captured Dock Barker, John Lafferty had called out Roscoe Gibbons and Byram Roland in a hotel corridor. Gibbons came out firing and was shot to pieces. Double O Buckshot in a hallway.

This morning Lafferty finds himself in Florida, twenty-five yards from the last of the Barker gang and for all he knows, Alvin Karpis is with them. Karpis is suspected in several killings.

Several very tough experienced men armed with submachine guns are probably inside that dark silent cottage.

John Lafferty touches the lump that the medal makes under his shirt. Then he slips his fingers inside the shirt and touches the medal itself.

He looks around. The mist is gone, it will be a nice morning. And here goes.

His heart is pounding, he breathes through his mouth, his chest is tight, the excitement makes him slightly dizzy.

That high school feeling, the All City Championship game is about to begin.

He stands up.

"All right!" he yells, surprised at the loudness of his own voice. "Come on out! Surrender!"

•

Ma Barker ducks back from the window.

"Fred, the street is fulla cops!"

"Goddammit!" Fred fumbles around, his head is ready to burst open.

He bumps the end of the bed. He can barely see.

"What the hell are those bastards doin' *here?*" There is a vile sour taste in his mouth. He is sure he is going to throw up. His undershirt is soaking wet. Come back tomorrow when I feel better.

"How in hell did those bastards find us?" he moans, scrambling over a suitcase open on the floor.

"The Tommy ain't loaded, I was gonna clean it." The bottom slides out of his stomach. I was gonna do all kinds of things. I was gonna clean the gun, quit the booze, apologize to Fatwitted. He grabs his .45 automatic and drops it. His hands are slippery with sweat. Holding it with both hands, he makes the window.

There is a goddam guy wearing a suit and hat standing in the front yard!

Fred aims the heavy .45 and fires three quick shots at Lafferty. He hits the porch of the house across the street.

Lafferty returns his fire and the FBI joins in with rifles and machine guns. A volley bursts forth from the twenty local law men, a flashing bombardment launched from behind trees and parked cars.

A rainstorm of lead rips into the cottage. Bullets spatter the trees and shrubs, breaking windows, rustling through branches, whacking into parked cars. On opposite sides, lawmen are sure they have been fired on. Their answer is a return volley, machine guns stuttering, rifles cracking, pistols banging away as wood and plaster scatter from the trembling cottage walls. An entire palm frond sags to the ground with a crash. A flower bed is splashed across the side of a garage. Firing slackens, there is a surprising amount of smoke still drifting through the trees. An Ocala deputy starts a half-hearted rebel yell. No one has been killed by the mad dogs yet; the law men are encouraged.

In a neighboring house, Mrs. D. H. Mathewson is wakened by the uproar. As she rolls out of bed, a burst of fire smashes through her closed bedroom door, ripping up her pillow and headboard. There is a sharp smell of gunpowder. She cautiously opens the shattered door a crack and more bullets rip the door-face over her head. There is a pop-popping of rapid fire from just outside in her yard, followed by a booming of shotguns and the deep mechanical racket from a submachine gun. Stunned by the sheer volume of the noise, she gets her daughter on her feet as more slugs whistle into the wall of the room, showering splinters over the bed.

A savage burst of fire tears a screen from a lower window. There is a crash of breaking glass.

A man is firing a hand gun from the upper window of the Broadwin house and a dozen determined men with rifles return his fire. Wrapped in bathrobes, Mrs. Mathewson and her daughter tumble out through the unscreened window and sprawl out of breath and frantic in the wet grass.

An Ocala sheriff stands right out into the road, firing a shotgun at the upper window. He blinks his eyes as his gun flashes and the Double O Buck smashes into the cottage second story. A section of screen tears free, tumbling end over end to the ground. A bullet breaks a car window. A headlight is shot loose, rolls backward down its sloping fender, bounces off the running board and hits the street with a crash.

Lafferty suddenly sees two dark shapes running across the lawn next to the Barker cottage. Somehow the Barkers have made it out the back windows and are getting away! It is every failed Dillinger ambush and Little Bohemia all over again. All those bungled traps in Chicago. From the frantic FBI, submachine guns and repeating rifles send a hail of slugs at the fleeing figures, missing by inches, ripping lawns, walls, trees and autos, smashing the windshield out of a Plymouth, puncturing all four tires.

Mrs. Mathewson and her daughter are caught in a wild dash for the house fifty yards back of their own. They are vaguely aware of the air around them screaming with lead as they make their frantic run, bathrobes flying and hurl themselves through their neighbor's hedge where a squad of Ocala lawmen are crouching.

Fred gets off a burst with the tommy gun and the Ocala sheriff crawls under a car. Water spouts from the smashed radiator. There is a steady pom-pom-pom from the gas-operated repeating rifles, as they shatter the flimsy wooden beach house construction.

Inside the cottage, the shots are much louder than expected. Loading the tommy gun drums, Ma feels the old-time excitement, bottles shattering on fenceposts, tin cans dancing in red dusty roads. Old Freddie is giving it to 'em in there, the Yankee sonofabitches. Ma laughs, struggling with the goddamn complicated L-50 metal drum (it's too heavy, it ain't woman's work), her five-dollar manicure all shot to hell on the steel drum magazine winding key. "Wind to 9 clicks," whatever that means.

A window explodes in a highpitched shower of glass fragments, the particles falling and falling, the echoing blast of Fred's .45 in contrapuntal to the pop-pop-pop of the Federals from the yard and street below. They must have worked around both sides by now. They've got us surrounded, the poor bastards. Give it to 'em, Fred.

"Let 'em have it!" she yells, laughing.

Quiet again, the torn window shade stirs in the soft morning breeze. Freddie moves around on hands and knees in the other room, the scrunch of broken glass, a curse as he brushes the tinkling shards from his trouser leg.

Close neighbors, aroused by the unbelievable noise, are running from their houses, out of the way of the zinging bullets. All around Lake Weir, others are out of their cottages, drawn to the staccato roar of gunfire from the Broadwin place. On the lake, a fisherman rows for the opposite shore. If they sink his rowboat, Old Joe the alligator will get him.

The firing increases, slackens, then stops. One shot, two more, and it builds up again.

As the fight continues sporadically, one hour, then two, word spreads through the area that a real honest-to-God gunbattle is taking place at Lake Weir. A Model T Ford, loaded with sightseers from Ocala, clatters down the Lake road narrowly missing people jogging toward the uproar. Men, women and children are pouring across lawns, trampling hedges and flowers in their haste to see real people firing live ammunition at each other. This could be better than the movies.

As three carloads of sightseers arrive at the lake, there is a sudden loud blast of machine-gun fire. They scatter from the road, ducking for cover behind cars and thick palms. The battle is still two blocks away.

A white-haired man wearing a fishing hat stands in his tiny yard, shooing the sightseers from his flower beds.

"There goes property values, by God! The crazy people, Harriet! The summer people must be back."

Harriet appears, rimless glasses, dentures, an old sweater around her shoulders, a coffee mug in her mottled hand.

"I knew it would happen. They rent to just anyone."

The man knocks his pipe against the small iron Negro holding a ring.

"It's the trashy ones from Miami," he says.

Two fat girls in slacks cut across his lawn.

"Hurry up!" one cries. "We'll miss it!"

He sails a stone after them, missing. Now his back hurts. Fat-butted sluts from Miami Beach. He will sue Carter Broadwin and the Lake Association.

Hundreds of people are on the road, coming from Ocala,

Belleview, Weirsdale, Leesburg and as far as Orlando to see the free show.

A man in a large straw hat is selling Snowballs, crushed ice in assorted flavors. Green, red and yellow coloring.

No local police are controlling traffic. They are all at the Broadwin house, emptying their weapons into the walls, vaguely aware of reward money.

A young boy and his girl arrive, drive right up into the line of fire, dismount and the windshield is shot out of their open Chevrolet. They dive into the grass.

The girl is blonde and angular, wearing a cheap cotton dress. Her eyebrows are pencil thin. She tries very hard to look like Jean Harlow.

"You damn crazy nut, Boyd Henry!" she screams. "What you bring me here for!"

"Shut up, Tula Mae!" The boy is wearing plusfours and white shoes. He snakes away on his belly under the car.

The barrage of lead poured into the house has prevented an escape from within; there is no mad dash for a car, no getaway, but the law is now low on ammunition. The Barkers and Karpis and whoever else must give up soon. Meanwhile, an urgent call from Oklawaha's only phone to Ocala, Leesburg and Orlando. More ammunition immediately, FBI, Federal Government, don't argue.

"You can stand on my lawn if you like, it'll cost you fifty cents apiece." A tall, calm woman in her sixties. Sweater, skirt, tennis shoes and sun visor. "We've a perfect view of the house. You can see everything from here. Fifty cents. Four bits."

There is a terrific burst of gunfire, palm fronds drop from trees, a flashing exchange of shots between house and FBI.

A Good Humor truck arrives, drawn by the crowds. Beautiful day, lots of people.

The crushed ice Snowball man glares at him. How can he compete with all that hightone city ice cream?

FBI men move slowly back and forth, tree to tree, keeping a distance. It will be a siege.

A man with sunglasses and a brand new flame-grain Kaywoodie pipe lies on his belly, watching the action, streaks of fire followed by the loud report as the guns go off a block away. He bats his eyes at the noise.

"Now that don't seem hardly fair. Fifteen or twenty law officers bangin' away at a couple o' people holed up like that. That ain't fair at all."

An emaciated boy, his face a battlefield of acne, gnaws on a Baby Ruth bar.

"If that's real gangsters in there, I hope they git away."

An unshaven man in overalls watches from beside a palm trunk. He squirts tobacco juice.

"You kin have 'em. You believe all that crap you read about 'em. These guys are killers. They'd blow your face off as soon as look at ye."

The boy is unconvinced.

"I still hope they git away." He concentrates on the peanuts in his bar.

A stray burst of machine gun slugs hits the brass bells of the Good Humor truck with a shrill crash. They ring.

The Good Humor man bounces heavily face down in the grass.

"Take all you want, I ain't goin' to stand up," he says to his fingers.

A newspaper reporter arrives from Orlando. He crouches at the command post behind a '32 Ford sedan and the local idiot, wearing white cowboy hat and Gene Autry shirt, explains everything.

"They been fightin' since early mornin'. They got the Barker gang, Alvin Karpis, Dillinger, Pretty Boy Floyd and Baby Face Nelson all cornered in there. They got ever damn big shot gunman holed up in there excep' Jesse *James*."

•

Ma chances a quick look out the back window.

The garage.

If we kin git to the car, we could run fer it. Freddie is a wonderful driver.

A submachine gun burst whacks through the flimsy garage,

punching ugly holes in the shiny lemon yellow Packard doors, tearing red leather, shattering a chromed headlight. The rich white sidewalls are ribboned, the silvery spokes tangled, and with a funereal hiss of escaping air the beautiful Sport Phaeton, bleeding gasoline from a dozen wounds, settles in a twenty degree list, dead in the water.

•

Fred fires a single shot from the window and slides a fresh clip into his .45. This damn gun is getting him nowhere.

"Come on, Ma, let's have the tommy gun."

Four FBI agents are firing at once from outside, the pop-popping of their weapons sounding like the Fourth of July.

Ma's green silk pillow, souvenir of CHICAGOLAND, QUEEN OF THE MIDWEST is shot to pieces. Rag stuffing and buckskin fringe. Sawdust. The store guaranteed cotton stuffing, too.

Fred is firing single shots out the window with a .45. His ears ache and he can smell his own stale sweat. His stomach is drawn up in a tight knot.

"Come on, Ma, change that drum and hurry up!"

"I'm a hurryin'. Don't rush me, boy."

There is a burst of gunfire from down the street. Fred fires one shot in return.

"Get that damn gun in here, Ma!"

"Hold yore horses, Fred Barker!"

A burst cuts close by his head. He ducks, angry now. Bits of wood are stuck to his bare shoulder with sweat.

"Come on Ma! Bring the damn gun in here. I'll change it myself!"

"If you practiced like I *told* ye, you could hit something with that hand gun."

Another burst from outside. The goddam snotty bastards down there don't know who he is. Ask that fatass sheriff in West Plains, Old Man Dunlop, that punk in the park, Goetz, that punk in the car, Doc McCoy, those jerks in the alley, the shyster lawyer, the bank guards, the messenger saps, every snotty goddam peckerhead that's been askin' for it for the last thirty years.

"If you practiced like I *told* ye!" yells Ma.

Fred jumps up, furious, and empties his .45 in a rage at a target below the window.

A terrific blast spins him around, chips of flesh and blood spraying the wall as he stumbles back the length of it, the bones are broken inside his shoulder, his lung is gone, and Freddie Barker, the baby of the family, the blameless misunderstood sensitive son of a poor Ozark woman alone, hounded and harried, persecuted all his poor miserable life, falls with a crash in the corner of the bedroom.

Ma yells from the other room.

"Hold the fort, Freddie. I got the thing in place."

BE NOT FAR FROM ME; FOR TROUBLE IS NEAR; FOR THERE IS NONE TO HELP.

"I'm countin' on ye, Freddie."

In the wreckage in the corner, Fred has eleven bullets in his shoulder, three in his head.

An FBI man runs across the lawn and hurls a tear gas grenade.

Inside the front room, there is a dull bumping explosion and thick bluish smoke curls slowly up from under the porch eaves.

Other agents move into better positions under cover of the smoke.

Ma is frightened. All that smoke. Second floor and one narrow stairway.

"They set the house on fire, Fred!"

Ma is alone in the back bedroom, struggling with the submachine gun. The locking lever sticks. Some damn fool has put too many rounds in the drum. She can hear yelling below.

"Fred, they're tryin' to get around this side!"

A machine gun burst hits the Kansas City bear. Ma's ears ring; she can't breathe. She has gone deaf.

"There was no need to do that," she says, her voice sounding far away. "That's a damn shame." The Kansas City bear is all over the floor.

(*Old Judge Parker, the Hangin' Judge, saved up his prisoners and hung 'em six at a time.*)

The room jumps and rolls with the gunfire.

•

A hurricane has struck the house, worse than any pig sty she ever lived in. Worse than Thayer, worse than the first shack in Tulsa. She is back where she started. Live in a cave in the hills with Jesse James and Cole Younger. She will never get that rug cleaned now. The coon was supposed to take it out yesterday and get it cleaned. She'll have to speak to him good and proper. Coons these days never listen.

Ma's purse is shot off the splintered table. She picks it up. The lining is torn, the hasp broken.

"Jesse used a grain sack, I use this old purse. It's my lucky purse."

Shots rip across the ceiling.

From a gouge in the plaster overhead, a thin steady trickle of plaster dust filters down like sand in an hourglass. She holds her hand open under it, catching a gritty rain in her palm.

Somewhere downstairs glass breaks with a high tinkling crash.

"Bust 'em all, you bluebelly bastards."

The sons of bitches she has hated all her life are right outside, right this minute, still hounding her. The effrontery to shoot at her when she's in her own house, minding her own business. Freddie will take care of them! They'll be sorry. Dock will be here soon. He and Alvin Karpis will come up behind the blue-bellies and shoot the daylights out of 'em. Jelly Nash will fix 'em.

She pulls a floor lamp out of the wreckage, brushes plaster and glass from it, and shakes her head.

"Ever damn thing I own. All my nice things."

A machine gun chops a line of holes across the wall to the picture of Jesse James.

(*Don't let 'em take ye alive, they'll tie a rope around yore neck.*)

A blast of gunfire opens a door, which swings in and falls off its hinges, carrying over a highboy with ceramic animals, stat-

204

ues, ash trays and a glass ball snowstorm scene with a fantastic crash.

"It took me thirty years to collect them things. Some of 'em belonged to my mother."

Ma, on her hands and knees, pushes her fingers through the rubble in a futile gesture, pieces spattering the floor.

In the wreckage there is a framed old-fashioned photo of her father. The glass is cracked and the frame broken.

(*You shoulda bin a boy, Kate. I often wished ye was.*)

WHOSO CURSETH HIS FATHER OR HIS MOTHER, HIS LAMP SHALL BE PUT OUT IN OBSCURE DARKNESS.

"Fred, I got the drum fer ye."

She crawls slowly into the other room, gashing her knee in the glass, wincing at sporadic bursts of fire. Nauseating blue smoke hangs in layers.

Freddie is on his back, sweaty bare arms, wet undershirt, ugly dark red gouges in his left shoulder and chest spilling blood. Ma chances a quick look out the back window.

"I got the gun fer ye."

Her tears begin.

"Ye kin stop hollerin' now."

She touches the wounds.

THE BLUENESS OF A WOUND CLEANSETH AWAY EVIL.

She continues to stare at Fred's body, slowly wiping her fingers on her plaster-smeary green skirt.

"Oh my Christ."

There is a blast of machine gun bullets close over her head. Weeping bitterly, she shakes her fat old head, her orange hair matted with sweat, plaster dust.

"Stop it, stop it."

In a daze, she stares at Fred.

MY STRENGTH IS DRIED UP LIKE A POTSHERD; AND MY TONGUE CLEAVETH TO MY JAWS; AND THOU HAST BROUGHT ME INTO THE DUST OF DEATH.

A burst of shots punches into the ceiling and wall.

"Look what the damn fools are doin' to us, Fred."

She is splattered with plaster, chips of wood stuck in her hair.

"I'm all alone, Fred."

FOR A JUST MAN FALLETH SEVEN TIMES, AND RISETH UP
AGAIN.

"Freddie can't be dead."

There is a short burst of shots, something breaks with a tinkling sound.

MY SON GIVE ME THINE HEART, AND LET THINE EYES OB-
SERVE MY WAYS.

(*My son Herman, he killed himself. You bet yore boots he
did, Katie; die with your boots on, that's the important thing.*)

"I'm goin' in the other room an' lay down a while, Freddie.
My head hurts like blazes."

(*Herman he killed himself.*)

THEY THAT BE SLAIN WITH THE SWORD ARE BETTER
THAN THEY THAT BE SLAIN WITH HUNGER; FOR THESE
PINE AWAY.

(*Herman is right in the next room, the cops made him kill
himself.*)

More tear gas explodes on the porch roof, below the windows.

(*Don't let 'em take ye alive, they'll hang ye. Sometimes a
hangin' pulls the head right off the body. Terrible things happen
to the body.*)

(*My daddy is gonna take me to the meetin'. One time he let
me fire the musket.*)

Ma crawls away, dragging the machine gun.

"I'm goin' to take a nap, Fred. You'll be all right."

In the hall, she closes the broken door to the front room,
leans against the wall gazing around at the wreckage, the tears
running down her battered face. She retrieves a scratched photograph of the boys from the floor, brushes plaster from it and
places it on the sideboard.

"Ever damn thing I got."

She shifts the machine gun to both hands, places her finger on the trigger. (*My daddy always liked me, I was his favorite.*)

There is a very loud single shot.

•

The palms stir in the faint breeze. Across the lake, a truck labors over a slight rise. A strange quiet falls over hundreds of spectators crouching behind trees and buildings. A car tilts on its flattened tire. In another, every window is broken. A punctured radiator dribbles a stream of rusty water on the sandy road.

The FBI hold their fire, gazing steadily at the house. The silence continues. Minutes pass, still no fire from the house.

"Maybe we got 'em."

"Hold up a minute," says Lafferty. "Let's see."

Ranged for blocks around, the sightseers are watching. Heads slowly appear behind hedges, palms.

At the stalled Good Humor truck, a hand slips into the rear compartment, reappears with a carton of ice cream. A dog howls. Barking begins across the lake.

Lawmen behind trees and automobiles and townspeople watching from windows wait. There is only the faint rustling of the palms in the silence.

An FBI agent glances at his watch. 11:18.

"Whaddya think?" He wipes sweat from his eyes. Five hours is hard work.

"Let's see." The tall man with the rifle slowly works his bolt, his eyes on the cottage.

"These babies are liable to try anything. Let's hang on a minute."

•

Lennie, the Negro cook, is with the FBI men and three deputies from Ocala.

A lean bony-faced man squirts tobacco juice into the sand of the road.

"Boy, you go on in there an' see what's what," he says.

"Me?"

"Come on, boy, move it."

"You mean me?"

"Boy, you get yore ass in there on the double," a sheriff says, "or I'll make you wish you had."

There is a pause.

"Take your choice, boy."

"OK, mister." Lennie starts for the house.

Behind the palm trunk, the sheriff says, "Boogies are just plain chicken."

It seems to take minutes for Lennie to cross the littered yard, stepping over palm fronds and broken window fittings from the house. He pauses on the porch. Everyone is watching. He pushes the front door and it swings open.

"Don't shoot now! It's only me . . . It's only me . . ." He clears his throat.

He eases himself into the silent living room. There is a strong smell of damp rot and plaster.

"Only just me, Mistuh Fred . . . Mizz Blackburn . . . Hello! Don't shoot now!"

He chokes on the tear gas in the dark room and it stings his skin. What will these white bastards think up next? He stumbles to a side window and shoves it open.

Immediately a sheriff stands up with aimed rifle to kill him. An FBI man grabs the barrel. The Negro gasps for air, tears streaming from his eyes, then ducks back into the house holding his breath.

Lafferty prowls around the yard, submachine gun ready, intently watching the upper windows. At Little Bohemia, Dillinger and the whole crowd crawled out the second story and disappeared; that's not going to happen here.

The Barkers might grab the cook and use him as a shield. Lafferty's finger moves to the trigger.

Inside the blasted cottage, tear gas stings Lennie's face, seeps into the sweat on his body. His armpits, his crotch are on fire. The white bastards got a new method. No more castration. Just march you through this bomb-smoke and burn it off you.

Agonizing up the wrecked stairs on tiptoe, choking on the gas,

Lennie enters the front bedroom. Over in the far corner, half covered with broken lathes and smashed junk, he sees the two-tone shoes, then the bloody torso.

"Ole Mistuh Fred . . . lookit that . . . like to tore that ole arm clean off . . . man oh man." He pushes aside the plaster-covered lathes. "Ole Fred don't look so tough at that . . . Looks like it caved him in . . ."

In the back bedroom, coughing again, crawling gingerly over a dresser on its side, broken glass and plaster crunching under his feet, he sees Ma Barker.

"Oh my . . . Ole lady Blackburn . . . Lord amighty."

Impassively, he stares down at the body. Thick square dead fingers curled around the trigger grip on the black oily submachine gun. He picks up a floor lamp and rights it, brushing glass splinters from the shade. Mr. Broadwin ain't gonna be pleased about this.

"What about it?" yells Lafferty from the yard below.

Lennie leans his head out the upper window. "They're all dead." His eyes are streaming from tear gas.

The FBI wearily get to their feet.

"Step back off the line and pick up your brass."

Lafferty takes a deep breath.

"Come on boys, let's go in."

An Ocala sheriff was just below Lennie.

"Did you see that? Did you see that nigger cryin'? He *loved* them people."

The word spreads quickly from the front lines back to the rear areas where the spectators watch. The war is over.

"The people inside the house are dead!"

"Well, I hope the cops are proud o' themselves."

"Fifteen cops. Fifteen cops and twenty deputies. It wasn't fair."

A man wearing Levis, white shirt and bow tie, shouts, "*I hope you're proud o' yourself!*" He drops behind his pickup truck. "Ooooh, I think the cop seen me!"

A silver-haired, neatly-dressed man stops an Ocala policeman.

"We've got to get all these people out of here. This is a private community." The cop lives in Ocala. A public community. He shrugs.

A gray-haired woman standing on her veranda shakes her head.

"I'll never know what Carter Broadwin could have been thinking of, renting to people like that."

Her neighbor, finishing a Coke, agrees.

"You just never can tell these days." The Coke was good, time for a little bourbon for the nerves.

Mr. Silverhair, smoothing his double-breasted navy blazer, says, "Officer, will you please get these people out of here? I'm sure none of them are members of the Lake Association."

He tightens the knot in his tie.

A small boy jumps up and down near the splintered Broadwin hedge.

"Are there dead people in there, Pa?"

The father grins, spattering tobacco juice across the azalea beds.

"They was the *Barker* gang, boy! They robbed from the rich an' they give to the poor."

"Kin we see 'em, Pa?"

"Show's over folks," says a local cop. "Break it up."

The boy's father stands his ground.

"Kin we see them corpses?"

"No," says the cop. "Get outa here. You're trespassin'."

The father is 5 feet 6.

"I'm a taxpayer."

"I'm a police officer an' you're trespassin'."

"I have some rights you know, officer."

"What you wanta see the bodies for? You wanta peek up her dress?"

"I could report you."

"That's right."

"C'mon," the father drags the boy away. "We'll see the corpses at the morgue. I'll call Delbert. He'll let us in."

The Good Humor man stands next to his ruined truck.

"Will everybody who took a Good Humor please pay up now? Please?" He has freckles and earns ten dollars a week.

The thin blonde girl is perched on the front bumper of the Chevrolet. She rubs her narrow hips across the double steel band. Jean Harlow at ninety pounds.

"Boyd Henry, you kin come out now, chicken."

Boyd Henry has lain with the transmission.

"I got grease on my plusfours."

She rubs her hips back across the bumper.

"You missed the whole show, chicken-liver."

"If my Ma sees this grease, she's gonna give me the dickens."

"Tell her it's something else."

"For that, you kin just walk home."

Miss Harlow glares.

"I was goin' to anyhow. And you're not gonna get to do it to me, ever, either."

Boyd Henry stuffs his grease-smeared hands deep into his pockets. Somewhere under the car, he has lost the ignition key.

The Good Humor man is on his feet, digging sticky sand from his money changer, dismayed at grass stains on his Good Humor white jacket.

"Will everybody who took a Good Humor please pay up now?" he calls. "Come on now, folks, the company'll take it outa my pay." The grass stains are permanent. "Come on, folks."

A sightseer finishes his ice cream, licks his lips, flips the stick away as he walks toward the house, a firm middle finger to the Good Humor man.

John Lafferty sits on the fender of a car, feeling suddenly very tired. Nothing to eat since he got off the plane. Twenty-four hours.

Inside the cottage, the local lawmen are talking to the reporter. All windows and doors opened, Lennie the cook mops his eyes on a dish towel, sits at the kitchen table and makes himself a sandwich. He places Ma's biscuits in the oven, adjusts the setting and goes to the Victrola on the dining room sideboard and puts on Ma's record of "Keep On The Sunny Side."

"Shame to shoot holes in all them purty tables an' chairs. Busted *hell* outa things."

There's a dark and a troubled side of life . . .

"Hey boy, will you turn off that phonograph?"

There's a bright and a sunny side too . . .

"I like that tune, Mister, it's kinda catchy."

It will help us ever day/ It will help us all the way . . .

"What you *doin'*, boy? Swipin' food?"

If we keep on the sunny side of life . . .

"I ain't swipin' *nothin'*. I work here."

"Not any more you don't."

"Take off, boy."

"I ain't hungry anyways, what with that there bomb-smoke."

The Negro cook slowly, elaborately gets to his feet, carrying a second sandwich in his mouth, goes over to the Victrola, cranks the machine and sets the needle back at the start of "Keep On The Sunny Side." Then he leaves.

Under the sheet lies Ma.

"So that's Ma Barker," the reporter says. "She wasn't very big, was she?"

. . . a bright and a sunny side too . . .

"Ma Barker had a Tommy gun. She was firing out the upper window at our men. It's a shame to shoot a woman but you have to understand she was a natural born killer."

"Yeah? Is that right?"

"Oh, she gunned down many a police officer in her day. Bank guards, innocent bystanders . . . women, children . . ."

"Yes sir, 1500 rounds fired all told. They put up a real desperate fight . . . Thompson submachine guns, rifles, pistols, the works. Somebody said they threw a hand grenade out the back window."

"They hit any o' your men?"

"I don't believe so. We was dodgin' bullets all mornin', though, yes sir."

He twirls his six-shooter frontier style.

"Real tough fight but we got 'em . . . we surely did."

The white-jacketed men from the coroner's office have arrived. The male corpse is in the front room. Evidently killed instantly. One burst hitting his left chest and shoulder. One bullet struck him squarely in his left nostril. That'll teach him to pick his nose. The intern chuckles. Corpse looks to be in early thirties, large nose, scars on face, eyebrows odd looking, probably hack surgery. Bad bruise on right temple. An ugly son of a bitch. No two ways about it. One eye is open. He's peeking.

(*Was it Ole Jesse or was it Cole Younger said, "Don't mind me, boys, die game? Don't surrender, die game!"*)

"Yes sir, 1500 rounds fired in all."

(*Don't let them sorry fools tie a rope around yore neck.*)

"Well, I guess we won't have to indict anybody here." The agent laughs.

Ma Barker lies on her back. Her eyes are closed.

(*Hangin' Judge Parker saved 'em up and hung 'em six at a time. Bluebelly justice fer ye.*)

The intern takes a look at Ma. Second body, woman, short, heavyset, mid-fifties. Puffy face, ordinary features (nobody you'd ever remember), frizzled red hair, enormous powerful looking hands. Barrel-bellied, bowlegged, one bullet wound.

Funny, finding an old woman in a mess like this.

"Oh yes sir, desperate characters like Ma Barker you don't take chances."

Guitars banging away in country harmony, the phonograph grinds on . . . *The storm in its fury broke today* . . .

"No sir, I really couldn't say who it was shot Missus Barker."

. . . *crushing hopes that we cherished so dear* . . .

(*Never surrender, Ole Jesse James said. My boy Herman he killed himself.*)

. . . *clouds and storm will in time pass away* . . .

"Can't really say who did what in a pitched battle this size."

. . . *and the sun again will shine bright and clear.*

(*Ole Jesse, he said, "Die with yore boots on, that's the only way." Die with yore boots on.*)

Ma Barker is wearing bedroom slippers.

(*They is some traditions that is worth maintainin'.*)

Keep on the sunny side/ always on the sunny side . . .

The sheriff gazes around the living room.

"The Barker gang. They really left things a wreck."

He stretches out in the Florentine chair.

"Somebody shut off that Victrola!" he yells. "The record's got a nick in it, keeps skippin' back. 'Keep on, keep on, keep on!' "

He laughs.

"Anybody here got a bottle o' dope?"

•